Bello:
hidden talent rediscovered!

Bello is a digital only imprint of Pan Macmillan,
established to breathe new life into previously published,
classic books.

At Bello we believe in the timeless power of the imagination,
of good story, narrative and entertainment and we want to use
digital technology to ensure that many more readers
can enjoy these books into the future.

We publish in ebook and Print on Demand formats
to bring these wonderful books to new audiences.

About Bello:

www.panmacmillan.com/imprints/bello

About the author:

www.panmacmillan.com/author/rogerbax

Roger Bax

Roger Bax is the pen name of Paul Winterton (1908–2001). He was born in Leicester and educated at the Hulme Grammar School, Manchester and Purley County School, Surrey, after which he took a degree in Economics at London University. He was on the staff of *The Economist* for four years, and then worked for fourteen years for the *London News Chronicle* as reporter, leader writer and foreign correspondent. He was assigned to Moscow from 1942–5, where he was also the correspondent of the BBC's Overseas Service.

After the war he turned to full-time writing of detective and adventure novels and produced more than forty-five books. His work was serialized, televised, broadcast, filmed and translated into some twenty languages. He is noted for his varied and unusual backgrounds – which have included Russia, newspaper offices, the West Indies, ocean sailing, the Australian outback, politics, mountaineering and forestry – and for never repeating a plot.

Paul Winterton was a founder member and first joint secretary of the Crime Writers' Association.

Roger Bax

CAME THE *DAWN*

B E L L

First published in 1949 by Hutchinson & Co

This edition published 2012 by Bello
an imprint of Pan Macmillan, a division of Macmillan Publishers Limited
Pan Macmillan, 20 New Wharf Road, London N1 9RR
Basingstoke and Oxford
Associated companies throughout the world

www.panmacmillan.com/imprints/bello
www.curtisbrown.co.uk

ISBN 978-1-4472-2089-3 EPUB
ISBN 978-1-4472-2088-6 POD

Visit **www.panmacmillan.com** to read more about all our books
and to buy them. You will also find features, author interviews and
news of any author events, and you can sign up for e-newsletters
so that you're always first to hear about our new releases

Chapter One

It all began at a party given by a Soviet cultural society in Moscow in March 1943. Most of the foreign colony were invited. I forget what the occasion was, but it's of no importance, for these parties were all pretty much alike. They were usually held in vast houses once owned by Russian noblemen, with lots of gilt and mirrors and faked marble pillars in their high-ceilinged rooms. The food and drink were always staggering in quantity and variety. There were always more guests than the rooms could comfortably hold, and yet you hardly ever saw an unfamiliar face. The social life in wartime Moscow was narrow and inbred, rather like that of castaways on a desert island. Most people went to the parties because they could think of nothing better to do.

This particular gathering was no exception to the general rule. All the usual people were doing all the usual things. There wasn't even a convoy captain down from Murmansk or an inflown American air crew to break the monotony. It was just the old gang of diplomats, members of the various Military Missions and foreign correspondents, with a careful flavouring of Russians.

There was a crescendo of voices as the vodka and wine began to flow, but in everything but volume the talk was small. The military people—Russian and foreign—were avoiding the painful topic of the war, which the Russians were convinced they were fighting singlehanded. Avoidance was easy, since few of the British and American soldiers could speak much Russian and almost none of the Red Army officers could speak English. Conversation therefore bumped along in a series of imperfectly comprehended toasts. One or two recently-arrived correspondents hovered on the edge of the uniformed groups, hoping to pick up a little copy, but the more experienced Pressmen were content to drink. The civilian Russians were behaving like the well-trained professional hosts they were, and only an initiate could detect the wariness under their mask of official cordiality. One or two sly-eyed hostesses, tough Party members in private life, flirted self-consciously with diplomats of rank. Apart from them, there was the usual sprinkling of Russian poets, artists and writers who in wartime Russia enjoyed the unwritten privilege of mixing freely with foreigners.

To judge by the noise, anyone dropping in casually would probably have said it was a swell party. But the alcoholic joviality was only a facade. Tomorrow most of the foreigners would again be frustrated, bored or angry, and most of the Russians would be aloof and unapproachable.

I helped myself to food and drink and for a time added my voice to the babble. After a while I got tired of the heat and the crush and managed to find a pillar on the edge of the crowd which I thought would at least protect my rear. I had just lighted a cigarette when a girl appeared in front of me with a tray of glasses and offered me champagne. I knew she wasn't one of the Society's official hostesses, and yet there was something vaguely familiar about her. I supposed she had been drafted for the occasion to help by being nice to the foreign guests, and she certainly didn't have to make any effort. She was sweet. She had dark hair and almost violet eyes and she looked about twenty. As I took the glass of champagne I said in Russian, "Please don't go away!" She gave me an enchanting smile but she went away just the same. I only stopped following her with my eyes when I found I was pouring champagne on to my shoe.

Several times during the next hour or so I caught her glance as she passed lightly from guest to guest, and once she smiled at me again. As soon as the crowd began to thin out I collected two glasses of champagne from a waiter, walked over to her and asked her to sit down and talk to me. She did so with a composed simplicity which was most appealing. I learned that she was a ballet dancer—no doubt that was why her face had seemed familiar, for

I must have seen her at the ballet in some minor role. Her name was Marya Lamarkina. She seemed a different type from most of the young girls in the Moscow *corps-de-ballet*. I knew many of them by sight, and some by repute. They were a vigorous, fresh and amusing bunch who liked going about with foreigners. This girl was rather gentle and shy, with old-world manners which I found exquisite.

She asked me about myself and I told her that my name was Philip Sutherland, that I was the correspondent of a London newspaper, and that I'd been in Moscow for two years. She congratulated me on my Russian, and after a little more conversation she said she must leave. I said I hoped we should meet again, but she only smiled and said 'Perhaps'. I could hardly bear to see her go. The slight intoxication I felt as I walked back alone to my hotel was not entirely due to alcohol. I couldn't stop thinking of that dainty figure and that charming smile.

Next day I had to go off with a Press party to cover a big atrocity story in one of the liberated areas, and moving about among burned and tortured bodies I wasn't in the mood to think of daintiness and charm. I was pretty used to horrors, but this was a particularly appalling business and once I'd dispatched my story I felt a reaction and was sick for a couple of days. Altogether, it was nearly a week before I could seriously get down to the problem of Marya. I was determined to renew our acquaintance, but it wasn't at all easy to know how to begin. I was afraid that a direct approach might frighten her away for good, and yet I couldn't see any alternative. It might be months before I ran into her again by accident, or it might be never. In the end, I sent her a short note by messenger. The forty or fifty words it contained gave me a lot more trouble than the million or so I had written for my paper since I came to Moscow, which was odd, since all I wanted to do was to ask her to accompany me to the Moscow Art Theatre on her next free day. I felt certain that she would make some excuse, but to my delight she accepted in an old-fashioned little letter and appointed the following Sunday as the day.

I met her in the foyer of the theatre, feeling not in the least like a hard-boiled newspaper man. I had gone determined to make her feel at ease with me, but in fact I was much more nervous than she was. She was natural and friendly, and very soon we were both thoroughly enjoying ourselves. The play was *The Cherry Orchard*, and it was given with the traditional brilliance of the Art Theatre. Marya was enthralled. She rarely had the opportunity to see a straight play and I was touched by her rapt attention to the stage. For the first time since I came to Moscow I was grateful for what before had always seemed to me interminable *entr'actes*. Each time between the curtains we had half an hour or so to stroll round and round the foyer, as the Russians love to do, talking.

In the second of the intervals I learned a good deal more about Marya. As a small child she had been brought up deep in the country by parents who apparently preserved the old way of life. When she was eight she was brought back to Moscow by a ballet school which had visited her district in search of promising material. She couldn't remember just how it had happened, but it seemed her parents had not stood in her way. A little later she had had a letter from them, written from some remote spot in Central Russia but giving no address, and that was the last she had heard of them. All her later efforts to trace them had failed. From what she could remember it was easy to imagine that they had not taken to the new regime, and that they had provided for Marya as best they could before the intolerance of the post-Revolution years had swept them away.

During the weeks that followed that first pleasant evening together at the theatre it was only rarely that I was able to be alone with Marya, but I could often see her on the stage. I became an ardent balletomane. I had always enjoyed Russian ballet on its own ground—no one who has not seen it can easily imagine the gorgeousness and glitter of its settings and costumes, to say nothing of the dancing itself. Now I had a more personal reason for liking it. Except when I was out of Moscow on some Press trip, I hardly missed a performance when Marya was dancing. At this time she was only just emerging from the chorus, but she was regarded as a dancer of exceptional promise. She had grace and vitality and technique, and a hint of passion on the rare occasions when she was given an opportunity to show it. Ballet is a serious business in Moscow, and success comes slowly, but I felt sure Marya would one day become a great dancer. Naturally I wasn't the most objective of critics. I was dazzled by her dancing—spellbound. But it wasn't just the glamour of the stage that was making me crazy about her. She had just the same effect on me when sometimes we walked together in the Park of Culture and Rest—a grimly formal place totally devoid of glamour.

I liked everything about Marya. I liked the impulsive way she would put her arm in mine before shyly withdrawing it. I liked the way she moved, and the ready laughter in her eyes. She was a *shining* person, if you know what I mean. Although she looked so demure, she had a tremendous zest for living.

She completely transformed my life in Moscow as our friendship grew. Frustration and enforced inactivity had been making me a little morose—everyone said I had been in Russia too long. But Marya's gaiety had a magical effect. The vexations of the job no longer troubled me unduly. With Marya I could laugh at official stupidities and obstructions which a few months earlier would have started a rush of blood to the head. I told her that without her I should soon have become a sour old man. "How old *are* you, Philip Georgevitch?" she asked. I told her I was nearly thirty. Marya thought this over. "Old perhaps," she said kindly, "but—not sour."

I couldn't see nearly as much of her as I wanted to. Almost every day she was either practising or dancing. It was I who was comparatively leisured, for with the spring thaw a lull had come on the Russian front and there was little war news to send. When we did meet, it always seemed that our relationship had ripened. Of course I was head over heels in love with her, and by now I knew that she felt for me something more than the ordinary romantic interest in a foreigner.

One day in the middle of May, when the sun was warm and all Moscow had blossomed, we took a bus out to Khimki—a bathing beach on the Moscow river—hired two tiny canoes and paddled off upstream until we had left the city far behind us. Marya delighted in any form of exercise and it was all I could do to keep abreast of her flashing paddles. She kept breaking into little snatches of song—it was that sort of day. She looked bewitching and I just couldn't keep my eyes off her. Presently she suggested we should picnic on an attractive bit of grassy bank fringed with silver birches. We had come prepared to swim, but we soon found that the water was still cold from the thawed snow, and after a few minutes' splashing and racing we climbed out to sun ourselves on the bank.

"I didn't know you were such a good swimmer," I said, a little breathlessly.

Marya shook her wet curls. "I've always liked it," she said. "I adore the water."

"I've got a sailing-boat at home," I said. "Perhaps one day I'll take you out in her."

Instead of making some light reply or ignoring my remark, Marya looked at me quite seriously. I had forgotten the directness of the Russians. "I would like that," she said.

I couldn't stop, then. I said, "Marya, you know I'm desperately in love with you."

"I love you, too, Philip," she said simply.

"Then will you marry me and come to England?"

"Perhaps," she said. "We will think about it."

I took her in my arms. I hadn't gone to Khimki that day with the deliberate intention of making love to her, but it happened naturally and inevitably. We were both incredibly happy.

Back in town, of course, we had to face serious problems which I suppose both of us, in different degrees, had pushed aside until now. I had been long enough in Moscow to know that about the most foolish thing a foreigner and a Russian girl could do was to fall in love, and that the most foolish thing of all was to marry. I had known it equally, of course, the day I had first set eyes on Marya. If I had been sensible, or unselfish, I should have tried to put her out of my mind after that first party. It would have saved us both a lot of heartache in the end. But people aren't like that. I had seen many love-affairs and some tragic consequences in wartime Moscow, and in my time had given much sound advice to others, but I had never known any couple refrain from loving or marrying because of the difficulties ahead.

All the same, the difficulties were formidable. I knew that if Marya married me she would be risking official disfavour and possibly jeopardizing her career as long as she stayed in Russia. I knew, too, that there was no certainty that she would be granted an exit visa when the time came for me to leave. One or two Russian wives of foreigners had been permitted to leave, but by no means all. The attitude of the authorities to foreign marriages seemed to be hardening. It was never quite clear what their motives were, but they had a morbid fear and suspicion of the outside world and just didn't want any mixing. Marya naturally had an inkling of all this, but she wasn't—thank God—politically-minded and was inclined to assume that everything would be all right.

I tried to face up to the issues as honestly as anyone in love could do. Indeed, when Marya herself raised the subject of marriage at our next meeting I gave such a realistic account of the possible complications that I reduced her to tears and felt an absolute brute. She even accused me, with a rare flash of temper, of having changed my mind about her, and we got into a silly emotional tangle before everything was sorted out. One thing was plain and that was that Marya wasn't going to be intimidated by difficulties, political or otherwise. She knew that one or two wives had got visas and saw no reason why she shouldn't in time. She had read quite a bit about ballet abroad and seemed confident that she would be able to follow her profession in London if she were patient. I thought so, too. We went over everything. Finally she said she would sooner be married to me for two years than not married to me at all. I suppose the result was a foregone conclusion all the time, because we both wanted each other and that was all there was to it. We did what so many other couples had done and grasped at happiness while we could.

When I told the British Ambassador he called me 'a damned young fool', warned me that he wouldn't be able to do much to help me, and then shook me warmly by the hand and wished me luck. He married us in the Embassy in June, and afterwards we signed the necessary papers in a registry office to comply with Soviet law. In the evening we had one of the jolliest Anglo-American-Russian parties I had known in all my stay. A large part of the Moscow ballet seemed to be there, the head of the Soviet Press Department looked in and expressed his good wishes, the correspondents and diplomats were charming and cheerful and everybody was in the highest good humour. The Russians were particularly cordial and all the auspices seemed favourable.

Marya and I were marvellously happy, for we were very much in love. She went on with her ballet routine just as before, but her horizon had widened and she talked a great deal about England, which she was eager to see. Her dancing kept her away for long hours, and every now and again I would go off on a Press trip as the tide of battle surged westwards and great cities were liberated. But still we managed to be together most of the time. While the summer lasted we spent as much time as we could out of doors. We used to go off for picnics on the river or take the Metro to the outskirts of the town and walk for hours in the birch forests. Together we explored Moscow. In Marya's company I grew to love the old city, honey-coloured in the golden autumn, rose-pink under snow in winter. When time was short we had a special 'beat'—once round the Kremlin. On a crisp bright day in winter there isn't a finer short walk in the world.

When the cold weather settled in, Marya insisted on teaching me to ski. Marya, like most Russians, was very competent. I, on the contrary, was very conscious of my clumsiness. We used to go off through the Sokolniki woods on the outskirts of Moscow and seek out a quiet spot where I could practise unobserved. I remember scrambling up one day, covered with snow and indignity after failing to negotiate some nursery slope, to find a group of little Russian children watching me in silence, and their leader solemnly remarking, "From what small hills you fall!" Rather sheepishly I tried to explain that we seldom saw snow in England, and then Marya came up, brimming with laughter, to release me from further inquisition.

If Marya was the better skier, I was the better linguist. My Russian didn't go very deep, but what I knew I knew well, and Marya assured me that I could pass for a Russian anywhere. I even looked like one, she said. That, I suppose, is because of the high cheek-bones I have inherited from a Scandinavian great grandmother. But actually I'm much taller than the average Russian, and a lot slimmer.

At first we had always talked in Russian, but now Marya was eager to learn English and I encouraged her. She had a quick mind and a retentive memory and she made good progress. She was disappointed that she couldn't quite lose her Russian accent but I was glad, for it was one of her great charms.

We had our worries. Marya was aware of a change in her relationship with some members of the ballet company whom she had counted among her friends. There was no ostracizm, but from time to time there was a coolness which was almost equally distressing to anyone of Marya's affectionate and generous disposition. The ballet, like every Soviet organization, had its political side, and the girls perhaps unconsciously took their cue from the Party members whenever Anglo-Soviet relations ran into difficulties. Marya, though very much a Soviet citizen in the eyes of the law, was regarded by her fellow-Russians as virtually a foreigner. It seemed a little hard that she should sometimes be treated as though she were personally responsible for not having opened a Second Front, but these moments passed, and on the rare occasions when Britain was conceded to have earned Soviet praise she even basked in reflected glory. Poor Marya was a little bewildered by the swift and subtle changes. Happily, her career did not seem to be suffering as I had feared it might.

Our life together couldn't be very domestic. We had taken a small suite at the hotel, which in the daytime was cluttered up with papers, secretaries and messengers, as I had to use it as an office. Most of our meals were taken in the restaurant, but sometimes in the evening, when Marya wasn't dancing, she would go all housewifely and solemnly cook a meal on the single electric-ring. She insisted that the meals she cooked were Russian specialities, but they always seemed to taste and smell the same, whatever ingredients she used. As a cook, she was undoubtedly a most promising ballerina.

Marya found that her friends were more reluctant to visit her now that she was married to a foreigner. I had been afraid that this would happen, but she was too busy to be lonely, and she liked most of the correspondents who lived in the hotel and who were always dropping in. Her favourite was a good friend of mine, Steve Quillan, who had recently come to Moscow to broadcast for an American network. Steve was as different as could be from the strident and assertive American of caricature. He was an outwardly placid man, with a quizzical expression and a droll sense of humour. To look at, he was tall and loosely-built, with broad shoulders slightly bowed and hands perpetually thrust into his trousers pockets. Though I never heard him discourteous to anyone in Russia except a censor, and that only under the greatest provocation, he disapproved strongly of the Soviet set-up, and his great delight was to make cracks about the Russians over the air which the censors had failed to detect in the tangle of colloquial American. I first got to know him when I acted as a stand-in for a broadcaster who'd gone out of town on a trip. The studio was about a mile from the hotel, and Steve and I used to plod up there together through the snow at two o'clock in the morning to deliver our broadcasts. I was only an amateur, but Steve was an artist at the microphone. He had a fine low voice, which was no doubt one of the reasons why he had gone into the broadcasting side of foreign reporting. He'd give one or two 'H'rrrmps', which seemed to lower his voice about an octave, and then he'd start talking in a deep bass that fairly stroked you into agreement.

Marya and I found Steve a source of endless entertainment. When he had nothing in particular to do he would weave his way up to our room, greet me with a 'Hello, you Fascist beast!', cast an appreciative eye over Marya, and drape himself across our settee with a contented sigh, as though he'd found sanctuary from a madhouse. Sometimes he'd bring up with him the script of a broadcast he'd just given, seeking our praise. He was still fresh enough in Moscow to be keen on the job, and he made a great effort to keep his vast American audience interested. Our raw material was very scrappy. Since we rarely met Russians except on trips, we had to base our reports on the snippets of information contained in the Soviet newspapers, and build on them. But what a builder Steve was! He might be physically confined to Moscow, but his imagination was away campaigning with the Red Army and he was an adept at turning a hint into a two-minute flight of radio fancy. While the official Soviet reporters were still observing the Dnieper from a distant height, Steve would be watering his horses in the river, describing the flora and fauna on the banks and giving an emotional account of the feelings of the residents along its shores who were about to be liberated. The Red Army moved fast, but Steve always moved faster. He was quite shameless about these embellishments. Sometimes he would glance mischievously up from his script, trying to catch my eye, when he came to one of the more colourful passages. The censor was completely cynical about these stories, provided they could be considered good propaganda, and he rarely cut anything solely on the ground that it was imaginary. But Steve had a lot of copy slashed on political grounds, like most of us.

Apart from Steve, Marya and I became friendly with a man named Jack Denny, and his wife who was also a Russian girl. It was a natural friendship because we had common interests and apprehensions. Denny had come out to Russia in March 1943 to demonstrate some new British tanks, which the Russians characteristically denounced as death-traps while demanding that supplies should be increased. At that time he was a sergeant in the Royal Armoured Corps. He was a first-rate technician, but however hard he tried he could never look or behave much like a soldier. Moscow suited him because discipline was relaxed there and he was practically an autonomous unit. At first he had worn a straggling black moustache in the belief that it gave him a military appearance, but actually it made him look like a rather mournful grocer. He took it off at the approach of winter because he thought it might freeze on him, and I must say he looked a lot better without it.

Denny was a thickset chap with a large placid countenance. It took a long time to get him talking as a rule, but let him once start on a pet theme and the ponderous flood of his discourse would wear you down. He had come out to Moscow equipped with a wardrobe the like of which had never been seen there before. It was quite embarrassing to walk out with him in winter when he was wearing 'civvies', for small children would follow us for miles, fascinated by the deerstalker hat and the coat of many linings that Denny had been convinced he would need in deepest Russia. It was just as well the kids couldn't see his underwear.

The circumstances in which Denny met his Russian wife were unique. After many requests, the correspondents had managed to get permission to visit a tank training-school where British tanks were being used, and Denny was invited too. He couldn't speak a word of Russian at that time, so the authorities thoughtfully provided him with an interpreter, whose name I afterwards discovered was Svetlana. After we had looked over the tank school there was the usual banquet. Denny was sitting just opposite me, and Svetlana was next to him. She was attractive in a heavy Slav way, with flaxen hair and hazel eyes, a splendid Russian bosom and a complexion like a baby's. At the banquet our host, a Tank General, set a hard-drinking pace, and before long we were all pretty tight. Denny, still unused to vodka, succumbed completely, but Svetlana was quite unperturbed. When he finally slumped in his chair she rolled her beautiful lace sleeves above her elbows, picked him up bodily, and carried him out. A few weeks later they were married.

Because Denny was a bit heavy in his movements and in his conversation, some of the colony were inclined to write him off as stupid. But he certainly wasn't that. He was slow, which is a different thing. He would quietly take people to pieces and examine their works, as he took everything to pieces. He couldn't stand anything shoddy. I have a mental picture of Denny dismantling an electric-light switch in our room at the hotel just to see how a Russian switch worked, and I remember now the tone of shocked disbelief in which he said, 'Blimey, look at this contraption.'

Denny's great qualities were lots of common sense and an

absolutely unswerving loyalty. He was one of the most naturally upright men I'd ever met. He was the sort of chap who could be relied upon to say 'I will' only once in his life and to mean what he said about sticking to his girl for better or worse. Svetlana appreciated that. She was very straightforward and loyal herself—a good Soviet citizen, believing what she was told like everyone else. Actually she had reason to be grateful to the Revolution. Her paternal grandfather had been an illiterate peasant with more children than livestock and no prospect of improving his lot. In the social earthquake after 1917, Svetlana's mother had found her way to Moscow, and with the help of state scholarships had been educated up to university standard and had emerged with a diploma as a teacher of languages. She had married a minor Party intellectual who had died shortly after Svetlana's birth. In due course Svetlana had followed in her mother's footsteps and had herself become a teacher of English at the Moscow Institute. When she met Denny her mother had just died, leaving a big gap in her life which Denny—who so obviously needed looking after—filled admirably. Denny of course was warned about the dangers of such a marriage, but like the rest of us he decided to risk it.

Marya and Svetlana, in most respects complete opposites, took to each other very quickly and became close friends. Svetlana admired Marya's accomplishments, and Marya found Svetlana reliable and comforting. We all saw a good deal of each other and visited each other's homes. Denny and Svetlana were a devoted pair and, domestically speaking, Denny went quite native. They had one tiny room with the bed curtained off, and they had a fourth share in a communal kitchen and an eighth share in the usual offices. The place wasn't too bad by Russian standards—there were no bugs, and with his special privileges as a foreigner Denny was able to get enough fuel for their little iron stove, as well as adequate rations. When Svetlana had more work to do than he had, he would even go down to the market and do the shopping. In the end, he thought nothing of travelling on the Moscow trams, which was the supreme test of acclimatization for any foreigner.

Sometimes, when he and Svetlana came to visit us at the hotel and saw again the comparative luxury of our faded Louis Quinze suite, they would grumble a little about their squalid conditions. But mostly they were looking ahead. Denny's ideal was a neat little villa in Streatham, with a trim grass lawn and a small workshop in the garage, and he got a tremendous kick out of telling Svetlana what fun they would have setting up house in England. Svetlana made it plain that they hoped to raise a large family.

Then the war and the Russians dragged them apart. Early in 1944, when Denny had been in Russia a little under a year, he was recalled to England. Svetlana at once applied for an exit visa, which was neither refused nor granted. The Russians were still sullenly awaiting the Second Front, and we all tried to pretend that that was the reason for their silence and that when they felt better about their allies they'd grant the visa. There was nothing whatever to be done except be patient. Both Denny and Svetlana took the blow with outward composure, though Denny's sense of justice was deeply affronted. He had always got on well with the Russians at the technical level, he had taught them a great deal, and he felt he deserved something better from them. But he didn't moan and he didn't lose hope. Marya and I went with them to the airport on a bitter February day and afterwards we did our best to comfort Svetlana, though we weren't feeling any too happy ourselves. In the evening Steve dropped in for a drink and his remarks about the Soviet authorities were corrosive. His indignation increased under the influence of vodka. He was supposed to broadcast that night and he went off at about nine o'clock, muttering, to write his piece. It was never broadcast, however. Apparently Steve took it down to the Press Department himself, got involved in an argument with the censor about the Russian wives, and finally had his copy killed. He told me next morning, with a grin compounded of shame and complacency, that he thought it was because he had written 'Soviet Neroes' instead of 'Soviet heroes' and had denied that it was a typing error.

With the separation of Denny and Svetlana a darker shadow fell across the lives of Marya and myself. We didn't dare to talk much about our own prospects, but I was seized with new anxiety and even Marya's gaiety occasionally gave way to tears when we were alone. We had cause to be worried, too, about Svetlana. One night, about a week after Denny's departure, she was stopped and questioned as she left the hotel by a plain-clothes member of the N.K.V.D.—the Soviet Security Police. Two nights later she was stopped again, and this time she was taken to N.K.V.D. headquarters. She had nothing at all on her conscience and was able to answer all the questions honestly and apparently to the satisfaction of her inquisitors. All the same, it was very disturbing. Svetlana wouldn't have been the first Russian girl to find herself in Siberia after becoming friendly with a foreigner. I don't think anyone was surprised when she told us soon afterwards that she had been sacked from the Institute without an explanation. She applied for one or two jobs in other Soviet organizations, but it was apparent that she had been blacklisted for having a British husband and for having asked to go away with him.

It was Steve who came to the rescue. A correspondent—a *British* correspondent, he was at pains to tell me—had just bribed his secretary away from him. What made the blow more bitter to Steve was that part of the consideration had been three pairs of American nylons. Anyway, there was a job waiting for Svetlana. The arrangement proved extremely successful, for Svetlana made an admirable secretary, and there was no further trouble with the N.K.V.D. Svetlana soon became her cheerful self again, helped by regular letters from Denny through the diplomatic bag. He had been posted as instructor to a tank school in Wales.

Marya and I had some wonderful times in the summer of 1944, but the shadow never really lifted. Night after night the great guns boomed out their victory salutes as Russian towns and villages were liberated, but they carried no message of personal hope for us. I knew that my office would expect me to leave Moscow as soon as the war ended, and I knew that from the professional standpoint I ought to leave. I might be able to stall for a time, but the newspaper business expects a measure of discipline and I had always taken a pride in my job.

Theoretically, of course, I could become a Soviet citizen and try to scrape a living at Marya's side. I confess I never seriously considered such a step, nor did Marya ever hint that it might be a solution. She had seen one or two of the wretched creatures who had done it.

In the spring of 1945 we talked the whole position over and made preparatory moves about her visa application. I tried to enlist the support of the Soviet Press Department, pointing out quite justifiably that I had done a reasonably useful job of reporting in Russia and that I expected them to treat me decently in return. I didn't suppose it would do much good, for these matters are decided at the highest level, but I felt I had to try everything. I wrote to Molotov, who knew me at least by name and by sight and certainly knew of Marya, and I even dropped a carefully-phrased letter—as correspondents occasionally did—into Generalissimo Stalin's Kremlin letterbox. The British Ambassador refrained from saying 'I told you so' when I called on him, and rather wearily promised that he would try to raise the matter personally with Molotov.

Our spirits rose a little during the victory celebrations, when British and American nationals were mobbed in the streets by enthusiastic crowds and even the official Russians unfroze. But the goodwill bore no material fruit. Day after day I rang the Head of the Press Department—who assured me that he had put in a word with the authorities—but he never knew anything. I got a cable from my office congratulating me on the work I'd done and raising my salary. It was dust and ashes. I would readily have bartered all the money I should ever earn for a seal on a piece of paper. Presently I got another cable from the office saying they had assigned me to take charge of the New York bureau—perhaps the finest job a correspondent could have. They hoped I was having no difficulty about my wife's visa.

I cabled asking them to approach the Soviet Ambassador in London, though I knew it would be futile. I said I would need a little time to clear up my affairs and they were sympathetic. I called at the visa office but was refused an interview. Marya called, and was told by some underling that the matter was under consideration.

I knew we were wasting our time. All the doors were closed, and not by chance.

For the moment, there was nothing more to be done. I write that now, but I wasn't philosophical then. I was desperately heartsick and worried about what might happen to Marya. But there it was—we'd had two wonderful years and now we were going to pay. I wired the office that I was preparing to leave and stonily packed my bags. If I had to go, the sooner it was done the better—there was no joy for anyone in these last days. Once more Steve rallied round, though his eyes seemed for the moment to have lost their twinkle. He wasn't wholly to be envied—he would have to do probably two more years in Moscow before his network moved him. He promised to look after Marya for me. Once more we all assured each other that it was only a question of time. I clung to straws of comfort—the thought, for instance, that at least Marya would have her dancing to take her mind off things. But we both felt as though a partial death had come to us.

I said good-bye to Steve and Svetlana at the hotel. I would have left Marya there also, but she was too Russian to cut the knot sharply at the end and she insisted on coming to the airport with me.

The 'plane was already warming up when we got there and we didn't have long to wait. Marya clung to me, looking woefully lost and pathetic. She said, "Philip, if they won't let me out you *will* come back here, won't you . . . just to see me, I mean?" Her voice trembled. "I—I don't feel ready to say goodbye." She pressed her head against my shoulder and began to sob in a way that tore my heart.

I said: "I'll come back, darling, darling Marya. I promise."

"I wouldn't want you to stay . . ."

"I know, sweetheart. Don't let's talk about it. It won't come to that. We'll find a way."

Marya looked deep into my eyes and said slowly: "Whatever happens I shall always love you. Always. I shall wait for you if I wait all my life."

"And I shall always love you, Marya. You're not—sorry—about everything?"

The tears sprang to her eyes once more. "I would do it all again," she said earnestly. "I've been so happy."

The loudspeaker blared. Marya dabbed her face. She said, trying to smile: "I don't want you to remember me like this. I must look dreadful."

We got up and went to the barrier. I took her in my arms, kissed her and held her close for a moment. Then I grabbed my case and went blindly on to the tarmac, not knowing if I should ever see her again.

Chapter Two

I worked in New York for more than eighteen months. Marya and I kept as close as we could by correspondence but it was a heartbreaking business. The whole thing seemed so wickedly unnecessary and unfair. I don't think she was ever out of my mind for a moment. There was no difficulty about getting private messages carried to and fro, for newspaper men were frequently going in and coming out and I knew most of them. Once Steve came out by air for a short break. He was reassuring up to a point—he said that Marya, though a little subdued in private, was dancing better than ever, and he thought she was too popular to come to any harm. Otherwise, there was little he could tell me that I didn't know from her letters.

When the case of the Russian wives was taken up officially by the Foreign Office I did what little I could to help in the campaign. It was impossible not to go on hoping, but as the months went by and relations between Russia and the West grew worse, the hope faded. Every conceivable approach had been made to the Russians. They had been appealed to on the ground of common humanity, and on the ground that they themselves had sanctioned the marriages with foreigners, and on the ground that we had been their fighting allies and deserved something better at their hands. Well-known friends of the Soviet Union had interceded on our behalf. The Press had given publicity to our troubles; the subject had been raised repeatedly in Parliament and at the highest diplomatic levels. The plain fact was that the Soviet Government had decided that it had nothing to gain by giving way, and there was nothing on earth that could compel it to do so. It had even set the seal on its decision by enacting a decree making any future marriage of Russians with foreigners illegal. It had slammed and bolted the door, and my Marya was on the wrong side.

By the beginning of 1947 I felt that at all costs I must get back to Moscow and talk to Marya. I put the situation squarely to the office and they were very decent. They called me back to London, and after a long talk Barnes, the editor, suggested that I should return to Moscow as the paper's resident correspondent. It was all the more generous of them because in other circumstances I doubt if they would have gone to the expense of keeping a permanent man there. Of course, I jumped at the offer. I applied for a visa, with a supporting letter from the paper, and in a week I got a reply. The application was refused. No reason was given, except that I was no longer *persona grata* to the Soviet authorities.

I broke the news to Marya by letter and, as one does, I urged her not to despair. But she wrote back in words of anguish and I couldn't think of any way to cheer her. I was helpless—we were all helpless.

Good colleagues of mine told me that the only thing to do now was to try to forget. I suppose it was sound advice—it was certainly well-meant—but it was advice I couldn't follow. It would have been different if Marya had been dead—that was something I could have taken on the chin like any other man. But the knowledge that nothing separated us except fifteen hundred miles and the harsh obstinacy of a bunch of bureaucrats just gnawed at me. When I dwelt on the brutal injustice of their action—as I did about a dozen times a day—I fairly choked with anger. I had got pretty low in health as well as in spirits by this time, and I wasn't much use about the office. Barnes realized I was in a bad state, gave me a fatherly lecture, and urged me to take some leave. The prospect wasn't very attractive at the end of March 1947, when London was still gripped by the worst winter for about fifty years, but a couple of weeks later the weather did a complete somersault and I could hardly get out of London quickly enough.

What I needed was fresh air, hard physical exercise and a change of scene. I thought without much enthusiasm of walking or climbing, and then I suddenly remembered the little sailing-boat that I'd told Marya about. I didn't know whether it would still float after being completely neglected for the best part of eight years, but at least I could go and see. So on a delicious spring morning early in April I travelled down to Southfleet in the Essex flats with a week's rations in my rucksack, a pair of sea-boots, and a determination to follow Barnes's advice and 'snap out of it' if I possibly could.

The boat, *Wayfarer*, was a three-tonner with a tiny cabin. I had stripped her of all her gear and contents just before war broke out and had left her high up on the saltings where only an extraordinary spring tide could reach her. The sails and spars I had given into the care of a young chap named Joe Brooks, to whom life and boats were interchangeable terms. As it happened, Joe was almost the first person I saw on the saltings—he hailed me as I was struggling to negotiate the deep glutinous mud of the creek at low water and directed me to a better route. I was really glad to see him, and he seemed pleased to see me. I had known him for only a short while before the war, and not very well at that, for he was quiet and reserved. But he was one of those naturally amiable fellows whom you can't help getting along with. He was about my age, spare and very brown, with frank eyes as blue as the sea and hair already a little grizzled at the temples.

When I'd cleaned some of the mud off myself we sat down on the gunwale of a dinghy he'd been scraping and had a talk and a smoke. He told me he'd joined the Navy at the outbreak of war but had been invalided out a couple of years later. Since then he'd been slowly building up a one-man business on the saltings, repairing yachts, looking after other people's boats, and doing a bit of brokerage when an opportunity offered.

I asked him about *Wayfarer*. The creek was dotted with yachts and dinghies, barges and fishing-boats, all dried out in the mud, and I hadn't been able to spot her.

Joe stood up and pointed across the saltings to a little rill. "There she is. She's in rather a bad state. I moved her when I came back so that she'd be under my eye."

"Will she do up all right?"

"I should think so," said Joe cautiously.

I told him that I had some leave and that if the weather kept fair I planned to stay down on the saltings for a few days and fit the boat out.

"It's very nice just now," Joe said approvingly. He was always in favour of anybody spending time on the saltings. "I live in the workshop over there." He pointed to a spacious but dilapidated houseboat like a Noah's Ark.

"You're not married, Joe?"

He smiled a trifle cynically and shook his head. "Boats are enough trouble," he said. "And women aren't usually very keen on my sort of life. They like water to come out of taps."

I wanted to tell him about Marya, but I didn't—not then. Instead we went over to have a look at *Wayfarer*.

Her condition, it seemed to me, was not too bad. Of course, she'd lost almost every scrap of paint and varnish and the wood was a bit soft in places, but I felt sure she'd do up sufficiently to give me some good sailing again. She'd never be the sort of boat to take to sea in a blow, but then I wasn't competent to take anything out in really bad weather. I had no illusions about my seamanship.

"Her gear's all right," said Joe encouragingly. "We'd better bail her out and see if she'll float on the afternoon tide. I'll get a bucket." And he plodded off cheerfully to the workshop. His time was his own, and he gave the impression of enjoying every minute of it.

During the next few days I threw myself with savage zest into hard physical activity. I wanted to tire myself out so that I could sleep at nights. Stripped down to a pair of old flannels, I scraped and painted and stopped leaks and rove new ropes from dawn till dusk. Joe lent me the tools and materials I needed, and often a helping hand as well. He also let me shake down in his workshop until *Wayfarer* was sufficiently dry for me to sleep in her. The weather was heavenly, with sunshine and soft air and larks twittering away like mad, and I soon began to feel a new man. The days passed very quickly. There was always something fresh to look at when the muscles got tired. It was the 'fitting-out' season, and from morning till night you could hear the sounds of hammering and sawing, the clank of steel cable, and the cheerful rattle of rope running through blocks. Boats changed colour rapidly as owners applied new paint with skill and pride, and the creek was soon as bright as a rainbow.

Joe seemed to be everywhere at once. He got through an immense amount of work, but all in his own way. He was an individualist, the monarch of his estate, which was about three acres of saltings. His jobs were as varied as the tools and stores in his workshop. One day he would go out and navigate a boat up the tricky channel from the Estuary; the next he would be burning off or painting a hull or fitting an auxiliary engine. He knew a good deal about engines, but sail was his passion. He was incredibly conscientious. He had quite a lot of boats under his charge and if a bit of wind got up during the night and the tide happened to be high Joe would turn out and row around in his dinghy, loosening a warp here or heaving in a bit of anchor chain there, until all was safe. He enjoyed it. I think he felt that he really owned the creek at night, when everyone else was asleep.

It took me just over a week to finish *Wayfarer*. I was rather proud of the transformation and was looking forward to taking her out, but first I went up to the flat which I rented in Chelsea to get some clean clothes and collect my correspondence. There was a letter from Marya that put me right back to Square One. Joe must have noticed my change of mood when I reached Southfleet that night but he didn't say anything. Later, when he was brewing the pot of tea we usually had before turning in, I felt I had to talk about Marya or burst, and I told him the whole story. He didn't say much, but he looked at her picture for longer than mere politeness demanded. When he handed it back there was a firmness about his chin which left no doubt where his sympathies lay, and he muttered something about 'bastards', which I thought showed exactly the right spirit.

The next day we had a short but exhilarating sail in *Wayfarer* and then I took some stores aboard and went down the creek on my own for a few days. That wasn't so good. It was all right while I was actually sailing, for in those difficult shoal waters off the Essex coast I was fully occupied trying not to go aground or getting off once I had grounded. There are a hundred-and-one things you can do wrong in a small boat and I did them all. But it got dark early in the evenings and then there was nothing to do but find a quiet berth for the night, cook a meal, and turn in. Those saltings and mud-flats were lonely at dusk. After the tide had gone out and *Wayfarer* had been left high and dry, there'd be nothing visible in any direction except mud and a low shoreline and a wide sky, and nothing audible except the depressing cries of sea-birds. At such times I told myself I'd been a fool to creep away from the lights and companionship of the town.

Sometimes I would be wakened in the night by a moaning wind, and then I would lie thinking—always the same thoughts. After two years, the ache for Marya was as hard to bear as when we had first parted. I saw her in my mind continually—Marya coming in breathless from her practices, bright-eyed and laughing, with the first snow sparkling on her little fur hat and muff; Marya singing for all she was worth on a long sleigh ride we had taken out into the country; Marya dancing impromptu to amuse the little shaven-headed children in the war orphans' home; Marya hopefully stirring a concoction on the stove. God, how I missed her! I tried to tell myself, as others had told me, that the only sensible thing to do was to write the marriage off and hope that perhaps someone else would turn up for each of us later on and that the pain would grow less sharp. Marya, after all, was still only twenty-two. She would fall in love again, and she would be much better off with a Russian. Such thoughts tortured me, without convincing. I didn't want her to fall in love with anyone else, and for all my experience of the world I couldn't believe she would. As for me, I knew I couldn't work up the faintest interest in any other woman. I wanted Marya. I wanted her so much I felt there was nothing I wouldn't do to get her.

Thinking about it all was just a mental treadmill. If there had been a single effective action I could have taken it would have been different. It was the prospect of living for years on slowly fading recollections of happiness that was intolerable. I knew I was in a desperate state. I couldn't forget, and yet I had to forget. I must discipline myself not to recall things best forgotten, yet the tricks of memory could not be disciplined. What was the good of pretending? For better or for worse, Marya was my life.

I sailed back to Southfleet much more depressed than when I left it. Physically, I was in splendid shape. I was as tanned as Joe himself. My hands were calloused from hauling on sheets and halyards, and my muscles were hard. I was bursting with energy. I could have throttled a Commissar easily! But my mind was like tangled rope.

I turned *Wayfarer* into the wind opposite the workshop and had the anchor down and the sails furled as smartly as even Joe could have required. When I had made all snug aboard I went ashore to see what he was doing. I found him in what was, for him, a bit of a temper. It seemed that a client with an expensive new boat and no knowledge had been throwing his weight about, and that always made Joe mad. He had a craftsman's pride and dignity and he didn't like being treated like a long-shoreman. He used some nautical language about spivs with luxury yachts and no manners that cheered me up considerably. It felt good to have a companion again. I made some tea and we sat down on the short grey grass of the saltings and idly watched the creek filling up.

If my mind had been easy, I could have watched that creek quite happily all day long. It was interesting even when it was dry. I liked the way the mud hissed as all the life beneath it breathed. It was intriguing to let the shadow of a hand move across the mud and to watch hundreds of sea-lice draw back into the putty-like substance as though they had been drilled. I loved to watch a spring tide pouring in, with its fringe of brown foam and bubbles and its hint of power. Joe felt the same. He was a dreamer. He had plans for a bigger and better workshop. He wanted to make some money so that he could buy the right sort of boat and go off round the world. He didn't want money for anything else, as far as I could see. To most people the creeks and channels which ran through the saltings like veins in a leaf were nothing but smelly beds of rather disgusting mud. To Joe, they were a gateway. He knew he was nearer real freedom sitting on the deck of a small boat dried out in one of those muddy creeks than he would have been in a suite at the Ritz. For when the tide came in the little boat suddenly became a living thing, eager to move, and the gate was unlocked to the open sea. You didn't have to ask permission or buy a licence or depend on anybody else's efforts. You could just up-anchor and sail away to the ends of the earth if you had the right boat and the knowledge and the guts. I felt pretty sure Joe would sail away one day.

We drained the teapot for a second cup, and watched a boat come in that I hadn't seen in the creek before. She was a gaff-rigged cutter, rather old-fashioned in her lines and sturdily built by modern standards, but very easy on the eye. As she turned into the wind I saw that she was roomy and broad in the beam. Her spars were heavy, and so was her gear. She looked like a much-used working boat in need of a coat of paint.

"That's a nice little ship," I said, with proper diffidence. I was always hesitant about voicing too emphatic an opinion on any nautical subject when Joe was about. But this time I could see by the quiet gleam in his eye that he fully shared my view.

"She's a husky job," he said.

"She must be pretty old."

"Thirty or forty years—but no one can build like that these days. There isn't the timber. She's well-seasoned oak and teak, and nothing scamped. I'd sooner have her than any modern yacht."

The cutter swung a little in the wind and I saw her name. It was *Dawn*.

I said, "Do you know the boat, Joe?"

Joe nodded. "She's from Mersea. That old boy stowing her sails is the owner. He's brought her here to sell her."

My interest was still no more than academic. I said:

"She looks a fine sea-boat. Nice and dry, I should think."

"Yes," said Joe, "she's what sailing chaps call sea-kindly. I was out in her once or twice before I joined up. You could go anywhere in *Dawn*."

"Anywhere?" I said, a shade surprised. She didn't look all that big. "What do you suppose she is—ten tons?"

"Just under, I should think. But she'd weather any storm, properly handled."

I said, "Would she sail to the Baltic?"

"Of course, if she were handled right. She's built to keep the seas."

I felt suddenly queer. I heard my voice saying, rather distantly, "Joe, I think I'd like to buy her."

Joe was looking at me strangely. He said: "Are you sure you're all right? You've gone quite white."

I said: "I'm all right. How much does the old boy want for her?"

"He's asking a thousand, but he might take less."

"Do you think I could handle her ... ?"

"Well ..." Joe began cautiously.

I jumped up. "Come on. Let's go and have a look at her."

We took his dinghy and rowed across to *Dawn*. Joe introduced me to the owner and we were invited aboard. The cutter was very snug inside. There wasn't a lot of head-room for a tall fellow like me but there were four berths, two in the fo'c's'le, as well as a small toilet and a galley. She seemed to be fairly well-found. I made some technical inquiries and learned that she had an iron keel and a draught of three-foot six. She had several suits of sails and what looked like a rather ancient pattern of auxiliary motor. I had a hunch, and was eager to buy her. I knew this wasn't the right way to buy a boat; I knew I was behaving like an idiot and that I should probably regret it when I came to my senses. All the same, I arranged to meet the owner in the Anchor Inn at six o'clock that evening and make him an offer. Then I rowed Joe back to the workshop, without talking. In fact, I avoided his eye. There was something about his expression that I didn't very much like.

When we got back to the saltings I said: "What's the matter, Joe? What's on your mind? She's a sound boat, isn't she?"

"Oh yes, she's sound," said Joe. He spoke as though soundness were a mere trifle. "Mind you, she'd need a good bit of spending on her. Her engine's no good. But the hull is first-rate."

Coming from Joe, that was as good as a survey for me. I said: "Could you get her ready for sea? Quickly?"

Joe wriggled uneasily. It was the first time I had ever seen him really disconcerted. If I'd been suggesting a particularly shady black-market deal he couldn't have looked more uncomfortable. If I'd known him a bit better I'd have seen that in his unassertive way he was waving a red light as hard as he could.

"I suppose so," he said. "It would take about a couple of months to do her up properly. There might be a bit of difficulty getting the right engine, but I expect we could pick one up somewhere."

"Good," I said. "The job's yours. Joe, what's it like sailing a 10-tonner alone?"

I suppose I knew what he really wanted to say as well as he did. If ever honesty struggled with an obvious desire to please, it was doing so now on Joe's face. But I just didn't want to hear his real opinion. He knew that too. After an eloquent pause he grinned a bit sheepishly and said, "Well, it's all right if the weather's good."

"I could find someone else to come along too," I said defensively. "I know a chap who's in the same boat as I am—matrimonially speaking, I mean. I'm sure he'd come."

"Does he know anything about sailing?"

"No, but he can learn."

Joe sighed. "I shall get a commission on this sale," he said, "but I shouldn't like you to feel you'd been hurried into it. P'raps you'd better think it over."

I couldn't help laughing. "If your sales talk is always like this," I said, "you'll never get that new workshop. Of course, I agree it's a long way to the Baltic ..."

"It's a long way to Southend Pier," said Joe darkly, "on a bad day."

I came down to earth then and spoke what was in my mind. It wasn't a question of heroics, it was a question of having no alternative. I said: "Joe, I'm going to recover my wife. If I can't, then frankly I'd sooner drown."

Joe looked worried. "It's not my business," he said, "but have you worked it all out? It'll be very difficult, won't it?"

"Let's get the boat first, and we'll work it out afterwards. All I want to know now is whether this boat, with reasonable luck and skill, will have a fair chance of making a safe passage across the sea."

"You wouldn't find a better boat," said Joe obstinately.

"Then let's buy her," I said, and we set off for the village. I wanted to do it before I had time to get cold feet. We found the old boy in the pub, and I ordered three pints and offered him eight hundred and fifty pounds. He looked at Joe and knew that was Joe's figure. He said, "Make it nine hundred." I said, "Right." I asked the landlord to find us a sheet of paper, and while the owner wrote out the receipt I wrote out the cheque. Joe provided the stamp and in a couple of minutes the deal was done.

"Well," I said, lifting my glass, "here's to *Dawn*."

Joe raised his glass with a thin smile, took a drink, and choked.

Chapter Three

Next day I travelled up to town by an early train. There was a letter from Steve saying that he'd got short leave and was planning to spend it in London, but giving no other news of any consequence. I rang up Jack Denny's lodgings and left a message asking him to come round to my flat in the evening. I hadn't seen very much of him since my return to England, but we had kept in touch. He was working in a jet-engine factory in Brixton.

I'd done some pretty hard thinking on the way up to town, and the results weren't very encouraging. I didn't for a moment regret the impulse which had led me to buy *Dawn*, but I wasn't crazy enough to imagine that my project—if you could call it that at such an early stage—had more than an outside chance of success. What I felt was that if I could sell the scheme to the practical and prosaic Denny, I should have moved from the fantastic to the merely improbable.

His very appearance, when at last he sat opposite me in the flat clasping a double whisky, was solid and reassuring. He must have been the only man in England who still wore boots from choice. I asked him for his news of Svetlana, which was negligible, and then I took a deep breath and said, "Denny, I've got a proposition to make."

"Oh?" said Denny noncommittally.

"Yes. I think you and I together could fetch Svetlana and Marya out of Russia."

Denny took a sip of whisky and put the glass down. Then he took out his pipe, blew through it, filled it, lighted it, and very deliberately put the matches back in his pocket.

"How?" he asked.

"I've bought a boat. I think we could sail it to the Baltic and pick them up somewhere on the coast this summer." I added hopefully that the boat had an engine.

"How big's the boat?"

"Oh, about twice the length of this room."

Denny said he couldn't swim.

I could see he wasn't taking me very seriously, and I couldn't blame him. To a man who has never been on anything rougher than the Serpentine and who doesn't really like the water anyway, the idea of a long sea passage in a small boat can't be very engaging. I did my best to make the proposition sound rational. I pointed out that I'd done quite a bit of sailing before the war, and that because a boat was small it didn't mean that it wasn't seaworthy, and that sailing was perfectly safe if you chose your weather carefully, and that anyway we'd be in sheltered waters for a good part of the time. I drew an idyllic word-picture of the pleasures of summer cruising; I tried to impress him with a lot of technical jargon about anchors and spinnakers and sailing on the wind; I said that in any case we both needed a holiday.

I built up what I thought was an almost irresistible case, and waited anxiously for the reaction. At last Denny said, "I think it would be a lot safer to smuggle them out in a large box."

I didn't think he meant it, but he just might have, and that shows how fantastic this whole affair was. One person *had* tried that method of leaving Moscow, as part of the diplomatic luggage of some country or other. However, Denny was apparently joking about the box. He said, "How would they get to the coast?"

"There aren't any restrictions on travel inside the country," I said. "Not for Russians."

"No," said Denny, "but there aren't any spare seats on the trains either. You know what a job it is getting a ticket unless you're an official."

"Oh, come, Denny," I said, "I'm sure they could find a way to get over that." I felt he was making difficulties.

"There's another thing," said Denny. "Suppose they got picked up by the N.K.V.D. while they were hanging about on some beach waiting for us? They wouldn't have much of a future then."

"They may not have much of a future anyway if we can't get them out," I said.

"M'm." Denny chewed reflectively on his pipe. You could almost hear the wheels going round in his mind. Presently he said: "I don't see how you'd manage to do all the arranging—with them, I mean. The timing would have to be very good—practically like a military operation. We'd need continuous contact with them. How would we tell them everything? Write it through the post for the censor to read?"

"Steve Quillan will be in London soon," I said. "We could talk to him about that. I believe there's a way. I haven't thought it all out—damn it, I only bought the boat last night. Obviously we'll have to go into all the details, and if we find the idea's not practicable we'll just have to drop it. I don't want to rush you into anything—I just want your help in exploring possibilities. I agree our plans have got to be just about one hundred per cent watertight before we make any serious move."

"Yes," said Denny with heavy humour, "and so's the boat."

For a while he sat there stolidly smoking. I've never seen a man look less convinced. He said, "When would you think of making the attempt—and where?"

"Well," I said, "it would have to be some time in August or early September. Before then, the nights wouldn't be long enough. If we left it any later we couldn't reasonably expect good weather. As for the place, we'd have to go into all that with maps and charts. I should think any quiet spot between Leningrad and Riga would do, provided it were accessible for the girls. There'd be nothing at all unusual in their strolling down to the seashore after dark on a warm summer night. We'd row ashore in a dinghy, pick them up, and be well away from the coast before morning."

"It sounds easy," said Danny, "the way you put it. I can't think why it's not been done more often. Aren't you forgetting the guards they're bound to have on the coast? I remember somebody at the Mission once saying that in 1940, when the Russians took over the Baltic States, there were some bits of the shore where they had a man posted every hundred and fifty yards."

"I'm sure that was exceptional. That was a time when every second Balt was trying to get to Sweden in a small boat. I don't suppose they've got more than a normal coastguard service these days. We'll have to find out."

Denny grinned. "That's right," he said. "We'll take a day trip to Leningrad and walk along the shore and ask the first N.K.V.D. chap we meet to give us the dispositions."

"There must be other ways," I said, a bit lamely. "Anyhow, I'm sure you're exaggerating that particular danger. We might be unlucky, of course, but they can't possibly watch every inch of that long coastline."

"They'd get very suspicious," said Denny, "when they saw your boat stooging about in the Gulf of Finland or wherever it was. They'd probably keep tabs on you the whole time."

"Well," I said, "that's something we can find out only by going there. After all, there wouldn't be much danger for anyone unless we actually made the rescue attempt and failed. We could perfect our plans and be all ready to carry them out. If at the last minute we weren't able to turn up, the girls would just have to go back to Moscow. It would be pretty shattering for them, naturally, but they'd be no worse off than before. They'd just have had a short holiday at the seaside."

"I suppose so," said Denny dubiously. "Of course, if they did get away in your boat the Russians would take it out of their relatives."

"I don't know who they'd find except third cousins," I said. "Svetlana's mother and father are dead, and she's an only child. Marya hasn't seen anything of her parents since she joined the ballet school—they're probably dead too. I can't think of anyone who'd suffer."

"What about the other wives?" Denny asked. "It wouldn't do their case much good if we kidnapped Svetlana and Marya."

I said: "I know. I thought of that. But do you honestly think, Denny, at this stage, that there's any chance whatever that the

Russians will change their minds, however well the wives behave? I don't. Of course, in ten or fifteen years, if there isn't a war, the situation may be different, but that's not going to be much use to anyone. I think we're justified in getting ours out if we can. Come on, Denny. What about it?"

Denny slowly shook his head. "I don't feel so completely hopeless as you do about a Russian change of mind," he said. "You can never tell. And anyway, I just don't see this plan of yours coming off. I think your boat would be spotted and followed wherever it went, as long as it was anywhere near the Russian coast. I think they'd sound the alarm all over the Baltic. I don't believe you could count on getting a dinghy to the shore so quietly that no one would notice. There'd probably be a scrap, and all four of us would be shot. And suppose the weather was bad. Think of the lousy summer we had last year—just one storm after another. Of course, I don't want to dissuade you . . ."

By that time I'd had about as much as I could take. The trouble was that in Denny's place I'd have felt the same as he did. There was nothing much to argue about, because we both knew the conditions and the risks. It was really a question of temperament—and on my part, I suppose, of wishful thinking. When *my* imagination got to work, the difficulties went down like ninepins; when Denny approached them they stood up like Eiffel Towers.

All the same, I got a couple of concessions out of him before we dropped the subject. He said he'd give the idea more thought, and he also said he'd come sailing with me in *Wayfarer* the next week-end—'without prejudice'. For the time being we left it at that.

I felt very dashed as I travelled down to Southfleet with another week's rations in my rucksack. I couldn't help thinking that I'd made a tactical error in not working out a plan in greater detail before approaching Denny. As an engineer, he'd have liked to see a working model or at least a blueprint. All I'd offered him was a pretty bedtime story.

Belatedly, I began in my mind to clothe the bare skeleton of the idea with a little flesh. I imagined us setting out from Southfleet in *Dawn* at about the end of May or in early June. We should have a long and tricky passage to Gothenburg in Sweden—three or four hundred miles of open water. That would mean several nights at sea, and would require that each of us should be able to handle the boat in order to relieve the other. It would obviously be impossible for Denny to learn more than the rudiments of sailing in so short a time, and it would therefore be a further condition of success that the weather should be absolutely perfect. That wasn't as unreasonable as it sounded, because within limits we could wait for a fair spell.

Once we reached Sweden we could make our way to the Baltic at our own pace through the Gota Canal, as I'd once thought of doing by steamer on a pre-war holiday. We should be in sheltered waters all the time, and perfectly safe. The real snag was the Baltic itself. The ideal thing would be to dash into the Gulf of Finland and dash out again, but sailing-boats—even with auxiliary engines—aren't equipped for that sort of operation. They're just about the slowest things on earth. However harmless our expedition appeared—and ostensibly of course it would be just a case of two mad Englishmen on a slightly risky holiday cruise—Denny was certainly right in thinking we shouldn't be allowed to poke our noses deep inside the Finnish Gulf without being watched. And that seemed to rule out any place as far east as the approaches to Leningrad—it would take altogether too long to get in and get out again. Probably the Russians would claim all the sea around there as territorial waters anyway, and would insist on putting someone aboard us for inspection. I doubted if any foreign yacht had been in those parts since the Revolution. From the point of view of Denny and myself, somewhere much farther to the west, like Riga, was more promising, for a night's sail from there would see us well on the high seas and on our way to Sweden. On the other hand, the girls would have much more difficulty in getting to Riga than to Leningrad.

I tried to visualize the actual escape, and the scene my imagination conjured up wasn't very comforting. *Dawn*, whether she went in under sail or engine, would obviously have to anchor a good way off the coast to avoid the risk of being seen or heard. That meant that one of us would have to stay with her, while the other would have to row the dinghy to the shore and back again. It would be a very exhausting row, even if everything else went smoothly. And then, as Denny had pointed out, however carefully one studied the topography of the place beforehand there was no guarantee that the dinghy wouldn't touch down on a bit of coast that happened to be guarded that night. Someone might hear it as it came close in. And how would the rower make certain of finding the right bit of shore in the dark?

By the time I reached Southfleet I had thought myself back into a state of inspissated gloom. I won't say I was thinking of abandoning the project, because that wouldn't be true. I was in the mood for any risks, providing they didn't unreasonably involve the safety of Marya. But the physical difficulties were certainly formidable.

The sight of Joe hard at work on *Dawn* cheered me a lot. He had brought her over to our side of the creek on the night tide and she was dried out on the mud just opposite the workshop. I was soon helping him to scrub her free of weed and barnacles and for the time being I forgot some of my worries. Joe had put aside most of his other jobs and for the next few days we worked on her from morning till night. It was a rewarding task, fitting her out, for she was in splendid condition in all essentials. Joe told me that he'd begun to put out some feelers locally for a suitable engine, but he didn't say another word about my projected trip. There was something ominous about the way he avoided the subject—he was like a Victorian father steering a conversation round the fringe of the family skeleton.

Early on Saturday morning Denny came down from town to go for his first sail. I may as well say at once that from my point of view it was a disaster. The visit started well enough—I introduced him to Joe and was glad to see that they didn't take an instant dislike to each other. In fact, they soon found some common ground. They were both experts in their own field—it didn't take Joe long to realize that what Denny didn't know about engines wasn't worth knowing. Denny gave barely half a glance at *Dawn's* pleasing lines and stout timbers and his comment was a derogatory, "So *this* is the ocean liner!" But when he went aboard and Joe showed him the old engine it took him only a couple of minutes to get grease up to his elbows. He and Joe both looked at the engine as though it were something the cat had brought in, and then they went into a technical huddle about the sort of engine *Dawn* really needed. Denny had no special knowledge about marine engines but I could see he was learning fast.

That was all quite satisfactory. The trouble began when the tide came in and I took Denny aboard *Wayfarer*. I realized afterwards, when it was too late, that I had been foolish to give him his nautical baptism in so small a boat. Though he was marvellous with his hands, and could fish a small nut out of an oil-bath with two fingers, he never knew what to do with his feet, and in that tiny cabin and cockpit his feet seemed to be everywhere. He would obviously have preferred to stay and talk to Joe, but I was determined to take him down the creek now that I'd got him there. So as soon as *Wayfarer* swung to her anchor I had the sails up and we were slipping down towards the sea over the tide.

There was a nice sailing breeze and it was a lovely spring day. In fact, conditions seemed to me to be perfect. I knew the channel through the mudbanks very well by this time and we reached deep water without incident. I tried to give Denny an explanation of all I was doing as I did it, but he had an abstracted air which I interpreted as meaning that he had already made up his mind to have nothing to do with my wildcat scheme. However, I was wrong about the cause of his abstraction. It soon appeared that he was feeling seasick. I had become so used to messing about on the water myself that I had quite forgotten that there were people who couldn't stand the slightest motion. But the expression on Denny's face was becoming more and more that of a man who is working out a complicated arithmetical problem in his head and suddenly he went ominously green and practically threw himself out of the boat in his effort to get his head over the gunwale in time.

He looked so bad that I hadn't the heart to go on, and his relief as I put *Wayfarer's* head round was unmistakable. He picked up slowly as we returned to the quieter waters of the creek and became rather shamefacedly apologetic. Naturally I assured him that most people were like that at first, and that after one or two trips he'd get his sea-legs, but he obviously disbelieved me. There was a stony look in his eye which said as clearly as anything could that it would be a long time before he left *terra firma* again. He positively staggered when he set foot once more on the saltings.

Joe grinned when we told him about it, but he backed me up loyally. He said he'd never known anyone yet who didn't vow that the first trip to sea in a small boat would be the last, and that nine people out of ten felt like making a second attempt after they'd been a few days ashore. But Denny was not to be persuaded. He was full of apologies about the whole episode, but when I put him on the train back to town he said he thought I'd better try to find someone else if I meant to go on with my plan. He didn't feel he'd be much use as a companion, and in any case he'd decided that the whole scheme was far too risky.

In spite of what Denny said I couldn't bring myself quite to give up hope of him. I knew that he had lots of guts, and that being seasick once wouldn't have been sufficient by itself to decide the issue. However, it would have been unrealistic to rely on him now. I was all the more disappointed because Joe had rather taken to him and I valued Joe's judgement. Actually Joe's attitude rather surprised me, because although Denny had shown himself good with engines he hadn't a clue about sail, and it was odd that Joe should think it a pity such an obvious landlubber couldn't accompany me.

I really didn't know what to do next. I was in a curious mood. From every practical point of view there seemed less chance of carrying out the plan than ever, and yet in my own mind it was steadily taking shape. Perhaps it was due to the fact that the fitting-out of *Dawn* was proceeding so satisfactorily. Her solid hull was for me the tangible evidence that the scheme wasn't all moonshine. Although there was no doubt at all that Joe took a poor view of the trip he was determined to send me off—if I finally insisted on going—with a boat that was fit to do the job, and *Dawn* had become the apple of his eye.

It was quite clear that I should have to have a companion, but I had no one in mind. I knew one or two sailing men, but it was most unlikely that they'd be able to get away for half the summer, and in any case I didn't feel I could ask them. At the very best our mission would be dangerous. Denny and I had everything at stake, but I could hardly ask a colleague or casual acquaintance to risk his neck in such an adventure for the sake of me and my wife. Denny's refusal was really most depressing. I felt sure that if he had gone into the matter a little more deeply, or been a bit more realistic about the Russians, he'd have come to a different decision.

Then, when I was sunk in gloom, something happened which altered everything. From a narrowly selfish point of view it was a stroke of luck, though it came in a very disguised form. I had gone back to the flat for the week-end, as I usually did, to collect clean clothes and food, and on this occasion to buy the best map I could get of the Baltic countries, particularly those along the Finnish Gulf—which actually wasn't very good. I was poring over this on the Saturday night, making some preliminary calculations of distances and possible lines of approach, when my telephone rang. It was Denny, and he wanted to see me urgently. I told him to come over right away, and he arrived in a taxi, which suggested a desperate state of mind.

Almost before he was inside the door he held out a letter for me to read. It was from Svetlana, in Russian, and had come through the ordinary post. It began with rather formal expressions of affection and then went on to say that as there now seemed to be no likelihood that she would ever get out of Russia, or that he would ever be able to see her again, she thought the only thing to do was to face the fact and call the marriage off. The letter wound up by saying, rather bleakly, that she had already applied to the Soviet registrar for a divorce, which would no doubt be granted, and that she hoped Denny would find another girl and be very happy.

I read the letter through twice. I felt grieved and shocked. I had known Svetlana pretty well, and this didn't sound like her.

I handed the letter back. "What are you going to do?" I asked.

Denny said, "What would *you* do if you got a letter like that from Marya?"

The mere suggestion was like a blow between the eyes. If I'd had a letter like that from Marya I wouldn't have believed it. Other wives might want to divorce their husbands, but mine wouldn't! I felt ashamed of myself for so readily taking the thing at its face value. I said, "May I have another look at it"

It was Svetlana's handwriting and signature, of course. It was genuine enough, in the sense that she'd undoubtedly written it. But what had made her write it? Had she done it spontaneously? That opened up a field of speculation which I felt it was better not to explore. There were worse things even than divorce and parting.

I poured out a drink for Denny, who needed it badly. "Look," I said, "Steve will be here this week. I 'phoned his office today. He's probably on his way now. He'll have all the news. This letter was posted nearly three weeks ago—he'll be more up-to-date than that. I shouldn't worry too much until you've seen him."

Denny crumpled the letter and thrust it into his pocket with a gesture of hopelessness. I could see he didn't know what to believe. He had been remarkably philosophical through the long years of separation, but he looked more unhappy now than I had ever seen him. I told him I'd let him know directly Steve arrived, and we agreed to meet at the flat. We had a couple more drinks and then Denny went off, looking as hurt and helpless as a dancing bear with sore feet.

I stayed on at the flat so that no time would be wasted once Steve had arrived, for I could imagine what Denny was going through. A couple of days later Steve's office rang me to say that his 'plane had touched down at Heath Row. I could hardly contain my impatience. Not long afterwards Steve himself 'phoned from the Savoy to say that he was having a bath and a meal and would be round for a drink at about nine. I managed to contact Denny at his lodgings without difficulty—he was probably sitting at the end of the telephone—and the two of them arrived at about the same time.

Steve had a letter for Denny, and two or three for me. He didn't look very happy. He took the drink I poured out for him with an absentminded "Thanks, *tovarisch*," and we watched Denny begin to read. It was a tense moment for me; Steve, of course, knew the facts already.

Denny doesn't show emotion readily, but his face flushed a dark red, and his long chin stuck out, and presently he muttered an obscenity which I should hardly have thought him capable of using. He said, "Listen to this!" and read out:

"They took me to the N.K.V.D. headquarters where I had been before and they told me I was a worthless person and had no sense of Soviet patriotism to want to be the wife of a foreigner, and they said I would never be allowed to leave Russia and that I might as well give up the idea. They asked me a lot of questions for hours and hours as though I was a criminal until I was so tired I could hardly keep awake, and then they said I must divorce you right away or else I should have to go and work in Kazakstan in a camp. They dictated a letter which I had to write out and they made me sign it and then they said they'd post it, but I didn't mean a word of it, and all I want is to come to you."

He stopped reading, and a silence fell on the room. The shadow of the Russian Security Police was over us all. Steve avoided my eye. Presently Denny got up and shambled over to the window—I could well imagine the tumult of his feelings. He stood there quietly for a few moments. Then he turned, and with a hard look on his face he said, "If that trip's still on, Philip, I'll come with you, if it's the last thing I do."

Chapter Four

Steve naturally said, "What trip?"

I told him that Denny and I had decided to fetch the girls away.

Steve looked a little startled, but only for a moment. He said, "No kidding!" Then the old mischievous grin spread over his face. "You couple of Fascist beasts," he said. He seemed to accept the idea as quite natural and reasonable. It was a bit of an act, perhaps, for he knew the odds against us just as well as we did. But it was heartening all the same. What had seemed like desperate lunacy when Denny and I had first talked about it could obviously be discussed with Steve as a straightforward problem in logistics.

I gave him a very rough outline of the plan in a few sentences. He was quite neutral about the sea hazards—he didn't know the first thing about boats and was prepared to assume that if we had the boat it would naturally get us without difficulty to whatever destination we happened to choose. I explained how necessary it was that the rendezvous we picked should be as far west along the Baltic coast as possible so that we shouldn't have to do much hanging about in Russian waters, and I said that late August seemed about the best time for the attempt.

"Gosh!" he ejaculated suddenly. "I've just recollected something. Marya told me about a week ago that she was scheduled to go on tour this summer. It would be just too bad if she was dated up for Omsk in August. Maybe there's something about it in her letters."

So far I hadn't had an opportunity to do more than glance at them, but this was something that had to be cleared up right away. I soon found what I wanted. In the last letter but one Marya wrote at length about the projected tour. She was definitely going, she said, always supposing that she didn't get her exit visa first, but she was a little vague about details. It was to be a fairly extensive trip, apparently, starting in Kharkov in May, going on to Odessa and Kiev and up through Byelorussia to Minsk and finishing at Leningrad in the late autumn.

"I don't much like the sound of it," I said. "She's practically bound to be in the wrong place at the wrong time, and it'll be very difficult to keep in touch with her."

"She could fall sick and not go," said Steve.

I shook my head. "I can't ask her to do that at this stage. It might be different if we had a firm plan." I could imagine how she would be looking forward to the trip, and how it would help to take her mind off things. I turned the pages of her last letter a little disconsolately. She was still writing about the tour, and how she hoped that in the provinces she might be given an opportunity to dance Aurora in the *Sleeping Princess*, which she had always wanted to do. As I thumbed over the last page a slip of paper dropped out. I picked it up, and when I saw what it was my heart gave a leap.

It was a little printed bill advertising the tour. There was a list of the ballets which the company would present at the various towns, with the dates. It seemed that Marya would be at Tula from May 20–23, Kharkov for a week in early June, Kiev for a week, Odessa for several days early in July, Minsk from July 12–16, Riga at the end of July, Tallinn from August 12–15, and Leningrad for a fortnight in September. The gaps were presumably for travelling, rehearsals and recreation.

It was our first stroke of luck. If Marya was in Riga for several days in July and in Tallinn, the capital of Estonia, for four days in August, she would be accessible from the sea. The others gathered round and we studied the dates.

"July is too early," I said. "August will be quite soon enough. I was on to the meteorological people yesterday and they say sunset in the southern Baltic in the middle of August is about eight o'clock, local time. That means we could start operations in the neighbourhood about nine, which is quite late enough if we're to get clear before morning. I don't fancy Riga, anyhow. It's protected by a couple of big islands in a deep gulf. Tallinn is a much better proposition."

Steve thought so too. He and I had been to Tallinn on a Press trip just after its so-called 'liberation' by the Red Army. I had only a faint recollection of the topography of the place, but the people had struck me as being very civilized, and far from friendly to the Soviet authorities.

Denny was still slowly perusing the schedule. "There's one day at Tallinn," he said, "when they're not dancing. Look—*Swan Lake* on August 12, *Sleeping Princess* on August 13 and *Don Quixote* on August 15. Nothing at all on the 14th."

"That'll be the Day of Rest," said Steve, with a grin. We were to remember that later. It nearly proved to be the Night of the Long Knives for us.

Denny said: "Tallinn's a long way from Moscow. Svetlana could get into a lot of trouble on the journey. And it's just the sort of place where the N.K.V.D. would be keeping their eyes skinned."

We thought that over. It certainly wouldn't be safe for Svetlana to stay there long without proper papers. In fact, if she weren't on official business she'd have to go in more or less on the same day she was to be taken off. If only she could get to Leningrad for a legitimate stay, it would be a comparatively short journey on to Tallinn. I said, "Steve, do you think you could get her to Leningrad?"

"I don't figure there should be much difficulty about that," said Steve. "After all, she's my secretary. I'm darned sure they wouldn't let *me* go to Tallinn—not after what I wrote about it last time—but they'd let me go to Leningrad. I could say I wanted to do a couple of broadcasts on the progress of reconstruction. Naturally I should have her come along. Then all we'd want would be a single ticket and she could travel on alone to Tallinn."

I suddenly realized that Steve was going to get himself into pretty bad trouble on our account if he wasn't very careful. "You'll have to keep out of it," I said. "If Svetlana escapes and they can pin anything on you, they'll jail you for a certainty."

"That's okay," said Steve. "Believe me, I won't do anything that'll get me in trouble. I'm in the dog-house already and I'm not going to make things worse. I'm due to leave for good in October and oh boy, have I got my eye on the date!"

"Well," I said, "it'll be Christmas in the Lubianka for you if you're not careful."

Steve patted my shoulder. "Now take it easy, *tovarisch*. What could be more innocent and normal than for me to have my secretary go with me on a business trip to Leningrad? It's always done. They know my Russian is pretty cock-eyed. And if she likes to clear off without telling me when we get to Leningrad—hell, that's her affair, not mine."

I wasn't convinced, but if Steve thought he could face the N.K.V.D. with that story I wasn't going to do any more dissuading. I thought he'd probably get away with it so long as he was careful. After all, he was an American of some repute, and they wouldn't dare to jail him without something fairly substantial in the way of proof. I didn't raise the subject of what would happen to him if they caught Svetlana actually making the attempt and questioned her. That was one of the things that didn't bear thinking of by any of us, though no doubt it was in all our minds.

Denny was still a bit worried about the last stage of the journey for Svetlana—how she'd manage about the railway ticket and what she'd do when she got to Tallinn. Then Steve gave an exclamation of disgust. "I'm a dope," he said. "I *know* a woman in Tallinn—at least, I used to. Hell, though, I can't recall her address. Maybe Svetlana knows."

I remembered now whom he meant. It was a woman he'd met on our trip and got a lot of information from about what happened when the Russians went into Tallinn. I said, "You mean the dressmaker—Rosa?"

"That's the dame. I delivered a letter for her to some friends of hers in Texas. My, was she bitter about the Russians! I wish I could remember her second name."

"She could be very useful," I said. "Definitely worth trying to trace. She might help with the ticket, and she'd be someone to go to in a jam."

"I expect Svetlana will remember her address," said Denny confidently. For the moment, we left it at that.

"What worries me most," I told Steve, "is the difficulty of communicating with you after you're back in Moscow. However carefully we make our arrangements before you leave here there are bound to be a lot of uncertainties until the very last minute. We can hardly conspire through the open post or by cable. It seems to me we should need to have a long talk with you about once a week."

"It's a bit far to commute," said Steve, with a grin.

The difficulty loomed larger the more we thought about it. We should have to depend on Steve for making all the arrangements and for letting us know that they were made. Suppose, for instance, that in the last week or so Marya found she wouldn't be going to Tallinn after all, or Svetlana fell ill, or the time of the rendezvous had to be changed. How could he let us know?

I poured Steve out some more whisky, and the sight of it must have stimulated him. He said: "I wouldn't have any trouble sending you short messages while you were still in London. I could send service cables to my bureau here and you could pick them up. They'd play. There could be a key word at the beginning of the cables which showed they were for you. I shouldn't be able to give you a lot of information, unless we worked out an elaborate code, but I could give you the answers on some of the points we'd left open."

"I don't see how," said Denny. "I thought the censor always stopped cables he didn't understand."

"Ah, but he would understand. Let's take an example. You'll want to know that I've fixed up something satisfactory about, say, Svetlana's ticket. I can't cable that in so many words, but I can cable asking our chap Donovan to send me out a couple of silk shirts. We can arrange beforehand that that means it's okay about the ticket. Or I could cable the bureau to send flowers to an old friend in Bootle. That could mean I was having trouble. If we make a list in advance of all the main items of information on which you'll need assurance, with the alternative answers, we can cover all the chief possibilities without risk. How's that for an idea?"

It seemed fine to us, but it didn't get us over the main problem. I said, "That's going to be all right while we're in touch with your office, but if all goes well we'll be on the high seas in a few weeks from now, and we'll have to allow ourselves at least two months to get to the Baltic."

"Hell," said Steve, "the *Mayflower* got to America in three months!"

Denny and I laughed. I said: "Well, we're not the *Mayflower*. We shan't dare stick our noses out except in a flat calm."

I could see Steve wasn't inclined to accept our own estimate of our sailing abilities, but he didn't try to argue about our proposed timetable. He was wrestling with another idea, and when he produced it it was something worth waiting for.

"Why shouldn't we use my broadcasts for communicating?" he said. "I'm on a regular schedule, so you'd know just when you could get me."

"H'rrrmp!" I said. "It would be a pleasure. But I still don't get it. What about the censor?"

"We'd have a real code. I've always wanted to try that sort of thing." Steve's eyes shone. He was right back to the days when *Treasure Island* had been the real world to him. "I'll have to work it out, but it'll be something quite simple. How's your shorthand, Philip?"

"Rusty," I said, "but I think I could get you down if you spoke slowly."

"That's all I need. Of course, there wouldn't be a message in every broadcast. I should give you a harmless keyword at the beginning of the talk if there was something coming that you needed to hear, and if I didn't give it you could switch off. For instance, I could start the broadcast with the word 'today' if there was meat in it. 'Today all Moscow is in holiday mood'—that sort of thing. Then you'd take it down verbatim and extract what you needed. Say every ninth word, counting the keyword 'today' as the first word. The censors are pretty dumb—look how they always

47

pass anything ironical that we send. If they can't smell out a simple subtlety like saying 'all the Russians simply love the N.K.V.D.' they're not likely to start counting words."

"I'm getting carried away," I said. "For heaven's sake let's not get over-confident."

I took a drink and thought about Steve's plan. I knew the Moscow censors as well as anyone, and I realized that Steve was right. They didn't look much below the surface and they certainly wouldn't search for a code unless they suspected that one existed. The fact that messages would be comparatively rare would be an additional safeguard.

"It's a cinch," said Steve. "I'll knock something out tonight—a trial message of some sort—and we'll give the system the once-over tomorrow. I'm sure it'll work. If it does, you'll be kept informed right up to the last minute. You'll have to take a good portable radio to sea with you. If I go to Leningrad I'll even be able to broadcast from there. I'll be able to give you an eleventh-hour situation report. Gee, what a story it's going to be!"

A picture flashed through my mind of Denny trying to hold *Dawn* in half a gale while I bounced about in the bilge trying to get a broadcast down in shorthand by the light of a hurricane lamp. It would be a story all right!

There wasn't very much more we could discuss that night. I felt we'd made good progress, particularly in deciding on the general area of operations. The next thing was to get hold of a chart of the Tallinn district and some good guide-books about the town and neighbourhood, and to give a little more thought to the nautical side of the undertaking. We talked for a while about general matters and then the party broke up. We arranged to meet again the following evening at the same time. Steve said he planned to be in London for just under a fortnight, but naturally he'd got a lot of people to see.

Next morning early I went along to the Admiralty chart agents and bought a copy of the *Baltic Pilot*. I also got some fairly large-scale charts of the Tallinn approaches and of the entrance to the Gulf of Finland, showing the northern coast. We should need a lot more charts later on, but these seemed to be the essential ones for preliminary planning. I was very happy about the way circumstances had conspired to make us choose Tallinn. To reach it, we shouldn't have to go very far into the Gulf or to spend long there. It was within comparatively easy sailing of Stockholm if we had a fair wind, and though it was set in a bay, like so many ports, its approaches didn't look quite such an obvious trap as the approaches to Riga.

I was eager to settle down to serious study of the charts, but I thought I had better assemble as much raw material as possible before we went into a huddle again that night. By the late afternoon I had acquired half a dozen books about the Baltic States, the Baltic Sea and Tallinn. As it happened, they turned out to be either very much out of date or much too slight and general for my purposes. There was no recent *Baedeker*, and most of the books related to the time when Estonia had been either a part of old Tsarist Russia or—for a brief period—an independent State. But after all it was topography rather than history that we were interested in, and I managed to find one passable map of the district.

Steve arrived at the flat just before nine looking disgustingly pleased with himself, and I concluded that he'd made progress with his cypher. He could barely wait until Denny arrived before producing a couple of sheets of manuscript and settling himself down to read out what was written there. I grabbed a pencil, and after a preliminary 'H'rrrmp' Steve started off in his rich bass.

"Hello, X.Y.Z.," he said, "this is Steve Quillan calling you from Leningrad." He stopped reading and said: "That's the stock introduction. It doesn't count for words." Then he went on: "Today I've been touring this battered city, studying all the reconstruction work in progress. Leningraders have sure set themselves tremendous tasks. One of the architects, a blonde vital woman of about forty, told me that on all occasions Leningrad has reckoned to show the way to other parts of Soviet Russia in making good progress with its economic plans and that with luck and hard work it should keep its lead. Most of the buildings here that were blitzed during the long hard siege of 1942 and 1943 have now been completely rebuilt or renovated, and as you walk down the old Nevsky Prospekt you might think you were back in the 'thirties . . ."

Steve's voice trailed off. "Got that?" he asked.

"Easily," I said. "Now I know why Svetlana likes being your secretary. Carry on."

"That's all for now," said Steve, "unless you'd like me to tell you more about the Nevsky Prospekt. You've got all you need. I'm afraid it's a bit rough but I had to dash it off rather quickly."

I made a quick transcription of my shorthand and underlined every ninth word, reckoning 'today' as the first word just as Steve had instructed. Then I wrote out the underlined words consecutively. They read ALL SET BLONDE ON WAY GOOD LUCK and after that there was a lot of rubbish which showed that the message was ended.

I felt shaky with excitement. Although I had known what was supposed to happen it did seem rather a miracle that so terse and relevant a communication should have emerged from Steve's easy and colloquial chatter.

"You see," said Steve, "it works. This is the night of August 13. You and Denny are lying somewhere off the coast of Estonia, waiting to go in the next day. Your nerves are all to bits with anxiety. You wonder what's happened to Svetlana. You pick me up on your radio and you get that message. You feel like a million dollars and turn in with easy minds."

"Steve," I said, "you're a wizard. I wouldn't have believed it. The only snag I can think of is that if you make many of these propaganda broadcasts your network will give you the sack."

Steve grinned amiably. "Don't forget I'm due for a new assignment in October anyway. My chief'll put it down to Moscow madness—he knows that everyone goes screwy there sooner or later. My predecessor set his room on fire! After all, I shall have to make the messages pretty friendly so as to be sure nothing will be censored out of them."

That was something I hadn't thought of. I remembered how, if a censor happened to be in a bad mood, he'd knock out a word here and there just to show his authority—and that would spoil the order of the code. But Steve wasn't worried.

"In the first place," he said, "I'll behave myself so well from now on that they'll think I've undergone a political conversion. I'll be polite and considerate even to the censors. And I'll give myself plenty of time before important broadcasts so that if they do cut out anything I'll still be able to suggest an alternative wording. I don't see any prospect of real trouble there."

"Don't overdo the friendliness, that's all!" I said. "Remember they're as suspicious of their friends as of their enemies."

Denny had been studying the simple cryptogram with some care. He said: "I don't want to be a wet blanket, but that message *is* rather an easy one. If you were trying to tell us something really complicated it would be much more difficult. If you were giving us new instructions, for instance, you might have to become quite technical."

But Steve was confident. "You leave it to Uncle," he said. "This is just a trial run. Before long I'll be giving you the specifications of the latest Russian tank in a broadcast on the virtues of the Heroine Mother!"

I was more than content to leave it to him. There was no doubt that Steve's ingenuity had swept away a big barrier. With a two-way conversation by cable in the early stages, and a one-way information service on the last lap, we should have at least a sporting chance of doing the right thing at the right time.

In good spirits we turned to examine the chart of the Tallinn approaches.

Chapter Five

We spent the next hour planning in detail how best to break another country's laws. I sat at the table with the atlas and charts, and the other two shared the pile of guide-books. There was quite a library atmosphere about the place.

The first thing was to choose the exact spot where the attempt was to be made. We had little personal knowledge of local conditions. The best we could do was to build up some sort of picture of the Tallinn area from the rather sketchy information in the guide-books and hope that our reconstruction wouldn't prove too different from the reality.

I've drawn a rough map of the area to make the position clearer. It will be seen that Tallinn lies in a bay about eight miles deep, and that the width across the entrance, between Cape Sourop in the west and Aegna Island in the east, is about ten miles. The whole bay faces roughly north-west. The single large island of Nais lies across the approaches, but there's plenty of sea room on either side of it for ships coming into harbour. The eastern side of the bay is formed by the five-mile-long neck of land called the Viimsi Peninsula, which stretches out to Aegna Island.

In choosing a landfall there were three things to take into account. From the girls' point of view, the nearer it was to Tallinn the better. They would have less difficulty in reaching the spot and would be less likely to attract unwelcome attention. For Denny and me, however, the exact opposite was true. An incoming dinghy would stand a greater risk of being seen near Tallinn than if it aimed to make contact some miles outside the town. Also there would be farther to row, for *Dawn* herself must obviously be anchored well away from the harbour to escape notice and to be ready for a quick getaway. Finally, whatever rendezvous we chose must be easily identifiable from the sea in the dark. We couldn't afford any hide-and-seek business on the beach. We must do without any preliminary rehearsal or reconnaissance, and yet go in with the precision of a commando raid, hitting the exact spot.

We ruled out the two chief bights that make up Tallinn Harbour proper on the ground that they looked too much like the lion's mouth. Kakomiag Bay, in the extreme west, was invitingly open to the sea, but I didn't see anything there suggesting itself as a suitable meeting-point. I regretted, not for the first time, that I hadn't used my few days in Tallinn more profitably.

Suddenly Steve took his head out of his guide-book and said: "Say, I guess we want to choose a location where the girls would have a good reason for being on a warm August night. What about this place Kadriorg? Just outside the town on the eastern outskirts. There's an old palace and park there, and a fine bathing beach. So the book says. Maybe the girls could be bathing."

"What, at ten o'clock at night?" said Denny.

Steve looked a bit dashed. "You never can tell with these darned Russians," he said. He sank deeper into his chair and went on reading, making little growling noises to himself. But soon he was bolt upright again. "Just listen to this, folks." He cleared his throat and read out, "'On warm summer nights the whole of Tallinn goes out in cars to swim at Pirita'." See what I mean—they *do* swim at night. The trouble with you British is that your minds are closed to new ideas. Where *is* Pirita, anyway?"

We found that easily enough. According to the chart it was a little coastal place on the south bank of a river about a couple of miles east of the town. From it a road or track turned northwards up the Viimsi Peninsula. Just across the river the ruins of an old monastery were marked. Since they were on the chart they must be a navigation aid but they wouldn't be any use to us at night.

"Pirita's about the right distance from Tallinn," said Denny. "The girls could take an evening stroll with all the other people and then slip away somewhere."

"That's right," said Steve, "it's a pushover." He had that 'human interest' look on his face that I'd seen so often when he was broadcasting. "This Pirita place sounds just what we want. Imagine the scene on the night of August 14. . . . It's a warm dry evening. The air is scented with dog-roses . . ." He caught my eye. "Well, with something, anyway. There are streams of young girls walking out along that road. Some are with their Red Army lovers, going off to canoodle on the banks of the river. Some are walking in pairs, hoping for a pick-up. There's an atmosphere of holiday and gaiety. There's a lighted café by the sea, maybe a band and dancing. Everybody's having fun and making lots of noise. Some people are having a moonlight dip . . ."

"It'll be a moonless night," I said.

"All right, a starlight dip. You'll allow there may be stars? Right. Our girls go out from Tallinn with the mob, their swimming things tucked conspicuously under their arms. They give the air to any fellows who may try to get fresh and they find their own quiet spot on the beach. That shouldn't be difficult—you know most folks make for the same ten-yard strip on any beach, just to be sociable. The girls have a little swim, and then they wait for you to come in with the dinghy. How's that?"

I said, "M'm." I was seeing more and more clearly the crux of our problem. The only point on the beach we could be certain of hitting accurately was a distinctively lighted one. From that point of view Pirita would be all right—we could find it. But it was precisely such lighted places which would be most dangerous. There'd probably be a glow over the water from all the lights. Even if the girls were a couple of hundred yards away from the crowd there might be swimmers in the water or odd couples on the beach. I voiced my misgivings.

"Okay," said Steve. "Let's say the girls take a tram out to Pirita to save their feet—there is one, according to my book—and then they feel like a bit of a stroll up the Viimsi Peninsula. They walk along this coastal track. They might be going to one of the farmhouses out on the Peninsula. They keep going for a couple of miles and presently they reach a swell little bay half-way up the

Peninsula, which doesn't seem to have a name. Got it? It's probably quite deserted. They sit down on the beach and shine a torch out to sea to guide you in. What about that?"

I found the little bay on the chart and on the map. I was just going to point out that shining a light out to sea was probably about the most suspicious thing anybody could do in those parts, when I saw something that set me tingling with excitement. On the shore above the bay the chart showed a pair of navigational leading lights.

I explained the significance of the discovery to the others. The idea is that a ship approaching a harbour through waters where there are dangerous shoals can be led in on a safe course by keeping two specially-erected shore lights in a vertical line. One light is some distance in front of the other and the rear one is higher. As long as the lights are kept in line a ship is as safe as though it were on a radio beam. Directly the lights get out of line the ship knows she is off her course. If our dinghy kept the lights in line it could reach this particular bit of beach with complete certainty on the blackest night.

Steve was impressed, but still a bit puzzled. He said: "If the lights lead *you* in there, they'll lead other ships in too. It must be quite a populated spot, that bay."

I explained that on the contrary there was probably nothing there at all except the two light structures, which the chart said were automatic and unattended. It was clear that their purpose was to guide ships approaching Tallinn Roads away from a dangerous shoal called the Vake. But once the ships were safely past the shoal, and long before they approached the Viimsi coast, they would bring another pair of leading lights into line from the south and would alter course for the harbour. If our dinghy continued on its way to the Peninsula it would be away from all shipping.

A great burden had rolled off my mind. The problem of making contact with the girls in the dark seemed solved. They couldn't possibly fail to find the Viimsi lights, which were considerable structures near the beach. They could sit down in the dark near the water's edge and talk about the Five-Year Plan until we arrived.

Then Steve had a bright idea. "If the dinghy's going to come in on a fixed track," he said, "I don't see why it need come right inshore. Why shouldn't the girls swim out to meet you, with the lights in line behind them? After all, it's only a matter of timing."

"That's all," said Denny sardonically, "just a matter of timing! All we have to do is to meet a couple of girls swimming in the dark at a certain split second four months ahead, and the whole thing's in the bag!"

We laughed. All the same, it was an idea which enormously reduced certain obvious risks. If there did happen to be coast-guards about, a dinghy coming in at night and taking two girls off the beach would arouse instant suspicion. But nothing could look less like an illegal attempt to leave the country than two girls undressing on a beach on a summer night, piling their clothes on the sand, and swimming off gaily into the darkness. They could do it under the very nose of a coastguard and get away with it.

There were hazards in this swimming project, of course. Denny, the landsman, said he'd never seen Svetlana swim, and he thought that in any case she'd need a lot of practice. Steve, with alacrity, said he'd see to that. Then again, none of us knew whether it was practicable to swim out from a shore keeping two lights in line behind you, but I could imagine myself doing if it I swam on my back or trod water occasionally. The girls could hardly come to any harm—the sea would be warm, and in the Baltic there wouldn't be any strong tides at that time of the year. There was, I supposed, just an outside chance that they might miss the dinghy, though if we all conscientiously kept the lights in line I couldn't see how. Even if we did miss each other no harm would be done. They would simply swim back and meet us ashore. Personally, I thought the idea an excellent one.

Then the cautious Denny had to raise a new doubt. He said, "I suppose those Viimsi lights are still there?"

How did I know? The chart was the best I could get, but still an old one. Now that I studied it more closely I found a warning panel which read, "The existence and position of many of the lights, buoys and other aids to navigation shown on this chart and formerly maintained by the Russian Government cannot be relied on." That was twenty years ago. It was difficult to know what the secretive Russians had done since then. For one thing, there'd been a war. On the other hand, leading lights of some sort on Viimsi were vital to the safety of Tallinn Harbour and could scarcely have been dispensed with. But it was plain that we should have to make certain, for our whole plan was beginning to turn on the lights. They would have to be checked on the spot. There was clearly a lot of work in store for Steve's Estonian dressmaker, if he could trace her.

There was not much more that we could usefully discuss together. Denny and I would have to tackle the major problem of reaching Viimsi, but over that Steve couldn't help. Nor could we help as far as the girls were concerned. Steve would have to handle the Russian end alone and give us the 'all clear' if he could. I felt we had made a good job of the outline plan—it was full of hazards that couldn't be eliminated but there was nothing on which one could put a finger and say 'That's impossible.' After a little more discussion we agreed that contact with the girls should be established a quarter of a mile off the Viimsi lights at 10 p.m. local time on the night to August 14. That was something to work to. I undertook of give Steve a list of the matters on which we should want assurance by cable.

Just before we broke up Denny said: "Suppose at the last minute either we or they can't make it. Do we have an arrangement to try again?"

That was a poser. The most likely reason for last-minute failure would be bad weather, and over that we were going to need all the luck in the world. We didn't know then, of course, that the summer of 1947 was going to be the finest of the century. Our 'second string' plans were rather half-hearted from the beginning, chiefly because the obstacles to a second attempt seemed almost insuperable. For us, it would mean taking *Dawn* out of Tallinn Bay and hanging about conspicuously in the approaches for an extra day. The girls might have much greater difficulty in keeping the appointment on the second night. All the same, if necessary we should have to make the attempt. We agreed that if we failed to make contact at the set time on the first night we should all try again the night after, and that if we were again unsuccessful we would abandon the undertaking. However remote the prospect might be that a second attempt could succeed, it was good for morale to know that the possibility existed.

We had one more meeting with Steve before he left, and cleared up some minor points. He told us that he'd fixed up with his bureau in London to keep in touch with me about cables. We gave him a provisional sailing date for *Dawn*—June 15. He took short noncommittal letters back with him for Marya and Svetlana. Most of the news, of course, he would tell them. After a rather depressing discussion we agreed that Svetlana should go through with her divorce—which cut no ice in British law anyway—to keep the Soviet authorities sweet and herself out of Kazakstan.

Denny had to be at work on the day Steve left, but I went down to the airport to see him off. He was in buoyant spirits. Over a last drink at the buffet he urged me not to worry about his end of the affair. "From now on, *tovarisch*," he said, "your job is to be at the rendezvous on the tick. My job is to do all that's humanly possible to see that the girls are there. If we both keep our eye on the ball, we'll be okay."

I said: "I don't know why you're doing this, Steve. It's damned dangerous, and you don't have to."

His eyes creased up in the old quizzical smile. He said: "Maybe I find life too uneventful. Maybe I just like you and Marya and the others." He put his glass down. "Or maybe," he added, "I'm just tired of watching Uncle Joe push people around. Say, we'll make a date. We'll have a party in your flat on October 15—that's my birthday. There'll be—five of us, and the drinks'll be on you. Okay?"

"Right," I said, and gripped his hand. Passengers were being called for the 'plane. Just before he went out on to the tarmac he said, "Don't forget to keep careful track of all my broadcasts all the time." And as an afterthought he added, "Shall I give Marya a kiss for you?"

I called, "Just one!" I've never known a correspondent yet who knew when to stop.

Well, that was that. I put up a little prayer for his safe landing and went off to the flat to pack some things. The next item on the agenda was obviously to get back to Southfleet and see how Joe was getting on with *Dawn*. If we were to sail on June 15 or thereabouts we had little more than six weeks left, and there was so much to do that it hardly bore thinking of. Denny had given a week's notice to his firm—much to their annoyance—and was determined to devote himself exclusively to boats for the rest of the time. There was one thing about Denny—having taken his decision he never looked back. He'd already begun to swot up navigation, and to my great relief he seemed completely at home with logarithms and angles and stuff that made my head reel. I suppose that was the result of his technical training. I felt I could safely leave all that part of the trip to him.

Dawn was changed out of all recognition and I wasn't surprised that Joe looked pleased with himself. He'd painted her a smart grey—he would have preferred white but I thought grey would be less conspicuous—and he'd had the white sails tanned a red-brown for the same reason. Joe said the mainsail was a bit old but there was certainly no time to have a new one made and he thought it would do unless we had a particularly hard blow. In any case, there was a storm-jib and trysail in the locker for emergency. All the ropes and rigging had been renewed and most of the gear. Altogether, *Dawn* was beginning to look as though she'd soon be ready for sea. Joe couldn't have regarded her more affectionately if she'd been his own boat. He was very much on his mettle, not just to have *Dawn* ready for us in time but to make her one of the finest boats in the creek. All his pals were watching his progress, of course, and in that small, highly-skilled community he felt his reputation was at stake. He needn't have worried.

The days raced by. Joe had found a reconditioned engine that he thought would be suitable and Denny came down to help him fix it. I bought a new metal alloy dinghy which was roomy and yet light to handle and Joe snugged it down on the foredeck. While

I was in town choosing the dinghy I bought a whole sheaf of additional charts. I felt no end of an old salt, but the chap behind the counter handed them over as nonchalantly as though they'd been a guide to the Tower of London. After that I rushed around making inquiries about how you cleared for foreign ports and arranging for special supplies of food and petrol.

I told Joe of our plans in more detail, and he was as interested as though he'd been coming with us. He bent gravely over the chart of Tallinn and I pointed out the Viimsi leading lights and told him the part they were going to play. He studied the chart with an experienced nautical eye. Then he asked me where we proposed to anchor *Dawn* while we were making the journey in the dinghy.

I said I hadn't decided yet. "It mustn't be too far from the shore if we're to get back to her and clear territorial waters before daylight."

He pondered. "You haven't a lot of choice," he said. He indicated the wide stretch of deepish water opposite Viimsi. "You can't drop your hook in twenty fathoms." Then he suddenly said: "There's another thing. How are you going to find *Dawn* again in the dark?"

That was something we hadn't thought of at all. The idea of combing Tallinn Bay at midnight looking for an unlighted yacht wasn't exactly pleasing—and she'd certainly have to be unlighted. The solution was really obvious, and it came to me as I stared at the chart. "Why," I said, "we'll anchor *Dawn* in line with the Viimsi lights. Then as long as the rower keeps the lights in line on his way back he's bound to reach her sooner or later."

Joe nodded. He studied the chart intently for a while and took some measurements. Then he said: "I think I've got a better idea. Why not anchor *Dawn* actually over the Vake shoal? The least depth is two fathoms, so she'd be in no danger. The shoal is lit by a lighted buoy with a flash every four seconds, so the dinghy couldn't miss it. If *Dawn* were left close up against the buoy you could row straight for the flash without bothering about keeping the leading lights in line. It's about the right distance—four miles from the shore—and handy for a quick run out to sea."

That was about the longest speech I'd ever heard Joe make, but every word of it was sound sense. His plan solved several problems at once. We could sail confidently into Tallinn Bay in the dark, knowing precisely where we were going. We could anchor at a spot which other ships would steer clear of because of the shoal, and we should thus avoid the danger of being either seen or run down in the dark. I made a mental note that Steve must be asked to check up somehow on the Vake buoy.

I congratulated Joe on his ingenuity, and we rolled up the charts. I said, "Well, what do you think of the plan now that you've heard it all?"

The light of battle—for it was almost that—faded from Joe's eyes, and the old cautious look took possession again. "It's fine," he said, "on paper."

"You think we'll run into trouble in Tallinn?"

"I wasn't thinking so much about Tallinn," said Joe.

"What, then?"

"Well, I was thinking about a young fellow who was here last summer—an N.C.O. in the Army, I think he was, just demobbed. He'd made up his mind to sail to South America, single-handed, in a 22-foot ketch. He spent months fitting her out and laying in stores and getting everything shipshape and he was full of confidence about the trip."

"Well?"

Joe grinned broadly. "He ran aground on a sandbank about ten miles from here and the boat broke up. He was taken off by the Margate lifeboat and got a shore job with a fishmonger at Canvey!"

I realized that even Joe could be highly objectionable at times.

Chapter Six

As soon as his week's notice had expired Denny came down to Southfleet to stay, and our preparations moved forward much faster. He applied himself to all his tasks with a doggedness which aroused my admiration, and he was quite impervious to the sly digs Joe used sometimes to make at his expense. Having decided that summer had come, and that the long woollen underpants he usually wore in winter were no longer necessary, he now wore a very short pair of shorts, and Joe said that with those knobbly knees he only needed a long pole to make him look like an overgrown boy scout. He had sought the advice of a chemist about his tendency to seasickness. I can imagine it was a most earnest interview. The result was that he arrived at Southfleet equipped with three different nostrums, one of which he took every time he went out in a boat. I don't know whether it was the pills, or smoother water, or sheer will-power, but he had no more misadventures of that type. His worst trouble was clumsiness. His feet were still a constant menace. He was always standing on a rope end, or stepping back into a pot of paint, or giving his head an almighty crack on some projection in the cabin. No doubt he would learn to move more cautiously once we were at sea, but he was obviously going to learn the hard way.

Just because he was so awkward aboard, I was uncomfortable about his inability to swim. He was just the kind of chap to trip over something and take a header into the sea. I tried to give him a few lessons in the creek. He did his best but it was hopeless. It went against his deepest instincts to take both feet off the ground at the same time. In the end we decided that the time would be more profitably spent in sailing.

Denny always fetched the papers in the morning, and one day he came back with a rather grim look on his face. He said: "More trouble. Have a look at this."

Joe and I gathered round. What had caught Denny's eye was a short paragraph from a correspondent in one of the Scandinavian capitals reporting that a couple of small ships had been mysteriously involved with the Russians in the Baltic. One of them had disappeared altogether with her crew, and it was believed that she had either been sunk or taken by the Russians into some port. The other boat was found floating but damaged, and minus her crew. The report said it was considered possible that a Russian patrol boat had intercepted both ships on the high seas.

The story was a little disturbing, but I wasn't inclined to attach too much importance to it. The report was no doubt published in good faith, but there was a good deal of hypothesis about it, and the facts might be quite different. At various times a good deal of unreliable news about Russia had come out of Scandinavia. This story might be on a par with reports of 'flying saucers' in the Baltic, which didn't seem to have amounted to much in the end.

"Anyway," I said, "even if the Russians are behaving like that, I don't see that there's very much we can do about it except keep a sharp lookout and hope for the best."

A mischievous look came over Joe's face. He said, "You'd better take the old punt gun."

I said, "What punt gun?"

Joe led us round to the back of his workshop, where there was a lot of old junk. Fastened to a stake driven into the saltings was a light skiff which he said had once been used for wild-fowling. It had evidently been long neglected and was in bad shape. "I thought I might use it," Joe said, "but I've been too busy. I bought it last year. The owner was anxious to get rid of it, so I did him a favour."

"Why was he anxious to get rid of it?" asked Denny suspiciously.

"As a matter of fact," said Joe, "he blew a finger off messing about with a charge. Put too much powder in or something. Look, this is the gun." He undid the canvas cover and disclosed a rusty metal barrel, a good ten feet long, lying in the bottom.

"Blimey!" said Denny, staring at it.

Personally, I didn't like the look of it at all, but Denny was intrigued. The weapon was fantastically old—under the rust you could see the metal had once been chased. Someone had cherished it in days gone by. It had a bore of about two inches, and a heavy trigger.

Although I'd been a war correspondent, what I knew about the actual operation of weapons of any sort would barely have covered a sixpence. I'd been more interested in the chaps who fired them. But Denny had been through a gunnery course during his tank training, and was in any case always fascinated by bits of metal.

Soon he had the thing out of the skiff and was examining it with intense interest. "It's an old muzzle-loader," he said. "See, you put the powder down the muzzle, then a wad of oakum or something, then you pour in the shot and shove in another wad, and she's loaded. The trigger explodes a cap and detonates the powder and everything blows up. It must take quite a while to load, Joe."

"Not as long as you'd think," said Joe. "A couple of minutes, perhaps. The fellow who owned it used to load it before he put it aboard. That was one of the troubles—once he'd fired it he had to go ashore and unsling it and start from the beginning again. He couldn't afford to miss. I remember he used to say it cost him five bob every time he fired it, but he used to get a lot of duck and widgeon."

"What does it fire?" I asked.

"Oh," said Denny, "small shot, bent nails, old bedsteads! Practically anything. What about the recoil, Joe? What did he do about that?"

"He had it slung in a sort of rope cradle," said Joe. "I think it was his own idea. He said it worked all right."

"You're not seriously thinking of taking this along, Denny?" I asked. "Damn it, aren't the perils of the sea bad enough without adding to them?"

"It's a useful weapon," said Denny thoughtfully. "You could do a lot of damage with it, you know. And what's more natural than that we should do a bit of duck-shooting on our holiday?"

"Not in August," said Joe, with a grin.

"No? Well, I don't know much about duck anyway," said the urban Denny. "But we could still take the gun aboard and keep it hidden." He looked across at *Dawn* and then back again at the stout steel gun. "Couldn't we rig it up as a dummy bowsprit, Joe? Take the wooden one off and put this on instead? It's about the right length and diameter, and nobody would know it wasn't the real thing unless they inspected it closely. We could paint it the colour of the wood and varnish it."

Joe considered. He and Denny together were a menace. "I dare say we could," he said. "But what about the recoil?"

They became all technical again. I heard them discussing something about a sliding tube, and then they thought of springs, and Joe wondered about the effect of so much weight in the bows. Of course, the more they discussed it the more interested they became, until in the end they felt they just had to fix the gun to see if their ideas worked out all right. Altogether, what with cleaning and oiling the gun, and then fixing it and painting it, I reckon it kept both of them busy for the best part of three days. I had no part in it—I went up to town on business and left them to it.

One of my first calls was at Steve's office to see if there were any messages. There were no cables, but he'd already done five broadcasts, and two of them were interesting. One was an account of the progress of the Russian ballet. It described how the Russians were anxious to keep up the flow of new talent by means of their ballet schools, and how some of the younger girls were coming along nicely. Then it mentioned half a dozen names, including Lamarkina—that was Marya—who was being given a big chance this year by going on tour with some of the stars and perhaps dancing some of the lead parts in the provinces. I took that broadcast as confirmation of what we already knew about the tour and as Steve's way of showing that he had the situation well in hand. I noticed that Donovan took a gloomy view of his colleague's new-found interest in the Russian ballet.

The other broadcast made me laugh. It was a lighthearted colourful piece about Soviet youth and Soviet sport. It said among other things that after an exceptionally good winter for ski-ing the young people were now turning to summer activities, and were getting very interested in what Steve called 'aquatics'. Swimming was as popular as ever. "Any fine day," said the broadcast, "if you go along to the famous bathing beach at Khimki you can see scores of blonde and well-built young Russians girls practising new strokes for the strenuous sporting events ahead." Steve was certainly enjoying himself. I hoped for Svetlana's sake that the water in the Moskva river was warmer than that in Southfleet creek.

Meanwhile, I had my own communication problem. Somehow, I had to ask Steve to make sure that the light buoy on the Vake shoal was still functioning. I thought at first that if I sent him a cable starting with his own keyword 'today' and using his own cypher system I might be able to get the message through, but when I tried to draft such a cable I had trouble. The word Vake in a short cable stuck out like a sore thumb, and I couldn't think of any descriptive circumlocution which would leave Steve in no doubt about what I wanted. Finally, I decided that the safest way would be to wrap my requirements up in a long letter and send it through the open post. Bang in the middle of a rigmarole of personal news I wrote:

By the way, do you remember meeting old Vake at my flat this summer—the fellow with the flashing eyes? His boy was over here a couple of days ago—a nice young fellow whom I'd like you to meet some time. He used to be rather a spoilt kid, but it seemed to me he'd changed a good deal lately and now he wants to go into the newspaper business. I'm interested in the boy and some time when you're around I'd like to know what you think of him.

I didn't think a censor would make anything of that, but I felt sure

Steve would remember the Vake light and would get the idea without difficulty.

When I got back to Southfleet I found that Denny and Joe had got the punt gun in place, and I had to admit that they'd made it look remarkably like a real bowsprit. Denny had combed the local garages until he had found the springs he wanted, and Joe had ingeniously adapted the metal barrel so that it was actually capable of doing the work of a bowsprit in carrying the foot of the jib. Denny had fixed a rubber cap over the muzzle to keep the barrel free from water, and the firing mechanism and springs were securely covered with a piece of waterproof sheet. The barrel had been painted a light brown and varnished. The whole thing looked very normal and innocuous. Denny had managed to make contact with the former owner of the gun by telephone, and had briefed himself about the right amount of powder and shot to use. I couldn't feel that he'd gone to the best sources for his information, but it transpired that the accident to the owner's finger had been only indirectly concerned with the gun—at least, so Denny assured me. Denny had laid in a store of small roundshot and powder, as well as a box of caps to detonate the charge, and he told me proudly that the gun was loaded and that we were ready for battle! He was keen to go off somewhere and fire it right away, just to make sure that it worked, but Joe was fitting a second fresh-water tank and had his tools all over the place, so we decided to wait for a more convenient moment.

Joe said, what about secondary armament? Weren't we taking a couple of revolvers? I squashed that idea before Denny could focus his attention on it. We should have to spend a good deal of time in the territorial waters of friendly countries, and we might even have to claim the right of innocent passage in Estonian waters at some time, and I didn't like all these bellicose preparations. It seemed to me that if we couldn't succeed in our mission by skill and secrecy there was no chance of succeeding by force, and that if we tried to do so we should be asking for the worst sort of-trouble. I regarded the punt gun as nothing more than the eccentricity of a man who by his hard work had earned the right to be humoured, and I hoped profoundly that no one would ever notice it.

We were now almost into June and our preparations were nearing completion. All but a few perishable stores were aboard, and a colossal inventory it was. In the quietness of the short nights I went over and over in my mind the list of things we should need, trying to visualize while there was still time the demands that each emergency might make on us. If there was the least element of doubt I added to the list. To show how thorough we had to be, one of the things we had to think of was a complete outfit for each of the two girls. According to our plan they'd be swimming out to the dinghy in nothing but costumes, and for quite a while after that—at least until we reached Stockholm—they'd have nothing at all except what we took for them. That was a responsibility which involved a whip-round among our friends for coupons, a lot of guessing about measurements, and a quite fantastic shopping expedition. Denny explained to the slightly puzzled shop assistant that it was to be a surprise for our wives. The assistant regarded the pile of silk stockings, slips and sou'westers and said she was sure it would be.

On June 3, a glorious day, Joe formally pronounced *Dawn* ready for sea. Apart from her hull, she was virtually a new boat, and in her solid way she looked magnificent. We all three went aboard that afternoon when the tide began to flow, because Joe wanted to try her himself under sail before Denny and I took her down the estuary. We spent the rest of the day out in her, and when we finally brought up in the old spot Joe declared himself completely satisfied with her performance. So, judging by the comments I heard in the creek, was everybody else. Nobody had the least idea of our real destination, of course. It had been impossible to conceal the large quantities of stores we had taken aboard and the meticulous preparations we had made, but our story was that we were going through the French canals to the Mediterranean.

The next day, June 4, was the real test. Denny and I slept aboard so that we could get away as soon as the ship floated. We planned to have a long day's sail out to the Nore and back, and I felt very much on my mettle, but confident. After *Wayfarer, Dawn* seemed as safe and comfortable as a liner. All her gear, of course, was much heavier to handle than anything I'd been used to, and the brand new ropes were hard on the hands. But Denny, who had learned a good deal by now even if a lot of it was book knowledge, proved far more useful than he had been at first. It is true he was more interested in the compass and the course we were sailing and the buoys we had to identify than he was in the set of the sails and the niceties of pointing, but we had agreed that his main job should be navigation. All the same, I was determined that he should actually sail the boat himself for a spell and get the feel of her.

It was a lovely day and we had a splendid beat to the Nore. Conditions were so good that I almost wished we were on our way instead of merely having a practice sail. If we could be blessed with three days of such weather for our passage to Sweden it would put us in good heart for the more difficult task to follow.

Just before noon, when we were far out to sea, Denny said, "What about trying the gun?" He assured me that the firearm was in splendid condition and he could positively guarantee that nothing untoward would happen. There wasn't, of course, anything in particular to fire at. The only objects in sight were the big iron navigation buoys, and Denny was much too law-abiding by nature to think of using those as a target. However, he said he only wanted to make sure the gun actually worked, and that it would be sufficient to fire it off into space.

Denny went forward to operate the contrivance while I stood by with one eye on the life-buoy and the other on the fire extinguisher. There was no means of taking off the rubber cap at the end of the muzzle since it was far out over the water, but Denny had laid in some spares and was content to shoot through it. He took the waterproof cover off the breech, or whatever the thing was called, placed a cap in the little pan provided for the purpose, crouched down behind the mast with his face turned away, and pulled the trigger. There was a noise like a bomb going off, and a lot of smoke from the breech and the muzzle. The whole ship shuddered, and I couldn't blame it. A fragment of rubber hanging from the muzzle showed that the shot had gone on its way, and Denny said he had seen some of it spattering the surface of the water, though I suspect that was his imagination. His ingenious recoil gadget had worked admirably, and altogether he seemed rather pleased with himself.

"That cost you ten bob," he said. He gave the barrel an affectionate pat and replaced the waterproof cover. As far as I could see, the boat had suffered no harm.

After a snack lunch we made a wide circle round the Nore and turned for home. Denny had had a spell at the tiller while we were close-hauled, and now I wanted him to take over while we were running. The breeze had stiffened a little, and was just strong enough to give us a smart sail back. It was almost dead aft, and I warned Denny to keep his eye on the boom and to look out for a gybe, for his steering was a bit erratic. He concentrated on the job and we began to make fine progress, with a creditably straight wake. Southend Pier soon emerged out of the warm afternoon haze and I reckoned we were doing a good five knots through the water.

Apart from a little trouble with his feet and the main-sheet Denny seemed quite at ease. He was sitting with the tiller in his left hand and the sheet tightly grasped in his right and looking very composed, and I was just congratulating myself that he'd soon make a fine sailing companion, when unbelievable disaster hit us.

The wind was backing a little in gusts and I saw the boom lift once or twice as the pressure got round behind the sail. I was just thinking that perhaps I'd better take over for a spell when Denny—so he told me afterwards—saw a heavy balk of timber floating right ahead of us and put the tiller down to miss it. A gust got forward of the mainsail and in a moment we were gybing all standing. It wasn't a serious gybe—there was no real weight in the wind. But as the boom swung across Denny gave a loud cry, almost a scream. Then, with an expression of surprise and horror on his face, he held up his hand for me to see. It was almost flayed!

I knew what he'd done on the instant. As the boom had travelled across it had dragged the coarse new rope through his hand, and instead of letting go, as he should have done, he had tried desperately to hang on. There was nothing to do but get to a doctor at the earliest possible moment. I dived for the first-aid chest and found a roll of bandage. Poor old Denny was in pretty bad pain, for the palm was burned as well as torn. I made him stretch out in the cabin, and gave him some brandy. Then I got the sails down and headed *Dawn* for home again. It took us over an hour to motor back, and it was one of the longest hours I can remember. There was nothing more I could do for Denny and nothing I could do to increase our speed. It was with immense relief that I finally brought *Dawn* to rest against the wharf. I shouted to a chap sitting on a bollard that we'd had an accident, and he came aboard and looked after the boat while I helped Denny along to the doctor in the main street.

Luckily the doctor was at home. He took one look at Denny's hand and said we'd better go up to the hospital, where it could be properly treated and dressed. He ran us up in his own car, and the hospital surgeon and nurse soon got to work on the hand. The fingers were pretty well cut to the bone and there was almost no skin on the palm. They did a bit of stitching and put on a dressing, and told Denny to come back the next morning.

Before we left I asked the surgeon how long he thought it would be before Denny could touch a rope again. He considered a moment, while we stood tensely waiting. Then he said: "If everything goes right, I should say two months. Not before."

To us it sounded almost like a sentence of death.

The doctor dropped us at the saltings, and we walked across to the workshop in silence. There didn't seem to be anything I could usefully say, and though Denny looked a bit less like a ghost he obviously wasn't in the mood for talking. Joe had noticed *Dawn* at the wharf and had just fetched her over to our side. He looked deeply concerned as he came to meet us. I told him briefly about the accident, and could see he knew perfectly well what Denny's hand must be like without looking at it. It wasn't the first time such an accident had happened in sailing history.

I blamed myself savagely for not having warned Denny about letting go, but there it was. It was an elementary thing I'd overlooked, but the damage was done. All our wonderful plans were wrecked;

all our hopes were shattered. As far as Denny and I were concerned, the bottom had fallen out of our world. I knew I couldn't possibly manage *Dawn* singlehanded, and for a long time to come Denny would be a hindrance rather than a help. By the time the hand was healed we should be well into August, and it would be September before we reached the Baltic. It was hopeless. We had been prepared for failure at the other end, and perhaps worse than failure—but to be prevented even from starting was unendurable. I looked helplessly at Denny, but he was staring moodily into space.

Joe, inevitably, had brewed a pot of tea, and he handed out the mugs. He said: "Cheer up! You'll still make it."

I said bitterly, "I don't see how."

Joe said, "It looks as though I'll have to come with you."

Chapter Seven

Joe confessed afterwards that he'd been thinking for a long time of offering to accompany us. It wasn't just that he was afraid we should come to grief on our own—the fact was that he was attracted by the prospect of adventure and of a long cruise in a boat he'd fitted out himself. I think he also rather fancied himself in the romantic role of a marriage-mender. But however much he might be pleasing himself by coming, his offer seemed to us magnificently generous and neither of us could find words in which to thank him. A beatific expression had settled on Denny's pale face, and I myself felt almost lightheaded with reaction and relief.

All the same, we couldn't let Joe come without stressing once more the risks of the trip. I emphasized—though he knew it already—that we might run into trouble with the Russians. I repeated that we should be breaking their laws, that for a time we should be inside their territorial waters, and that if they could catch us they'd have the right to jail us and would almost certainly do so. I drew a most unattractive picture of our likely prospects. But I don't think Joe was even listening. He went on reflectively sipping his tea while I talked, and I'm sure that in his mind's eye he was already crossing oceans.

I said, "Besides, Joe, what about your business here?"

"It'll be all right," Joe said. "As a matter of fact ..." he had the grace to look a little embarrassed. "I did put out some feelers. I've a pal who'll look after all the boats while I'm away, and the rest of the work will just have to wait. If the trip's successful, you can build me a proper workshop when we get back."

That seemed fair enough, and we shook hands on it. Then Joe

said: "There's just one other thing we ought to get clear before we start. Who's going to be skipper of this expedition?"

I thought for a moment. I said: "Suppose we fix it this way, Joe—you'll be in charge of everything to do with sailing the boat. I'll be responsible for the expedition as a whole, subject to what's nautically possible. How's that?"

"It suits me," said Joe. "As long as we know. The only time in my life I was nearly drowned was when two chaps gave orders at once."

I said, "What happened?" I always liked Joe's happy reminiscences.

Joe said: "One of them shouted 'Port your helm!' The other one shouted 'Starboard your helm!' So we kept going and hit a tug."

Now that Joe was coming with us the expedition took on a very different character. He had the quiet confidence of the professional, and though a passage to Sweden in a small boat was still a big undertaking, particularly if the weather should turn against us, it no longer seemed lunatic. All preparations went ahead very smoothly in that last busy week. Joe took complete charge at Southfleet. Denny couldn't do much—he had to go every day to the outpatients' department to have his hand dressed. I was mainly up in town, for what with food and a passport there was quite a bit of extra arranging to do on Joe's account.

The day before we were due to sail, I paid a last visit to the X.Y.Z. office. There hadn't been any news for some time, but as it happened a message came through from Steve while I was still in the office. It was tacked on to the end of a cable to Donovan and said simply, *Please convey best wishes Uncle Philip and many happy returns.* Steve had evidently remembered the date and was on his toes. Donovan shook his head sadly as he handed me the cable and said, "That guy's sure headin' for a crack-up."

The last day at Southfleet was pretty nerve-racking, for we had nothing much to do but wait for the tide. Denny had his stitches out in the morning and in the afternoon he insisted on reloading the punt gun. It took him a long time, with one good hand and a swathe of bandage, but he wouldn't let anyone else do it. After that, we forgot about the gun's existence. It made an admirable bowsprit.

High tide at Southfleet was at ten o'clock, and we had decided to go down the creek under power over the last of the flood. As the mild and peaceful evening drew to a close I sat up on *Dawn's* foredeck smoking an after-supper pipe and thinking how lovely the creek looked. The wet mud reflected the colours of the sunset, the wide saltings were darkly purple under sea-lavender. I wondered if I would be looking on this scene again in a few months' time with Marya by my side. Perhaps, I thought, it was better to hope than to know.

Presently the church clock in the village began to strike nine and Joe said in a quiet matter-of-fact voice, "Well, let's get under way." He started the engine and I got the anchor. In a few moments we were gliding gently downstream. One or two people waved to us from their houseboats as we passed, and we waved back quite casually. From our appearance, we might just have been going out into the Estuary for another trial, but on board there was an almost tangible excitement. Joe was just a shade too-calm, Denny just a fraction too nonchalant. As for myself, I was speechless now that we were actually started on the great adventure.

As it turned out, sailing conditions during the next four days were so perfect that a tyro could have made the passage single-handed. A great anti-cyclone was stationary over the whole of Northern Europe, so our radio told us, and a light steady breeze on the starboard beam persisted almost to the end of the trip. Day after day *Dawn* just sailed herself, with the tiller lashed amidships and the sheet made fast. Joe said it was like sailing in the trade winds. Usually there are lots of chores to be done at sea, but we had to look for jobs to keep us occupied. It fell to me to keep *Dawn* well swabbed down and shipshape in accordance with Joe's exacting requirements, and usually I did the cooking. Joe attended to the navigation of the ship, though there was precious little for him to do. He and I shared watches at night. Denny's job was to get his hand better. We didn't talk much about our plans, for August and Tallinn were still far off. Most of the time we just lazed.

On alternate evenings we tuned in to Moscow radio and listened to Steve's broadcasts. The first talk had no interest for us—it was a piece about Soviet patriotism taken, I judged, straight from *pravda*. I could only suppose that Steve was carrying out his plan of getting on the right side of the Soviet Press Department by writing sympathetic pieces for a change. On the third evening, however, we had a most exciting message. Reception was particularly good, and the voice of the woman announcer came through so clearly and in tones so familiar to me that I could almost imagine myself back in the studio, waiting my turn. We listened tensely while she repeated several times, "This is Moscow radio calling X.Y.Z. for Steve Quillan," and finally, "Steve Quillan begins in thirty seconds from—*now*." It was the drill for synchronizing the broadcast with the X.Y.Z. transmission from New York, into which it had to be exactly fitted.

Then Steve began, and this time we got our signal with the word 'Today'. For the next two minutes I was scribbling hard, while the others stood by anxiously. Steve was on a political theme. I took down: "Today the ordinary Russian has U.N.O. very much in mind. He knows of course that it is touch and go whether the organization will deal successfully with its problems, but the man—and indeed the woman—in the street will not be put out by what may be temporary difficulties. They prefer to see how things go, and to hope that gradually there will be a greater desire among all nations to co-operate for their common good and to ensure the maintenance of peace ..."

So it went on, and it took me quite a while to transcribe the whole broadcast into legible longhand. It was the most awful drive!—what the Russian man-in-the-street thinks hasn't the slightest influence on Russian policy anyway—and it was chock full of dreary *clichés* and empty hopes. However, that didn't worry us. You could have heard a pin drop in the cabin as I ringed every ninth word, for we all knew that what emerged on any of these occasions might well mean the success or failure of our expedition.

There was so much bad news that might come Steve's way, and that he might have to transmit to us. But this message was heartening. It was all in the first few sentences of the broadcast and read IN TOUCH WITH WOMAN BY SEE. The 'SEE' was obviously 'SEA', and the meaning was plain. Steve had managed to contact Rosa, the dressmaker in Tallinn.

Joe was particularly impressed by the demonstration. Though he'd been told about the cypher, and had admired the idea, he hadn't seen the magic actually at work until now. He took off his peaked cap, scratched the grizzled hair over his right ear, and then read the whole message through, while a slow grin spread across his face.

"He wraps it up, doesn't he?"

I said: "I hope he wraps it up enough. They've only got to cotton on to one of these messages, and heads will roll."

Denny said thoughtfully: "That dressmaker is taking a big chance. I suppose she thinks it's worth it."

"She must know what she's doing," I said. "It's not the first risk she's taken. It was pretty dangerous for her to call on Steve at the hotel that morning in Tallinn, but she was past caring about herself. She lost practically all her family when twenty thousand Estonians were rounded up and deported to Siberia overnight."

We all sat silent for a moment. Then Joe brought us back to earth with, "What about a cup of tea?"

On the fourth day out the friendly breeze died away, and we ghosted along in the light airs with a spinnaker set. We knew we were not very far from Denmark. As night fell the wind was scarcely more than a coolness on the cheek and we made little progress. However, soon after daybreak Joe gave an eager shout from the foredeck and after inspection through his glasses a triumphant "Land-ho!" It was the Jutland coast, about seven miles off the starboard bow. We all had a good look at it, for there's no thrill greater than a successful landfall after a long passage in a small boat.

What we needed now was wind. Joe was in the highest spirits and nearly whistled his head off, but no wind came. In the end we decided to stow the sagging sails and rely on the engine to get us into Gothenberg before nightfall, just in case the luck of the weather should turn against us. We reckoned that we could fill up with petrol in Sweden. All afternoon we steamed north-east at a steady seven knots, helped by a favourable tide. By late evening we were dodging shipping in the Gota estuary, and before dark had been given a friendly welcome at the Royal Swedish Yacht Club and were safely tied up to one of their buoys in Langedrag Yacht Harbour.

The first long leg of our journey was over. We had a pleasant meal ashore and turned in with a delicious sense of relaxation.

Altogether we spent about four days in Gothenberg, and we found it a very welcome rest. The motion of the boat had been slight, but it was a relief to feel solid land under us again all the same. The Swedes were kindness itself, and their hospitality was almost embarrassing. We ate as we hadn't eaten for years, and I'm afraid we drank rather more schnapps than was good for us. We had to excuse ourselves from two parties because of the necessity to listen in to Moscow, but in fact there were no more messages. As we were supposed to be on a pleasure cruise we made a sightseeing tour of the city. But we were none of us really in holiday mood—the difficulties of our mission were never very far from our thoughts—and soon we began to prepare for the next stage of our journey.

There wasn't a great deal to do. *Dawn*, after a morning of spit-and-polish, looked as smart and clean as any yacht in the river, which was saying a good deal. We'd had such an easy passage to Sweden that there was almost nothing to be done in the way of repairs and renewals. We filled up with petrol and topped up the fresh-water tanks and the batteries, and laid in some additional stores. We also bought Swedish maps and charts of the Gota Canal and the lakes we should have to pass through, but we couldn't get anything better of the Tallinn area than the charts we'd brought with us. Joe thought we might be able to get some information locally about the lights in Tallinn Harbour, since at least an occasional ship must be trading to those parts. I was agreeable, provided an opportunity arose naturally, but was scared of letting anyone know that we were interested in Tallinn and was against raising the subject ourselves. We spent some time drinking and listening in dives along the waterfront, but we learned nothing useful from the few English conversations we had.

We had three hundred and fifty miles of rivers, lakes and artificial canals to negotiate before we reached the Gulf of Bothnia, not to mention more than sixty locks. There would be no more sailing until we reached the great inland lakes, so Denny came into his own with the engine. He had been to see a doctor in Gothenberg about his hand and the verdict had been quite encouraging. The wound was healing according to plan and in a week or two he'd be able to start doing finger exercises to get the stiff muscles and tendons into use again. With one sound hand and a much reduced bandage he was able to do most of the things that had to be done to the engine, and virtually took charge of our passage through the canals.

For the next week or two we all looked and behaved like tourists. Joe, in particular, was as carefree as a schoolboy. He had found on the library shelf a guide-book to Sweden, and he spent a lot of time up on the foredeck telling us about all the wonderful sights we were missing. There was plenty to see and plenty to occupy us. We could tie up practically anywhere we liked, and for long periods we spent more time ashore than afloat. We would chug a few miles in the morning, just for a change of scene, and for the rest of the day we would explore. Once we'd left the factories of Gothenberg behind it was a fertile and pleasant landscape that we passed through, and the further we went the more picturesque it became.

We pottered along to little Lake Akersjo, through a canal cut in the solid rock, and then out into Lake Vanern, which the guide-book told us was the third largest in Europe. We had a look round Vanersberg and took in some more stores. There was room to move about, now, and one night about an hour after dark we staged a sort of dinghy-rehearsal. We found a quiet spot, and I put Joe and Denny ashore on the lakeside. Then I rowed out to where *Dawn* was lying at anchor, muffled the oars, and rowed in again as quietly as I could towards the point where I'd left the other two. They agreed that they'd been unable to see the dinghy until it was nearly at the bank, but they'd heard faint noises while it was still quite a way out, possibly a quarter of a mile. But this was a lake. By the sea there were always covering noises, if only of wavelets splashing on pebbles. It didn't look as though we had much to worry about on the score of the dinghy.

Lake Vanern was nearly ninety miles long and fifty wide, so we were able to do some sailing again. The pilotage was intricate, for right across the centre of the lake there was an archipelago of tiny islets and underwater rocks. It was good practice for what was to come later. We had one unpleasant night when a freak storm got up, and it seemed for a time that we might be driven ashore, but we weathered it. Next day we passed a charming little place called Sjotorp and then began to climb the exciting staircase of locks to Lake Viken, the highest point on the route.

If only we had had the girls with us, cruising through the canals and lakes would have been an idyllic life. The scenery was getting better all the time, and for some miles the canal was so high up that we could look down from the deck of the boat upon rolling countryside stretching away far below us and all around. Pleasant though it was to laze, we didn't forget business. We had listened regularly to Steve's broadcasts and just before we entered Lake Vattern—the second big lake on the route—we got another message. This time the subject of the broadcast was a cocktail party that Molotov had given to foreign diplomats in Moscow and the relevant portion, when transcribed, read like this: "Today Mr. Molotov was host to all the leading lights of Moscow. The diplomats were all on holiday, and as a special treat young communists—girls and boys—gave a most delightful concert. One of the unchanged features of eternal Russia is the singing, which still has a unique charm. It is understandable that working Russians would as soon spend their hard-earned money on good concerts as use their roubles to buy tickets for the theatre, for the choral tradition is very strong indeed. However, that's all by the way. This party was a significant as well as a pleasant occasion ..."

I won't bore you with the rest of the stuff. It was a shockingly bad broadcast, and I felt pretty sure that Steve had sweated it out with a wet towel round his head in an atmosphere thick with vodka fumes. Indeed, we began to think that the party had been altogether too much for him, because when we applied the rule of thumb method we produced LEADING HOLIDAY AND THE WHICH THAT MONEY BUY IS. This was plaintive but unilluminating. Then I realized—as I should have done earlier if I'd been paying attention to the words instead of to the shorthand—that Steve, greatly daring, had meant 'leading-lights' to be taken as one word. We now got LEADING-LIGHTS AND BOYS UNCHANGED STILL WORKING ON TICKETS.

We drank Steve's health in schnapps. It was a most satisfactory message, for it showed that he'd received and understood my letter about the Vake shoal buoy, and also that he'd managed to get Rosa at work on the spot. I was beginning to have a superstitious feeling that everything was going much too smoothly, and a fear that our luck would break at a critical moment.

Chapter Eight

In fact, though, our luck and the weather still held. We crossed Lake Vattern under all possible sail in the merest of breezes. There was no point in pressing on too fast, because we certainly didn't want to find ourselves in the Baltic until well into August. We took in stores and refuelled at Motala on the eastern shore of the lake, and then began to bump our way down the long escalator of locks to the sea.

On July 20 we locked out of the Gota Canal at Mem and tied up at the old wharf. Once again we were in what passed in these parts for salt water, and the open sea lay ahead, though we had to reach it through a long fiord and by pilotage among hundreds of rocks and islands which lay scattered in our path. We had a little conference at Mem about the next stage of our journey. The alternatives were to sail direct for the Gulf of Finland—Hango, which guards the northern shore of the entrance, was about 220 miles away—or else to go north to Stockholm and then make the direct passage—a mere 175 miles—across the neck of the Gulf of Bothnia. Since we still had time to kill we all voted for Stockholm as a safe and civilized jumping-off point for the start of the final assault. A couple of days later, after an uneventful trip along an inland route, we tied up to a mooring in the Stockholm Yacht Basin among as fine an assortment of craft as I've seen anywhere. We still had just over a fortnight in hand.

To have sailed from England to Stockholm in a small yacht so soon after the end of the war was considered something of a local event, and we hadn't been there twenty-four hours before we had a newspaper man on board. I wasn't very happy about that, for publicity was the very last thing we sought. It was quite certain that the Russians had their ears to the ground in Stockholm, for they had always resented the smuggling of Balts to Finland and Sweden on private vessels and the sanctuary that the kindly Swedes usually provided for refugees. The juxtaposition of my name and Denny's would inevitably give the whole show away to them. It wouldn't take them long to add up two husbands and a private yacht in Baltic waters and decide that a relief expedition was under way. On the other hand we certainly didn't want to give anyone the impression that we had something to hide. For the purpose of the inescapable newspaper interview, therefore, I changed my name from Sutherland to Suthers, and Jack Denny became Mr. Jack. If the immigration people noticed that the published names were different from those in our ship's papers and passports they probably thought it was the result of bad newspaper reporting. Anyway, nobody complained. I said in the interview that we were on holiday, and that we planned to do a little sailing in the Stockholm archipelago before returning home through the Gota Canal. We were all ecstatic about the beauties of the Swedish scenery and the fascinating castles and monasteries that we'd seen on the way.

The interview, in fact, went off quite smoothly and there were no repercussions, but I felt that the sooner we left Stockholm the better. It was evident that, if we stuck around, the hospitality of the Swedes would again become embarrassing. After we'd refuelled, filled our water tanks and taken in stores, therefore, we slid out of the Yacht Basin towards dusk one evening and anchored in sheltered water in the lee of an unoccupied island at the eastern or seaward edge of the archipelago which covers the harbour. We were now spared the gaze of curious eyes and the questions of friendly fellow-yachtsmen, and were in a good position to make sail for the Gulf at any moment.

Here, in this quiet anchorage, we had our first real council of war. The chief problem—indeed, almost the only problem for us—was one of timing. We must be neither too soon nor too late. We had to be inside Tallinn Bay on the night of August 14—subject to any fresh instructions we might still get from Steve—and it lay

160 miles due east of us across open water. The trouble was that the distance was too great for an accurately-timed last-minute dash. Theoretically, we could steam across in something under twenty-four hours with fuel to spare, so that if we left our present anchorage on the night of the 13th we ought to arrive at Tallinn at dusk on the 14th. By making that quick passage we should reduce to a minimum the chance of being spotted on the way. But there were two objections. One was that it seemed unwise to use half our fuel before we even reached Tallinn, since we couldn't tell what insistent calls there might be on the engine later. The other was even more serious. Over so long a distance a small boat couldn't work with certainty to a timetable, and we felt we dared not bank on good weather just because it had been good for so long. We couldn't risk being blown a long way off our course, if a wind should get up, with no margin of time in hand. In the end we decided that for safety we needed a jumping-off point very much nearer Tallinn, even though it would mean exposing ourselves in the Gulf longer than we liked.

We got out the charts covering the western section of the Gulf of Finland and studied them carefully. The Gulf itself is about fifty miles wide. Tallinn lies on the southern shore, about fifty miles inside the neck, with the Finnish capital of Helsinki almost opposite to it on the northern shore. Slightly to the west of Helsinki, also on the northern shore, we found the Porkkala Peninsula, which the Russians had taken over as a naval base under the terms of their peace treaty with Finland. That base and its immediate vicinity were definitely places to avoid. But west of Porkkala there was another vast archipelago of fantastic complexity. There were thousands upon thousands of islands, many of them little more than rocks. It seemed to me that without venturing far into this maze, which would be dangerous without local knowledge, we could at least lie quietly just inside the outer fringe—perhaps for a couple of days—and then emerge and steam across the fifty miles of Gulf to Tallinn on the afternoon of the 14th with a good chance of reaching our objective at the right moment.

We weren't exactly happy about this plan, but on balance we

preferred it to the other. We should be in Finnish territorial waters, of course, but we looked innocent enough, and though the Finns were very much under the thumb of the Russians they still presumably controlled their own waters and were not likely to molest us. So, at least, we reasoned. In any case, however and whenever we entered the Finnish Gulf by daylight—and it would have to be by daylight if we were to find an island sanctuary—we could hardly fail to be seen. At least we should look less suspicious pottering about among islands, which yachtsmen always like to do, than sailing direct for the Estonian coast.

It was a crucial decision we had to make between the two alternatives, and rightly or wrongly we decided to lie up in the islands. The idea was to reach them in the evening of the 12th, forty-eight hours before our Tallinn rendezvous, and if possible find a sheltered spot just before nightfall. We planned to sail there, if conditions were favourable, so that we should have plenty of fuel left for our getaway. That meant leaving our present anchorage two or three days before the 12th.

It was after we had made our plans, and therefore felt that for a short time we could relax again, that Denny became interested in maritime law. All the talk about Finnish territorial waters and the right of innocent passage must have aroused his curiosity. Anyway, he began to browse in a textbook that I'd brought along with the rest of our small nautical library, and before long he was holding a sort of seminary. As we had absolutely nothing to do except keep *Dawn* shipshape and cook our meals and swim, it helped us to while away the time and it was certainly fascinating.

Like most people, I suppose, I had always believed that under international law territorial waters extended three miles out from any coast, and that after that distance the 'high seas' started, where no country had any jurisdiction, at least in peacetime. Joe, too, had the 'three-mile-limit' firmly in his head. However, what Denny found in the book was very different, and rather disturbing. He read out some interesting bits about how various States at various times had regarded the limit of territorial waters as 'two days' sailing' or 'the range of vision', or the 'range of cannon-shot'—which, in the latter part of the seventeenth century, was apparently about three sea miles. But it soon became clear from the book that while Britain and the United States, as the chief maritime nations, had done their best to get general recognition for the three mile limit, there wasn't in fact any universally recognized law on the subject at all. Some countries, it seemed, claimed a six-mile limit, and some even twelve miles, and I was interested to learn that Denmark, Norway and Russia had once tried to close the Baltic altogether. Russia had claimed a twelve-mile limit in 1909, but nobody seemed to know what she claimed now, which was not surprising. My guess was that she would claim whatever happened to suit her at any given moment, and that where she was concerned the less faith one put in international law the better. I was for putting the book back on its shelf.

"But we must know our rights," said Denny stubbornly.

"If we get away safely we shall have to answer to our own Government for whatever we've done. We ought to know what we're entitled to do."

I could see his point. If we got into trouble with the Russians inside what was indisputably territorial waters nobody would be able to help us anyway. But if there were any untoward incidents on the high seas, and we managed to get away safely, we'd have British law on our side. At least, I thought so.

Denny, however, was becoming less certain. He read out something about 'the right of hot pursuit'. "A vessel may be pursued upon the high seas and there seized" [he read] "when she or a person on board her commits a violation of the laws of a foreign state while within its territorial waters."

"That's what we're going to do," said Joe, a little unnecessarily.

"But it's all rather vague," said Denny. "One chap here says: 'The party in such cases seizes at his peril. If he establishes the forfeiture, he is justified.' I don't get that."

"Might is right," I said. "If he wins, he's right. If you win, you're right. I say, I don't very much like the sound of this. Where's the 'freedom of the seas' we always used to hear so much about? Does it say how far they can go after you?"

"There doesn't seem to be any limit," said Denny. "Wait a minute, though—it says here that the pursuit must be 'immediate, hot and continuous'. And it must start in territorial waters, not on the high seas."

"Ah! So if a Russian patrol boat, for the sake of argument, spotted us as we were leaving Tallinn Bay, it would be entitled to chase us out on to the high seas—supposing that we could get that far!—and make us hand the girls over?"

"That's about it," said Denny grimly. "But if we were already at sea, they wouldn't have the right to board us just on suspicion."

"They'd probably do it all the same," I said. "I hope we don't have to put them to the test. If we can leave Tallinn Bay around midnight, we should be practically out of the Finnish Gulf by daybreak and well on our way to Stockholm. Chuck the book overboard, Denny!"

He didn't, though. He put it carefully away. I knew Denny would never break a law if he could help it, even a vague one.

That night we had another message from Steve. It was skilfully wrapped up in a long-winded broadcast about a Soviet oilfield on the Volga, and it confirmed the time of the Tallinn rendezvous, which was all that we now needed to know. I would have loved a quiet hour with Steve just then. Though I trusted him implicitly I would have been glad to hear just how he had made his dispositions, and so would the others. The message had made the climax of our expedition seem near, and I knew Denny's thoughts were very much with Svetlana and the journey she would have to make alone from Leningrad—if that was still the plan. This last brief period of waiting was trying, and the strain showed in our long silences and our somewhat brittle spasms of conversation. I had seen men in the same mood before an attack. Joe alone was fairly unconcerned.

The long holiday voyage had made us all fighting fit, and we were deeply sunburned. Denny's hand was now quite healed, and we were all itching for departure, particularly as one or two yachting parties out of Stockholm had passed near by and waved to us in the last day or two.

It was on the evening of the 9th that the barometer, which had long been steady as a rock, gave a little downward flicker when Joe tapped it. The drop was slight, but we were all very conscious of our unbroken run of good luck. The wind, which for so long had been southerly, began to back a little and freshen.

We were now in a serious quandary. It looked as though we might be in for a bit of really dirty weather. It might amount to nothing more than a short hard blow finishing in a night, like the one which had given us such a tossing on Lake Vanern. In that case the thing to do was to remain at anchor until it blew itself out, since we still had time in hand. But who could forecast how long the storm would last? This might be the beginning of a break, in which case we should have to beat to windward all the way to the islands and should need every minute of time that remained. Whatever decision we took would be a gamble. Joe sniffed the air, and ran over the timetable again, and finally said he thought the risk of a bad dusting at sea was less than the risk of arriving late at the rendezvous. We accepted his decision. In a few minutes we had the anchor weighed and the sails hoisted and were on a course for a point ten miles south of Hango, close-hauled and reefed

It was grand to be moving again, but the possibility of bad weather pressed heavily on our minds. As night drew on the glass fell further and the wind headed us, so that we had to change course. Dark clouds were banking up ominously, and there was a rumble of thunder in the air. I was unable to sleep a wink during Joe's watch and was quite glad to take my turn at the tiller towards morning. I didn't at all like the metallic look of the sky at daybreak, or the very confused sea that was getting up. However, Joe seemed unconcerned. He told me to give him a shout if the wind strengthened appreciably, and then turned in for a short nap. Like all real sailors he could sleep under almost any conditions of wind and water if he had a mind to.

I let him have his sleep without disturbing him, but the wind was steadily rising, and when he came on deck again a couple of hours later he had a quick look round and decided that we'd better take in another reef. We had been making heavy weather of it for some time, and with shortened canvas the motion was much easier.

The storm was still grumbling away all around us but seemed unable to break. Towards noon there was a bright gleam of sunshine between two dark edges of cloud and Joe had a shot at taking sights, which was pretty difficult in view of the motion. Presently he emerged from the cabin with a new course, and what he said was our position, though he didn't look very happy about it. Fortunately we had plenty of sea-room, and for a boat of our draught there were no navigational hazards anywhere near.

As the day wore on conditions became much worse. The wind strengthened steadily from the north-east, the sea got up alarmingly, and *Dawn* began to plunge like a bucking horse. It wasn't a gale, or anything like it, but there was a lot of weight in the wind, and to my inexperienced eyes the black water looked very menacing as it rose above our bows and then raced away under our stern. After all these sybaritic weeks it was clear that we were going to get our real baptism. Joe was a new man. All this time he had been playing at sailing, but now he had something worthy of his skill. His eyes narrowed against the wind and he lost his faintly mocking grin. There was a fresh snap about his instructions. Previously he had been skipper only in a technical sense, but now he imposed his will both on us and on the boat. "Never be afraid of a boat," I had heard him say. "Always believe that you can make it do what you want it to do." The same thing obviously went for the crew. When Denny emerged from the cabin chockfull of pills and looking like a scared green ghost, Joe ordered him below without a second glance. Poor old Denny went gratefully.

Suddenly there was a crack of thunder right overhead and a fork of lightning split the sky. Rain swept down on us, reducing visibility to nothing. We were quite alone on a grey-black sea that smoked with spindrift. Joe and I had long since struggled into oilskins and sou'westers but there was no chance of keeping dry. *Dawn* was sailing well and we took very little green water, but the cabin-top streamed continuously. Time after time we buried our nose in the tops of the waves, and foam surged into the cockpit and flooded round our sea-boots. Joe kept me hard at work pumping, and I even had to use a bucket when the water got too deep.

A storm at sea experienced in a small boat is incredibly awe-inspiring and frightening. The waves rushed down on us like hungry animals, and the fury of the wind in gusts and its mad scream through the rigging was something I could never have imagined. *Dawn* seemed unbelievably tiny and I couldn't think she would survive if the sea got worse. But Joe was calm enough and I took my cue from him. He was watching each wave, easing the tiller occasionally to avoid a beam sea. Every now and again he glanced up at the sails. He had fitted out the ship and I know he thought she would stand up to pretty well anything with proper handling. He must have felt more than a bit disconcerted when the mainsail, reefed down though it was, suddenly split with a crack like a gunshot under the impact of a particularly ferocious gust. It began slatting about violently, and in a moment it had blown to shreds and a large triangle of canvas was being whirled away over the steaming sea.

There was plenty of excitement then. Joe yelled, "Get the trysail!" and went forward to wrestle with the remnants of the mainsail. The next few minutes were as mad as anything I've known. *Dawn* was at the mercy of the sea, and a good deal of water was coming aboard. I staggered about the cabin, indifferent to Denny's groans, too busy now to be scared, trying to hold the sail locker open long enough to get the storm-sails out. After that, of course, we had the devil of a job bending them on. Joe, with admirable foresight, had rigged a lifeline across the cabin top before we sailed—otherwise I doubt if we could have done it. As it was, Joe did most of the work. I managed to get the old foresail and jib in, with my legs knotted round the mast a good deal of the time and a prayer in my heart. Joe was having a private fight with the trysail and he seemed to be winning.

Just as I finished bending on the storm-jib we took one green sea which almost tore me from the ship and Joe yelled "Go and bail!" I practically swam back into the foaming cockpit and got to work again with the bucket. All hell seemed to have been let loose—the rain was lashing us, the wind was hammering at us, and *Dawn* was wallowing horribly and taking more and more water. But in a few minutes Joe had joined me in the cockpit, the storm-sails filled, and the little ship had gathered way again. I plied the bucket without pause until the water was no more than a slop around our feet. It seemed a miracle that *Dawn* was still floating; even more astonishing that in little more than five minutes we could have achieved so much.

Joe shook the water out of his eyes like a wet dog and grinned. He shouted, "I thought you were gone that last time!"

It seemed that we had had the worst of the storm. Slowly, through the evening, the wind moderated, and by supper-time I was able to prepare some hot food, and Denny was sufficiently recovered to join in eating it. He was a bit shamefaced about his sickness, but Joe told him amiably that he'd been far more use out of the way, and he cheered up when he realized that Joe hadn't expected anything else. By dusk we had bent on the spare mainsail and we all felt quite cheerful again. The barometer had risen a little and the wind had veered once more to the south. It had been a sharp storm, but there were no signs that the weather had broken for good. We were back on our course again, though with only a very approximate idea of our whereabouts.

Next day, August 11, was as bright and fair as we could have wished. We all had plenty to do cleaning up, drying clothes and sleeping-bags and making shipshape after *Dawn's* battering of the day before. What was annoying was that if we'd waited at the island for another twenty-four hours the storm would have passed and we would have had a fair passage to Hango. But no one could have foreseen that, and now that the storm was over I felt I wouldn't have missed it for anything.

When the sun got up Joe took careful sights and he and Denny checked our position. We had made lamentably little progress. Instead of being nearly at Hango, as in more favourable circumstances we might have been after thirty-six hours at sea, we had been driven far to the south of our original course and had still 150 miles to cover. But we now had the wind aft of the beam and were making excellent progress.

That night we received another message from Steve. It wasn't in cypher—it was merely a sentence introduced into the beginning of his broadcast for the benefit of his fans and saying that he was going off to Leningrad and would be broadcasting from there on the reconstruction of the city.

By midday on the 12th we had Hango on the port beam and were entering the Gulf. Our plan to approach the islands, if possible, unobserved, had taken insufficient account of the prevailing conditions. Visibility was much too good, and though we were ten miles off the Finnish coast as we slipped into the Gulf, we could see the shore quite plainly. The shore could also see us. After about half an hour a launch flying the Finnish flag came out of Hango and gave us a friendly salute as it passed. Any idea of secrecy clearly had to be abandoned. We could only hope that if we sailed in with colours flying and a brazen front, everyone would believe that we really were engaged in nothing but a holiday cruise.

In a dying breeze we ghosted along the Finnish shore, moving in gradually towards the land, but keeping well outside the line of islands. Just in case someone had a telescope trained on us from the shore we put on the right sort of act. Joe exchanged his old naval cap and blue trousers for an unfamiliar pair of khaki shorts, and Denny and I lay about on deck in the hot sun in nothing but swimming trunks. The weather was perfect for holiday-making. The glass was slowly rising to a new high and the cabin-top was getting almost too hot for comfort. So little wind was there that our wake was hardly noticeable as we glided over the water and, by the time we had reached the place where we had planned to seek shelter for the night, dusk was near at hand.

We didn't fancy an intricate pilotage, and our aim was to bring up at the first suitable spot. Cautiously we sounded our way between a couple of low green islands on the fringe of the archipelago. As soon as the water shoaled to five fathoms we let go the anchor. It was important that we should be able to get out to the open sea without difficulty in case another storm blew up during the night, for none of us put much trust in the holding power of this rocky sea-bottom. Otherwise, where we had stopped was the pleasantest place imaginable. The tiny islets between which we lay were lush and green, with a few low bushes and lots of wild flowers. After supper we went ashore in the dinghy to stretch our legs. The night was almost as warm as the day had been. After a stroll, we sat and smoked by the water's edge and discussed the storm that we'd weathered, and the alternative plans which we might have made and hadn't, and the friendly but curious Finnish launch, and the remarkable fact that we'd arrived here at all. Then Joe said that it was always a good thing to get a full night's sleep when there was no need to keep watches, so we turned in.

I don't know whether it was the result of a new sense of danger, born of our proximity to inhospitable shores, or whether it was the knowledge that Marya was lying asleep in Tallinn only fifty miles away at that very moment, but I was a long while dropping off and I woke several times during the night after vague but disturbing dreams. As soon as the first streak of light shone through the porthole I abandoned the effort to sleep. I dressed in shorts and a khaki shirt and went out on deck to sniff the air of yet another delectable morning.

I was just thinking of having a refreshing dip when my roving eye caught sight of something which froze me to the deck. There was a motor-launch anchored at the entrance of the channel through which we had come, and it was flying the flag of the Soviet Union at its stern.

Chapter Nine

I went below at once and woke the others. It was not yet six o'clock, and I thought there was just a chance that we might be able to slip away round the back of the island and out to sea while whoever was on board the Russian boat still slept. But Joe, fully awake on the instant and peering out of the open port, said he could see two figures already moving in the well of the launch. So that hope was shattered.

We were all deeply perturbed by the new development but not, I think, surprised. Our fear that we might have been kept under observation had proved well-founded. No doubt a patrol boat had been sent out from Porkkala right away to keep an eye on us.

"They've got a damned nerve sticking themselves right in the middle of the channel like that," said Denny, who was now almost an authority on maritime matters. "It's practically a hold-up. Do you think they'd stop us if we tried to leave?"

I said: "We'll find that out later. I shouldn't think they'll do more at this stage than keep us in sight. It may be just a routine check-up on their part—they've no grounds for any but the vaguest suspicions."

"They soon will have," said Joe.

"It depends," I said. "Our job is to disarm their suspicions. We've got to put on a convincing act—mad Englishmen having fun."

"It'll be an act, all right," said Denny grimly. "I can't see how we're going to shake them off."

"We'll think of something," I said, with a confidence I was far from feeling. "We'll have to make our own opportunity. The more harmless and friendly we can seem, the better chance we'll have.

94

But one slip will be fatal. Don't forget, Denny, you and I don't understand a word of Russian, we've never been to Russia, and we don't know anything about Russia except what we've read in the papers. If they see a spark of intelligence in our eyes when they talk to each other it'll be as good as a signed confession for them. Now I'm going to reconnoitre. There's nothing like keeping the initiative."

I launched the dinghy in leisurely fashion and rowed slowly towards the Russian boat. She was about the same length on the waterline as *Dawn* and had a large single cabin forward and an open cockpit aft. Her wooden hull looked rather lightly built, and her lines suggested that she was intended for fast patrolling in fairly sheltered waters rather than for bad-weather work. As I drew abreast of her I saw that her name was *Neva*. She had no visible armament and looked very inoffensive. All the same, I didn't see how she could claim the right of innocent passage that Denny's book had talked about. She was flying the flag of the Red Navy and she was clearly a naval auxiliary. We were many miles from Porkkala and quite definitely in Finnish waters, and it wasn't the job of a Russian patrol boat to exercise guard duties there. It looked as though we had overrated the amount of independence left to the Finns. Probably in the Gulf of Finland the Russians did as they liked.

I nosed slowly round to the stern of the launch and when I saw someone looking in my direction I gave a friendly wave and the man saluted. With a couple of sharp pulls I placed the dinghy alongside *Neva*, smiled a frank smile and said, "Good morning."

The man was in uniform, naval or of a naval type, and from what I could remember of Soviet badges of rank I judged him to be a lieutenant. He was short and burly, with fair hair, deep-blue eyes and a fresh open face. I had seen hundreds like him around Kharkov and Dniepropetrovsk; he, was practically the male counterpart of Svetlana. Whatever his present job might be I felt that he was fundamentally a good fellow.

He leaned over the stern of *Neva* and regarded me with grave curiosity. "Engleesh?" he asked.

I nodded. He knew our ensign, of course.

He shook his head sorrowfully from side to side and pointed to himself. "No speak. *Oy oy oy!*" He made a gesture of regret with his hands. "Engleesh—no." That seemed to be about as far as he could get. I tried him with German and French, but he still looked blank. He turned and spoke into the cabin, words which I couldn't catch. It seemed a bit odd that the Russians should have sent a patrol boat to intercept an English vessel without anyone aboard who could speak English. I was just beginning to think it a good sign when a little man emerged from the cabin, looked across at me and said "Good morning" in English. I took an instant dislike to him. He was slight and narrow-chested, like pictures one had seen of Goebbels. He had a thin, rodent face, with a sharp nose and bright little eyes. His hair was wispy and grey. He looked about fifty, and he wore a nondescript costume of semi-military cut but without insignia. I took him for an N.K.V.D. man, not very well disguised. He didn't smile, but he seemed prepared to be chatty. He said, "It is a swell morning, yes?" I recognized his type. Some time or other he had spent a few years in the United States, and remembered just enough of the more obvious idiom to be irritating.

I said it was a swell morning.

"You are on vacation, you and your friends?"

"That's right," I told him cheerfully. "We sailed out from England to Stockholm, and as we had a few days to spare we thought we'd like to look at these islands."

"It is unusual," he said. "Not many guys come here."

That made me smile. I said, "We Englishmen often go where other people don't go."

"Sure!" said the little man. He leaned over *Neva's* rail, quite motionless. "You build empires."

I didn't want to start a political argument at seven o'clock in the morning and I said: "Well, we're not building one here, you know. We're here for pleasure. It's very nice. We like Finland."

The little man looked surprised. "You have been ashore?"

"Oh no. I mean we like Finnish waters. These *are* Finnish waters, aren't they?"

He nodded slowly.

"The Finns don't mind you patrolling here?"

"They are our friends," he said. "We help them."

"Yes, I see."

He looked across at *Dawn*. "You stay long?"

I tried to look sad. "Unfortunately, no. The day after tomorrow we have to return to Stockholm. We're meeting some people there. It's a great pity—we'd like to stay."

"And what will you do while you are here?"

I shrugged. "Swim, eat, sleep, lie in the sun. We may have a look at one or two of the islands today. Do you know them well?"

"Yes," said the little man. "You must be careful of the goddam rocks. Very careful. They are dangerous."

I assured him that we should take no risks.

"You have charts?"

"Of course, but not of the channels. Only of the Gulf. We shall keep on the outside of the islands, where it's safe."

"You do not cross the Gulf? To Tallinn, for instance?"

I considered. "I don't think so. Is there much to see? Is it better than this?"

He shook his head. "Just a city—a fine city."

I said: "We're not very keen on towns. We like to get away from people." I feared it was unlikely he would take the hint. "Anyway, it's too far across to the other side. What is it, seventy or eighty miles?"

"Fifty miles."

"No." I dismissed the idea. "We'd never keep our appointment in Stockholm. Besides, these islands are marvellous. How do you like our boat?"

Again his glance travelled across to *Dawn*. I felt sure he didn't know anything about boats. He looked as though his spiritual home was the interrogation cellar. He gave a little shrug and said: "It is quite nice. Okay. Why do you paint it grey like a warship?"

I thought of Joe and his fancy for a smart white yacht. Perhaps I hadn't been so clever after all. I said: "The climate in England is very bad. Rain and fog all the time. Grey doesn't show the dirt."

He nodded slowly and looked again towards *Dawn*. "Has it an engine?"

"An auxiliary engine," I said. "But we don't often use it. We prefer sailing. It takes longer, but it's more restful." I pushed the dinghy off. "Well, I must get some breakfast." I rubbed my hand over my stomach for the benefit of the lieutenant, who all through the conversation had stood stolidly by the little man without a word. He grinned amiably and saluted.

"We shall perhaps see you again," said the little man as I shipped the oars. It was a statement of fact, if ever there was one. I nodded pleasantly and rowed away.

I gave the others a short report over the ham and eggs. I told them the little man seemed to be in charge. "He's suspicious, no doubt about that, and very inquisitive, but I think it's only routine. He doesn't seem to have anything to go on. I expect they've been told to keep us shadowed until we leave."

"Did you see what sort of engine they've got?" asked Denny.

"No. They didn't ask me aboard."

Denny grunted. "It looks as though we're in for plenty of trouble. What are we going to do? Don't forget we're supposed to leave for Tallinn about midday tomorrow."

I wasn't likely to forget. I said, "What we need is a bright idea."

Heavy silence at once enveloped the cabin.

I said: "One or two things seem clear enough. They won't let us out of their sight, and we can't run for it because they're faster than we are. The only chance seems to be that we may be able to slip off tonight in the darkness and be far enough away by tomorrow to do what we've got to do before they get on our tracks again."

Joe nodded. "It's a thin chance, but I don't see any other."

"We can't slip away," said Denny, "if we let them keep us hemmed in the way we are now."

"No," I said. "We must find a better anchorage. What I suggest is that we have a quiet morning here, as though we're in no hurry, and then after lunch we'll amble up the coast for a couple of miles and drop anchor on the seaward side of one of the islands, so that we can head straight out to sea when the moment comes. Is that all right, Joe?"

"If the weather holds," said Joe, "and we can find a good anchorage."

Actually, the weather had never looked more settled. Apart from the presence of the patrol boat, conditions couldn't have promised better for our enterprise. The sea was as calm as a pond, and we were obviously in for a roasting day.

After breakfast we tried to behave like the yachting party with no particular plans that we were supposed to be. It seemed an opportunity to do some long-overdue laundering. We rigged a clothes-line from the mast to the cockpit and soon there was a fine array of underpants and khaki shorts and brightly-coloured towels drying in the sun. I could see the little man watching every move we made. There was something sinister about his immobility.

While Denny checked over the engine and put the cabin to rights Joe and I had a swim. The lieutenant was taking a dip, too, and we swam towards him, but when he saw us coming he turned and made a bee-line for the launch. There wasn't to be any unofficial fraternizing, even in the water. The rodent had no doubt given his instructions.

After our swim we lazed on deck for a while, reading and smoking. Then we all three took the dinghy, with some food and drink, and went ashore on the neighbouring island in full view of *Neva*. Joe gathered some sticks and we lit a fire. We organized a little mild horseplay, in case it was expected of us. Joe made a ball out of brown paper and string, and for half an hour we played cricket, using a stumpy pine tree as a wicket. I would have given a lot to hear what the little man was saying to the lieutenant at that moment. He had changed his position, but never seemed to take his eyes off us. I suppose he was trying to make up his mind about us.

After lunch we lay on a bed of pine needles and discussed the situation in low tones. Our chances of getting away from *Neva* unseen, even at night, seemed poor. It wasn't likely that both the Russians would sleep at the same time. They would know that darkness was our only opportunity if we had any concealed plans;

the mere fact of our anchoring in the open when evening came would inevitably make them more watchful. They would certainly bring up somewhere near us again. If the night were quiet it would be impossible for us to get our anchor and make sail without their hearing. I couldn't see that we had an earthly chance. From the point of view of evading them, storm or fog was our best hope, but there was not the least sign of either.

It was evident that pretty soon we should have to make a big decision. If we couldn't break away from *Neva* our expedition would fail. None of us, in the last resort, was prepared to accept defeat—and particularly at this stage. We had known when we started that we weren't going on a picnic. Now it looked as though we should have to fight. As we lay there, morosely discussing the problem, we were all reluctantly approaching that conclusion, as hungry castaways might slowly form a resolution to eat the cabin boy when every other alternative appeared exhausted.

It was Denny who actually put the idea into words. He said thoughtfully, "Well, we're three to two."

I said: "The lieutenant has a chest like a barrel. He'd take a lot of holding. What's more, he has a gun. I saw the holster. I expect the little man has a gun too. I just thought I'd mention it."

"I knew we ought to bring guns," Joe said.

I said: "Don't forget we're in Finnish waters. I'm not saying we shan't have to fight if there's no other way—I'm just putting the facts. We should be hopelessly in the wrong if we attacked them. They're only watching us—they haven't molested us so far. If we lost the fight, anything could happen to us. Our best hope would be to catch them off guard and get them tied up before much harm could be done. For that I estimate we should only get about twelve years apiece in Siberia if we were subsequently caught."

"I don't like it," said Joe, very understandably.

I said: "Neither do I. Anyhow, I vote we wait until this evening before we start anything desperate. Something may turn up."

"Yes," said Denny, "probably another Russian boat." He was feeling very low.

We packed up our things without haste and rowed gently back

to *Dawn*. We took in the washing and made all shipshape. Finally we hoisted the sails and began to glide out to sea, through the narrow gap between *Neva* and the island. There was almost no wind, and no perceptible current. Our speed was about half a knot. As we edged past the launch the lieutenant again gave us a salute, but the little man only stared sardonically. I don't think he had a very high opinion of us from any point of view.

Joe, returning stare for stare, waited until we were safely out of earshot and then said: "She's certainly built for speed. She could make rings round us."

Denny said: "That little man gives me the creeps. He's got eyes like a lizard."

It seemed ages before we rounded the end of the island and lost sight of *Neva*. Even our spinnaker hardly drew. There was a slight heat haze, but nothing like enough to cover an escape. For hours we idled up the coast. There were no indications that *Neva* had moved yet, and indeed she had no need to. The Russians could probably see our tall mast. I had no doubt that the little man wouldn't let us get far without following, and that at the first sound of our motor he'd be after us like a stoat after a rabbit. It would be an understatement to say that we resented him. Any one of us could cheerfully have wrung his neck at that moment.

Denny kept looking across to the south, where with a little better visibility we might almost have seen the impressive silhouette of Tallinn. I knew just what he was thinking—so near and yet so far! It was maddening to be thwarted like this at the last moment. I avoided his eye, for I somehow felt as though he relied on me to produce a miracle and was disappointed that I showed no sign of doing so. Our nerves were all getting a bit frayed.

In the early evening I launched the dinghy and began to tow the yacht at a snail's pace towards a suitable anchorage. We had to be close in to an island, otherwise the water would not be shallow enough for our anchor to get a grip on the bottom. But we must also find a spot free from surrounding hazards, so that if during the night an opportunity came for us to leave we could do so without fear of running into some obstruction.

Denny lay on his stomach in the bows, keeping a lookout for rocks awash and shouting occasional directions to me. Joe kept the lead going as we felt our way towards the shore. Finally we let go in four fathoms, after Joe had reported that the lead brought up gravel. There wasn't even enough wind to tauten the anchor cable, and with her sails furled the yacht lay absolutely motionless on a glass-smooth sea, her every detail reflected in the water. I rowed up and down in the dinghy on the seaward side of *Dawn*, looking for rocks and taking soundings with the small lead. The results were satisfactory. As far as I could judge there was deep water and a complete absence of obstructions between *Dawn* and the open sea. It would be quite safe to set sail in the dark—if we were allowed to.

There was still no sign of *Neva*, and after a while I began to wonder whether it was our own sense of guilt which had made us so certain that we should be followed. Perhaps, having had converse with us, and watched us harmlessly amusing ourselves all day, the little man had decided that we weren't worth pursuing. It was a pleasant fancy, but I didn't really believe it, and of course I was right. After we had been at anchor for a little over half an hour we heard *Neva's* engine starting up and in about fifteen minutes she came into sight round the tip of one of the islands. She was moving quite slowly and appeared to be heading rather aimlessly out to sea. I would have liked to watch her through binoculars, but I was afraid that the rodent would be watching us in the same way, and I didn't want to appear interested in what *Neva* was doing. Complete unconcern was our best attitude. We saw her steam a couple of miles or so parallel to the shore and then turn in towards the land. After that we lost sight of her for about half an hour, though we could still hear her engine's powerful beat. The little man was undoubtedly playing with us.

Presently the engine note grew louder again and the launch came into view from the east and slowly approached us. The lieutenant was at the wheel and the little man was sitting nonchalantly in the cockpit. In a few minutes she was alongside and the lieutenant shut off his engine. The little man stood up. "You are not staying here?" he asked. He seemed very assured and his tone was insolent.

I felt like telling him it was none of his business and giving him a poke with the boat-hook, but decided reluctantly that tact was still called for. I offered him a cigarette, which he refused, and said we thought of doing so. Joe and Denny were listening, but saying nothing. They appeared to be playing a card game on the cabin-top.

"It is much better inside the islands," said the little man. I shrugged. "We happen to like it here."

"It is not a good place," he insisted. "Bad anchorage." He said something to the lieutenant, whom he addressed as Stepan Ivanovitch, and the lieutenant dutifully shook his head. "There is rock beneath—goddam rock," the little man went on. He would have been very funny had his appearance been less repulsive. He looked again at Stepan and the lieutenant nodded. "Rock," said the lieutenant, or something that sounded very like it.

I said, "No, gravel." I picked up our heavy lead and showed the bits of gravel sticking to the tallow. It didn't mean a thing to the little man, but there was a gleam of professional approval in the lieutenant's eye. He knew it was a good anchorage as well as we did, but he knew his duty also. He went on shaking his head.

Pressing our advantage I said coldly: "You have no *objection* to our staying here, I suppose? We are, of course, in Finnish waters, and shall be only too happy to obey any Finnish instructions. But you're not Finnish."

The little man looked angry, but he answered softly enough. "Of course we have no objection," he said. "If a guy wants to stop here, sure he can. We only wanted to help." He gave a sharp order to the lieutenant, who started *Neva's* engine. In a moment they were roaring out to sea.

Denny threw down his cards and watched *Neva's* departure with a scowl. "I bet they'll soon be back," he said. "I suppose they've gone off to work out the next move."

He wasn't far wrong. They were away for about an hour, but never far away, for we could hear their engine clearly all the time. They seemed to be stooging around quite pointlessly. Finally they returned and came alongside again. I had expected them to anchor near us, but the next gambit fairly took my breath away. The little man said calmly: "Would you mind if we also used your anchor? My damfool man has let ours fall overboard, the son of a bitch."

It was about the coolest and clumsiest lie I had ever heard, in spite of the fact that the launch's cable hung uselessly over her bows, quite anchorless. I had no doubt whatever that the anchor had been deliberately unshackled and was safely stowed away in their boat. Unless the lieutenant was about a million times less competent than he looked, there was not the remotest chance that they could have lost their anchor. I looked at Joe, who winked broadly. Denny was making awful faces, which I hoped the little man couldn't see.

It was all very well for Denny to make faces, but what was I to say? Our job was to behave as an English holiday yachting party would be expected to behave, and so far I thought we had done so. We had faintly resented busybody interference, which was certainly in character. But we had no excuse for not being obliging, even if someone *had* been idiotically careless. On our own admission we were in no hurry, and we had already brought up for the night. If we now flatly refused to let them tie up to us they would assume the worst and would keep a closer watch on us than ever, if that were possible.

I tried to stall. I said mildly: "It won't be very safe for two of us on one anchor. But we can lend you a spare anchor."

That, however, didn't suit the little man at all. He was now quite certain that we were over a very good anchorage and that it would hold a liner in a gale. At least, that was the impression he gave. He settled the matter for us with an arbitrary order to Stepan. In a couple of minutes the lieutenant had a warp fastened to our cable with a most businesslike and convincing knot.

"There," said the little man with satisfaction, "now we shall be buddies for the night. Do not fear—the weather is good, there will be no storm. Now I have a proposition to make. We will have a party tonight. You will come on board our ship and we will show you what is Russian hospitality."

Denny had climbed down into the cockpit and was hacking at my ankles, but I knew that our only hope was to play along for the time being. I said: "That's very nice of you. Very nice indeed. At what time?"

"Oh"—the little man threw out his hands—"whenever you like. Say at nine o'clock. We will have a helluva party."

I tried to look enthusiastic. "Have you got any vodka?"

He said quickly: "Do you like vodka?" I suppose he'd been trained to set traps like that.

I said, "I've never tried it, but I'd like to."

"Very well, you shall try it. At nine o'clock, then." Now that he was having his own way he had become much more amiable. He let go of our cockpit and very gradually *Neva* swung away from us until she lay idly at the end of her warp about twenty feet away.

"Well," said Denny, throwing himself gloomily on to one of the bunks, "that's torn it. Tied up for the night and invited to dinner! We'll never get away now. Why didn't you tell them to go to hell?"

I explained, as patiently as I could, that there hadn't really been any alternative for us, and in the end Denny saw my point of view and became more reasonable. He said: "At least we'll be able to get at them now we're asked aboard. I don't see how we can avoid a fight."

I said: "Sh! Keep your voice down."

"You know what these Russian parties are," Denny went on. "They'll get us in there and fill us up with vodka and when we wake up it'll be noon and we'll wish we were dead."

That was true enough. I didn't have to be told how one felt after an all-night drinking bout with Russians.

"If only," I said, "we could get them drunk and keep sober ourselves!"

"If pigs could fly!" said Denny. "They'll watch every glass. If we're not careful it'll be the other way round."

It was at that point that I had the great idea. I said: "Listen, we can use this party. There's only one way to catch them off their guard. We'll *all* get drunk. We'll all get absolutely pickled."

"I suppose," said Denny with heavy sarcasm, "that the boat will sail herself over to Tallinn while we all lie unconscious on our bunks sleeping it off?"

"No," I said. "Joe will sail her over. He's the paid hand. English gentlemen don't take their paid hand out to a party!"

Joe grinned for the first time that afternoon, and I could see a great light dawning in Denny's mind. He said, "Blimey, do you think we could sell that to them?"

"We've got to. It's our one chance."

"It's a pity you didn't think of it earlier," said Joe. "They've seen the three of us hobnobbing all day."

"We'll start making up for it now," I said. "Seriously, if we can get them to swallow that, I'm sure the rest of the plan will work. Just put yourself in their place. All they want is to be sure that we don't get up to any mischief during the next twenty-four hours. If they see us getting visibly tight under their very eyes at a party that goes on all through the night, do you think they're going to worry about Joe? It just won't occur to them that our getting tight is all part of a carefully-worked-out plot. Why should it? After all, they haven't a single solid reason for suspecting us of anything. I bet you what you like that once they've got over the shock of our leaving Joe behind they'll get matey and finish up under the table with us."

"Yes," said Denny slowly. "I agree. There's a good chance, anyway."

"Good. Now for the details. First, there's Joe."

"What do I do?" asked Joe.

"You," I said, "will make yourself a nice hot cup of cocoa and read Denny's book on maritime law." We all laughed—it was such a relief to have even the rudiments of a plan again. Then I remembered we had to keep our voices down. I said, "Actually, Joe, you'll have to carry the whole burden of the night on your shoulders."

"It looks as though I'll have to carry you too," said Joe.

"That's quite likely. Now, here's the plan. Denny and I will go aboard *Neva* at nine and settle down to drink our friends into a coma—we hope. All you have to do is to keep awake. Some time before morning you *may* hear us shouting for you to come and fetch us in the dinghy. That's if we can still shout."

"I get you," said Joe.

"There'll be no play-acting, mind you. We shall be really stinking. You'll probably have a job getting us into the dinghy, and you may have to take us one at a time. That's your problem. If you have to drown anybody, drown Denny. If you don't hear anything from us at all by, say, two o'clock, you can assume that we've all passed out and then you'll have to come and drag us out without being called."

Joe nodded. "And then?"

"If we're not too far gone, give us lashings of black coffee and try to bring us round. If we're dead to the world, just leave us. If you can, make sail before it's light and slip away. When you're out of earshot—not that it'll matter much if our plans go well—start the engine and get right out into the middle of the Gulf. Don't go straight across, because when they come round they'll almost certainly look for us between here and Tallinn. Keep well out towards the entrance to the Gulf and we'll go in to Tallinn in the evening. Okay?"

Joe grinned and touched his forelock. "Aye, aye, sir!"

"Come on, Denny," I said. "Let's get ready for the party."

No bride can ever have prepared herself for the altar with greater care than Denny and I for our own peculiar ordeal during that next half hour in the cabin. At Denny's suggestion we started by swallowing a tablespoonful of salad oil, which he said would line our stomachs and enable us to keep sober longer. Joe said he thought it unsporting, like putting a piece of iron in a boxing glove. Actually, the oil made me feel pretty sick, but I managed to keep it down with an effort of will, and Denny said he liked it. Then we both shaved carefully, and put on the suits we'd brought with us for going ashore in respectable places, and Denny put some gluey stuff on his hair. We had white shirts and white collars, and Joe went up on the foredeck and conspicuously cleaned our shoes. When it was all over Denny looked like a Methodist sidesman about to take the collection. Joe was laughing so much he nearly fell off the ship trying to get into the dinghy, and I had to tell him sharply to remember his place.

He rowed us over just at nine, and the lieutenant was in the cockpit of the launch waiting for us. As I clambered aboard *Neva* at Denny's heels I called out, "All right, Joe, come back when we shout," and he pushed off before the surprised lieutenant could say a word.

Then the little man came out. He was surprised too—by everything. The transformation in ourselves must have been striking, to say the least. He stared at us open-mouthed for a moment, and then he remembered his manners and gave us what no doubt passed with him for a smile of welcome. Then he realized that Joe was missing. He looked round, puzzled, and saw Joe in his khaki shorts and shirt just climbing back aboard *Dawn*. He said protestingly, "But your friend . . ."

It was my turn to look puzzled. "He's not our *friend*," I said. "He's our paid hand. You understand—our servant. He has work to do."

The little man was right off balance. He said, "Gee, I expected him to come too." He still stared uncertainly across at *Dawn*.

I looked as shocked as I could. "Of course, if you'd said so . . . I'm sorry. We never thought of it. You see, in England we never take our servants out to dinner. It would be insulting to one's host."

"But you eat with him on the ship," said the little man. "You play cards with him. You all wear the same sort of clothes. You laugh and joke together. You do not treat him like a servant."

"That's different," I said. "I'll explain. You see, a boat is very small. It would be awkward to preserve class distinctions. But an *invitation*—that's another matter. It's formal. Oh no, it wouldn't do at all. If you wish, of course, I'll go back and fetch him, but—well, I think he'll feel rather uncomfortable."

The little man hesitated, and I trembled inwardly. But after a moment he shrugged his shoulders and said we knew best. The lieutenant asked him what it was all about, and Denny and I kept poker faces while the little man explained that this just showed what the exploiting *bourgeoisie* were really like. It was a potted political lecture, and I could see that they'd both swallowed our preposterous story, hook, line and sinker. The lieutenant kept giving us curious sidelong glances as though we were strange and slightly dangerous animals. Then the little man invited us into the cabin, and the last thing we saw of Joe was a figure up on *Dawn's* cabin-top in the twilight with something like an apron tied round his middle, washing up what must have been clean crockery with every appearance of diligence.

Chapter Ten

Neva's cabin was of a conventional pattern, with a long upholstered settee along each side and a table in the middle. There was a compartment forward which I guessed was the toilet, and just inside the cabin there was a small galley with a paraffin stove. I noticed that there was no provision for screwing the table legs to the floor and that the stove was not swung in gimbals, which confirmed my view that *Neva* was essentially a fair-weather ship.

If Denny and I hadn't been used to Russian ways we should have been staggered by the sight which met our eyes inside the cabin. The little man might have his defects, but like all his countrymen he believed in receiving guests royally. The cloth on the table was not as clean as it might have been, but there was an astonishing variety of food. It consisted of what the Russians call *zakuski* and we, for lack of our own word, call *hors d'oeuvres*. There was black and red caviare, smoked salmon and sardines and tinned crab, slices of fat bacon and lean ham, chopped onions and tomatoes, a sort of vegetable salad, little green peas, olives, and a dozen other dishes besides. Somebody—no doubt the lieutenant—must have spent a busy evening getting ready for us. I caught Denny's eye and couldn't help smiling. The very appearance of the table took us straight back to our Moscow days, when banquets of oriental lavishness had been just part of our routine.

The little man waved me to a seat on the port side of the boat, with the lieutenant beside me. Denny sat down opposite the lieutenant and our host opposite me. He said: "First let us get acquainted. My name is Alexander Kleinman. The lieutenant here is Stepan Gorbenko—Stepan Ivanovitch Gorbenko. You know we have patronymics in Russia?"

I said: "Patronymics? Oh, you mean that business of taking your father's name? Like Ivanovich? Yes, I read about that in a book. *War and Peace* it was called. A very good book, by a man named Tolstoy. You know it, I expect."

Kleinman nodded. So far he evidently couldn't make us out at all. He said, "You like literature?"

I smiled ruefully. "I'm afraid I can't say I know much about it," I said. I hadn't really intended to start a discussion on literature right at the beginning of the party. It would follow, I felt, a well-worn track. I quite expected that Kleinman would announce he was a great admirer of Dickens.

"In Russia we like your Dickens," said Kleinman.

"Yes," I said. "I mean, I can understand that. He is a very fine novelist, with a lot of sympathy for the under-dog." That seemed to dispose of Dickens to everyone's satisfaction. "By the way," I went on hurriedly, "my name is Philip Suthers. My friend's name is Jack—er—Henry Jack."

Denny beamed.

"Good," said Kleinman. "Now that we all know each other, let us have a highball, yes?" He grinned with difficulty, as though he had a sore face, and showed three gold teeth. On the whole I preferred his face in repose.

Stepan had selected one of a dozen half-litre bottles of Moscow vodka which adorned the table, and was jerking the waxed cardboard stopper out of it by hitting the bottom of the bottle with the palm of his hand. It was a simple little trick which Denny and I had ourselves often performed. Stepan looked pleased when we expressed interest, and demonstrated how it was done. Then he poured the vodka into four glasses in what appeared to me to be lethal quantities.

"Before we drink," said Kleinman, "please help yourselves to food." He waved his bony hand over the board.

Denny piled an assortment of *zakuski* on to his plate and I followed suit. The atmosphere up to now was far from free and easy—I felt that Kleinman was watching everything we did and was waiting to catch us out in some mistake. I knew there were plenty of mistakes we could make, and I couldn't reach Denny to kick him under the table even if I'd wanted to.

When our plates were stacked high with food, Kleinman raised his glass ceremoniously. "I propose you a toast," he said. "To an enjoyable vacation." So far he hadn't bothered to translate a word of the conversation—Stepan was evidently expected just to tag along quietly. We nodded our appreciation of the toast. I took a little sip of the colourless liquid and put down my glass. Foreigners, I had noticed, always approached vodka with a certain initial caution, and this was supposed to be our first experience of the stuff. Denny went one better in corroborative detail. He choked. Stepan bounced up and began thumping him on the back. Kleinman looked amused and I began to feel a little less constrained. I said: "It's pretty strong stuff. It would make a good varnish remover."

"Eh?" said Kleinman.

"Just a joke, Mr. Kleinman. Gosh, I can feel it burning now."

"The trouble," said Kleinman, "is that you are scared of it. It is not really strong—not so strong as your goddam visky. But you must know how to drink. One big swallow, it is gone, then you eat. Watch Stepan, he will show you."

Stepan had already emptied his glass, but he was very ready to demonstrate his technique. There was quite a ritual attached to it. He broke bread and nibbled a piece, then he flicked the side of his neck with the nail of his first finger, and clinked glasses with us. We all drank "bottoms up" without disaster, and Kleinman applauded.

"This is a magnificent banquet," I said.

"It is all from cans," said Kleinman. "On a boat it is the best we can do. But Russian food is good. Look at Stepan here—he is from the Ukraine, where the food is the best in Russia. What a man! What a stomach!" He patted the lieutenant's stomach playfully while Stepan poured another round. Kleinman seemed to treat Stepan as something between a puppet and a poor relation.

"If I may," I said, "I should like to propose a toast myself."

"Sure!" said Kleinman. "Please—go ahead."

"To your boat, then—the *Neva*." We drained glass number two, and I made two marks with my thumbnail on the tablecloth. I was glad to see that Denny was eating steadily through the various dishes—we had always found the important thing with vodka was to have plenty of blotting-paper to soak it up. I was also keeping an eye on both the Russians to make sure there was no heel-tapping. At Russian banquets—particularly when there were soldiers or sailors present—there was always an element of rivalry in the drinking. When foreign guests were being entertained it was almost a point of honour for the Russians to get them drunk without getting drunk themselves. But occasionally I had known the Russians cheat. At one banquet I had actually seen Vishinsky himself slip some water into his vodka glass when he thought no one was looking and then brazenly propose a toast. Tonight, however, nothing of the sort could happen, for there was no water on the table. We could all watch each other drinking level.

After we had drunk the toast to *Neva* Denny said: "I like your boat. I like the sound of her engine."

"Yes, it is a good engine," said Kleinman without enthusiasm. His little eyes focussed on Denny. "Do you know about engines?"

"A little," said Denny. "I am an engineer, you know."

Kleinman seemed rather surprised. I remembered that he had us pigeon-holed as English gentlemen. He said, "You work in a factory?"

I caught Denny's eye. He said: "Well—er—not exactly. I—I own one."

"Ah!" said Kleinman. "Of course." He grinned. "A capitalist."

"In a small way," said Denny modestly.

"Mr. Jack," I observed, "employs only about thirty workmen."

"What happens to the factory while you are away?" asked Kleinman.

"I have a good manager," said Denny. He looked very solemnly at Kleinman. "He does the work—I draw the money."

"Of course," said Kleinman. "And you, Mr. Suthers—what is your line of business?"

"I'm afraid I don't do anything very much," I said. "I just amuse myself, you know. I have a private income. I was born with a silver spoon in my mouth."

Kleinman looked startled. "I don't get you," he said.

I explained the phrase, and the three of us laughed. Kleinman seemed more satisfied now that he had us fitted into a social background. The lieutenant was twisting his glass round and round and his face had a fixed, mirthless grin as though he knew he had to look happy, but couldn't see why. I wondered what he was really thinking—it wasn't much of a party for him so far. I said: "It's a pity our friend, the lieutenant, doesn't speak English. He must feel out of it."

Kleinman gave a contemptuous downward flick with his hand. "*Nichevo*. Don't bother about him—he has vodka, he is quite content. Tell me, Mr. Suthers, do you visit many countries in your yacht?" It was clear he was determined to pump us dry before the real drinking began.

"Before the war," I said, "I went to France and Holland. But now, of course, it's not so simple. There are many shortages in England, and it's not easy to prepare a boat for sea. Also, my friend and I are not very experienced sailors, and it is difficult to find a good paid hand."

"Like Joe?" said Kleinman. He didn't miss anything, or forget anything.

"Exactly," I said.

"But you like visiting other countries, when you can do so?"

"Certainly."

"You have never been to Russia?"

There wasn't much finesse about that. I looked hard into his beady eyes. "Unfortunately, no," I said. "My friend hoped to go during the war, but they sent him to Egypt instead. It *was* Egypt, wasn't it, Henry?"

"It certainly was," said Denny, with a mouth full of caviare. He was beginning to get a vodka flush. "Don't ever go to Egypt, Mr. Kleinman. There's nothing but sand and camels."

"You were in the Army?"

Denny nodded. "Five years. In tanks."

"It was a great fight against the Hitlerite scoundrels," said Kleinman, rather unexpectedly. "You should have been at Stalingrad, where the outcome of the whole war was decided."

"What were you?" asked Denny tactlessly. "A political commissar?"

"I was guarding the rear," said our host. "Stepan-Ivanovitch, more vodka!" I scratched in number three as Kleinman raised his glass. "Another toast," he said. "To the day when you visit our great country, Russia."

We drank that with proper enthusiasm. If Kleinman had known how soon that day was to be he wouldn't have looked so pleased with himself. I said: "I've heard and read a good deal about your country, Mr. Kleinman. Of course, there are various views about it in England, as you probably know. Not everyone at home approves of what you do. But then, you don't always approve of us. It's a pity relations can't be better. We could do so much good in the world if we worked together."

That speech seemed to fit into the party line all right, for Kleinman nodded vigorously. "That is just it," he said. "All that is needed is co-operation between us, instead of disagreement. But we must have patience. One day your country will change its opinions and will agree that the Soviet Union is right, and then there will be co-operation." His voice dropped a little. "You know our great leader and teacher comrade Stalin has said that there is no reason why our country and yours should not be friends."

Denny leaned across the table and said twice, in a loud voice, "It's the right spirit." I wasn't quite sure at first to what spirit he was referring. His speech was getting rather thick and a lock of black hair was falling across his forehead. He said, "Let's drink to comrade Stalin."

I thought myself that there was a certain lack of reverence in his tone, but Kleinman didn't appear to notice it, and anyway we weren't posing as anything but plain outspoken Englishmen. The lieutenant struggled to his feet when he realized what the toast was about and stood rocking slightly as we clinked glasses. The pace was getting a bit gruelling. I had been pretty drunk several times in my life, but I had never before sat down at a table with the cold-blooded intention of finishing up underneath it.

That last glass seemed to loosen the lieutenant's tongue. He'd obviously been bottling up a lot of things all the evening out of deference to Kleinman, but the vodka had made him bold. He began to ask Kleinman various things about us. Kleinman was a bit impatient and tried to brush the questions aside, but the lieutenant persisted. This, of course, was where we had to appear out of the conversation. I looked inquiringly at Kleinman and presently he said, "The lieutenant is interested to know if you have ever studied dialectical materialism."

I shook my head. "I wouldn't understand it if I did," I said. Kleinman translated, and to my surprise the lieutenant looked rather relieved. He grinned self-consciously and said: "It is the same with me. For many months I have been studying the history of Marxism, to get a diploma, but I cannot get it." Kleinman wasn't interested in the lieutenant's academic failures and asked him to pour out some more vodka. I felt sorry for Stepan, who was plainly a simple soul in need of a friendly ear. I said to Kleinman: "Ask Stepan Ivanovitch to tell us about himself. Has he always been in the Navy?"

That started something. No sooner had Kleinman translated than Stepan planted his elbows on the table among the debris and plunged into the story of his life. I looked at Kleinman and went on eating unconcernedly, as though I expected to be put wise when the torrent of words was over. But I was fascinated, not only by the strength of the torrent, but by Stepan's vitality, and by a new boastfulness. It seemed that he had become a sailor only as a result of the war. "Before the war," he said, "I was a coal-miner in the Donbass." He made a gesture as though he were lifting a heavy pick, and an empty vodka bottle went crashing to the floor. "I was a shock-worker," he said, "a Stakhanovite." He threw out his chest and gave it one or two blows with his fist, making it rumble like a drum. "I was the strongest man in the pit."

Kleinman translated, though the pantomime made Stepan's drift fairly clear.

Denny said, "What's a Stakhanovite?" and we listened patiently while Kleinman explained how the original Stakhanov had made history by discovering that if you did less walking at work you saved time. But Stepan was now impatient of Kleinman's interventions. He was stabbing the air in front of Denny with a fork to give emphasis to his words. "In the Donbass," he said, "our pit in 1941 was the best in the whole of the Ukraine. We over-fulfilled our plan by thirty-five per cent. I myself produced at the coal-face half as much again as any other man." He held up his great fists, knotted his muscles. "I tell you, I am strong. I can tear a seam of coal to pieces. I can fill two buckets while my comrade fills one. That is heroic labour." He glanced at Kleinman. "That is Leninist-Stalinist work."

I spluttered and pretended it was the vodka, while Kleinman gave us a fair translation. Stepan was really wound up now. He was as full of his prowess as a child. He reeled off statistics of coal production and showed us a medal of the Order of the Red Banner of Labour that he'd received from President Kalinin. He seemed to be a model son of the Soviet Union, vigorous, earnest and unquestioning. Kleinman watched him with a slightly sardonic expression, as though he was finding the exhibition somewhat naive.

The party was now beginning to warm up appreciably. Denny and the lieutenant were both visibly oiled. Denny, a diligent mixer and a patient man, was soon engaged with Stepan in something that sounded like bilingual baby talk. 'Plate', Denny would say, holding it out rather shakily for another helping of smoked salmon. 'Ple-it', Stepan would echo after him. Presently I heard Denny trying to get his tongue round 'tarielka' as though he had never heard a Russian word pronounced in his life. I had to fight down a tendency to giggle helplessly, and concentrate on Kleinman, who was struggling hard to keep his wits about him. The effort had given his face an apoplectic hue but it had been largely successful. He said, alarmingly, "I am sorry for your man by himself on your boat."

I waved my hand airily. "He's quite happy," I said. "I told him he could help himself to our rum. He likes rum." I put my hand confidentially on Kleinman's arm. "Tomorrow," I said, "we will all have a party on board *Dawn*. Not like this, perhaps—with all this luxury—but still, a good party. And you shall try our rum."

"So you are not getting the hell out of it tomorrow?" said Kleinman.

I said with great intensity, "I beg your pardon?"

"You are not leaving tomorrow?"

I shook my head, raised my glass and waved it tipsily. "No," I said. "No, we are not leaving. Do you know what we are going to do tomorrow? You don't? Well, I'll tell you. We shall be drunk. Quite, quite drunk. All day long. We shall lie in our bunks and sleep. Won't that be lovely?"

Kleinman grinned, and reached for the vodka bottle. For him, that was the watershed—if you can call it that—between sobriety and intoxication. From that moment he seemed to stop worrying and really begin to drink. From that moment, too, my own recollections become a little hazy. I know that we began to get very matey. I asked him to tell me what Russian women were like, and the subject being very much to his taste he went into a lot of detail. He told me about an adventure he'd had with some girl in Kazan, and pretty soon the conversation at our end of the table had definitely taken a turn for the worse. He had picked up a good deal of smut in Chicago as well as his frightful accent and odd vocabulary, and he told me a lot of old stories. At some point in the night I remember noting with surprise that I'd chalked up twelve vodkas on the tablecloth, but that must have been comparatively early. I remember, too, in a vague sort of way, seeing Denny and the lieutenant get up and stagger out to have a look at *Neva's* engine, which I don't think Kleinman would have approved of at an earlier stage in the evening. They were talking and laughing a great deal, just as though they understood each other. I imagine they were merely repeating the same words over and over again, but they were evidently having a thoroughly good time.

I had been afraid that Kleinman might get political and quarrelsome in his cups but—perhaps significantly—he soon forgot his ideology when he began to get tight. Our toasts were becoming more frequent and more silly, and our relations were getting better and better. I began to think I had misjudged him—he now seemed to me a friendly little chap. I know I shook him by the hand several times and asked him to come and stay in my flat when he came to London. He tried without much success to write down my London address in a little book and I drew a sketch-map of the district. He also showed me a game which he said was a Russian variation of noughts and crosses, but you played it with nude blondes.

Then, inevitably, someone started to sing. I suppose it was the lieutenant. He had a strong tenor voice and no inhibitions. He started off with some rousing naval songs in which Kleinman tried to join, though he obviously didn't know the words. Then he gave us, of all things, 'The Miners' Song' and some dirge about 'bending our broad backs for Stalin'. Having got this required music off his chest he produced a *balalaika* from the forepeak—practically breaking up the cabin to get it—and began crooning old Ukrainian folk-songs. Vaguely I knew that I knew them, and vaguely I remembered that I was not supposed to know them. They brought back old nostalgic scenes and memories—frozen dug-outs on the Don, peasant huts and bomb-shattered provincial hotels, broken-down Russian buses and stranded Russian aeroplanes, early morning vodka parties with Red Army officers and Russian correspondents, and dancing with buxom Russian waitresses in the empty palaces of the Crimea. For me, these songs were part of the warp and weft of the war years and now I had to hum them and pretend they were new to me. I felt very sentimental and was sorry for myself in a maudlin way. I was getting very drunk.

We sang in turn, more or less, first a Russian song, then an English one. Denny and I rendered all the old standbyes like 'Tipperary' and 'Two Lovely Black Eyes' and 'Roll Out the Barrel', and we made a great hit with 'Polly Wolly Doodle' and 'My Bonny Lies over the Ocean'. Kleinman made us sing several of them twice—he thought them 'swell'. We must have made that quiet and beautiful night hideous with our raucous discords for I certainly had no pretensions as a singer even when sober, and Denny added volume rather than harmony. Also, he couldn't be dissuaded from beating on the table with his fists in time with the songs, so that he set all the plates and glasses dancing. No longer did he look like a Methodist sidesman. His face was scarlet, his eyes were bloodshot, his suit was rumpled and his once-neat white collar was unfastened at the neck to give him air.

I've a fairly clear recollection of a kind of hiatus in the noise, when we were all too hoarse and tired to sing any more, and then of Kleinman getting up on his side of the table and swaying a little, so that he reminded me of one of those little china figures with nodding heads, and saying something about 'Champanski'. I remember seeing four bottles of Russian champagne on the table, and then hearing a lot of popping. Champagne on top of vodka was murder, but it tasted fine. We sang a bit more—at least, Kleinman and I did—in a desultory way. Stepan was plucking rather ineffectually at his *balalaika* and appeared to be crying quietly to himself. I couldn't see the little man's eyes any more—the second round of champagne had made everything go misty. His face was just a vague round blob. Then the whole cabin began to rotate. It went over and over and over, and I felt dreadful, and that was the last thing I knew.

Never have I wakened to consciousness so reluctantly. When I first tried to move my head I doubted if I should live. My mouth felt as though it was full of sawdust. I was lying down and I wanted to go on lying down. But I also wanted to drink. With infinite caution I moved my head to the right and saw that Denny was lying motionless on the opposite bunk. We were back in *Dawn*. At that moment I could hardly have cared less.

I must have given a loud groan, for someone came into the cabin and I saw that it was Joe. He looked revolting—his grin was so wide that I thought his face would fall in two. He said, "Oh, what a beautiful morning!"

With a fearful effort I struggled into a sitting position. "Water," I croaked, "for the love of Mike!" Joe produced a jug, and I took a long swig. After I'd had the water I felt drunk all over again.

"Would you like some ham and eggs?" said Joe. He had a simple sense of humour. I shuddered and drank some more water. I could have drunk water for ever.

Then Denny began to stir, and I saw my own agony repeated. We were still wearing most of our overnight clothes, and they were in a shocking state. After a time, with infinite pain, we managed to throw them off and to struggle into shorts and shirts.

I sat on the edge of the bunk with my head in my hands. I said, "Where are we, Joe?" I knew somehow that it was important, but I couldn't remember why.

"At sea," said Joe cheerfully.

I said, "Good old Joe!" I had a feeling that he had given the right answer. I would have slapped him on the back except that there was a loose piece of iron in my head that kept dropping every time I moved.

Presently Joe made some black coffee and we drank a lot of it. I tried to collect my thoughts, but found it hard to concentrate. I said, "What time is it?"

Joe said it was one o'clock.

"What, in the afternoon?" asked Denny incredulously.

"Of course," said Joe.

"Good God," said Denny. "What time did we come home?"

Joe said: "I fetched you when the singing stopped. Just after three."

"Did we come quietly?" asked Denny.

Joe was still grinning. He said: "I thought you were both dead. What happened?"

I looked at Denny. "Tell him what happened," I said.

"What happened where?" said Denny.

"On that boat," I said.

"Never heard of it," said Denny. He looked at himself in the mirror and groaned. "And to think I'm going to meet my wife tonight!"

It was the hangover to end all hangovers. We sluiced ourselves and shaved with infinite care and still felt as fragile as old parchment. Then we stepped rather gingerly into the cockpit. The fresh air felt good, but the bright light was blinding. It was another warm summer day, but there was a pleasant breeze and I saw that *Dawn* was quietly sailing herself. I thought that in two or three hours I might begin to feel moderately human again. I gazed around, but could see no sign of land in any direction. I said, "Where exactly are we, Joe?"

He showed me the chart, on which our course and position were marked in pencil. We were about thirty miles north-west of Tallinn and bang in the middle of the Gulf. I still couldn't get my ideas into focus. I said, "Joe, I know we had some plan last night, but I can't remember what it was."

"I shouldn't try," said Joe. "It'll come back to you. Everything's under control."

I wound a wet towel round my head and said: "What happened, Joe? Tell us your story. P'raps it'll help us to remember."

"Well," said Joe, "after I'd got things shipshape in the cabin and had a meal I went up on deck for a smoke."

"And listened to us making beasts of ourselves," said Denny.

"Exactly. It was very warm and pleasant and I had a little rum to keep me in good spirits. I could hear quite a lot of what you said, particularly when the boats swung together. Then you began to shout and sing and the party got very noisy. I waited, and there was some more talking, and then I couldn't hear anything at all. So I rowed over."

"We must have been a fine spectacle," I said.

Joe nodded complacently. "You certainly were. It *looked* as though there'd been a free-for-all. You didn't actually fight, did you?"

"Fight? Good heavens, no. At least—I don't think so. We were all most friendly."

"Well, the little man had blood on his face and a black eye. He must have fallen against something pretty hard. The lieutenant was snoring on the floor—he seemed very comfortable on a lot of broken glass. Denny was curled up in the cockpit, and you were lying across the table with your head on your arms."

"Wonderful scene," I said. "Just like the 'Sleeping Beauty'."

"Well, not quite," said Joe. "I didn't feel like kissing any of you, believe me. I had a hell of a job getting you into the dinghy. Denny began to come round after I'd thrown some water over him, but he collapsed again when I got him aboard here. I had to lower *you* into the dinghy with a rope!"

"Poor old Joe! Didn't the other two show any sign of life at all?"

"Not a flicker. I didn't even have to be quiet. If I'd opened the seacocks they'd have gone down without a whimper."

"Vodka's dynamite," said Denny.

"I know," said Joe. "I tried it. I thought I might never have another chance. Their champagne's not bad, either. Anyway, I got you aboard here and tried to sober you up a bit, but you were too far gone. I couldn't get you to swallow anything. It was hopeless trying to undress you, so I decided you'd have to lie as you were and sleep it off. The rest was easy. I untied their warp, made sail, and here we are."

"Did you leave them adrift?" I asked.

Joe looked pained. "I couldn't do that," he said. "They might have been a danger to someone else. I found their anchor in the fo'c's'le—the one they were supposed to have lost—and left them all secure."

"Very considerate. I wonder how they're feeling at this moment."

"That lieutenant's tough," said Denny. "I bet he's having vodka for breakfast. When we went into the cockpit to look at the engine he started drinking out of a bottle. Did you see their engine, Joe?"

Joe nodded. "It must be fifty horsepower."

"At least," said Denny. "I bet they can do fifteen knots."

I was still struggling to get a clear mental picture of our situation, and that remark of Denny's helped to make things click into place. I said: "I suppose they'll be after us. Or maybe they'll put out a general alarm all over the Gulf. Do you think they have a radio transmitter on board?"

"They haven't," said the efficient Joe. "I looked."

I was beginning to focus again. I tried to imagine myself in Kleinman's position, and then I wasn't so sure about the general alarm. By N.K.V.D. standards he hadn't done so well—he'd hardly want to admit that we'd got away because both he and his lieutenant had got drunk. He'd be more likely to comb the Gulf for us in an attempt to retrieve his error. He'd know that with our engine we couldn't be more than sixty or seventy miles away. He'd also know that we were definitely up to mischief. He'd be after us. I couldn't imagine what we should do when *Neva* appeared. Perhaps it was the hangover, but I didn't see that we could do anything. It rather looked as though we'd merely postponed our failure by a few hours.

I gave Joe an outline of what was in my mind. He was puffing calmly at a cigarette and seemed at peace with the world. I said: "How long do you think we've got, Joe? An hour or two?"

"I think longer than that," said Joe, blowing a lovely smoke ring. "You see, before I left their boat I took a look round and saw a lot of cans of spare petrol in the cockpit. So I dropped them overboard in a couple of fathoms. The only petrol they've got at the moment is what's in their tank."

Well, that certainly made our prospects much brighter, and Joe deserved the cheer we gave him. It meant we had probably gained a day and a night free from pursuit. Kleinman and the lieutenant, coming out of their drunken sleep, would only now be discovering the loss of their petrol. They would have to put back into Porkkala or some other base to refuel—always supposing they had enough petrol in their tank to reach port. There was no chance that they could do all that and still seek us out before dark. We had regained our freedom of action.

The most urgent thing now was for Denny and me to get rid of our respective hangovers in readiness for the arduous night's work. We hove to at about three in the afternoon and I went overboard for a refreshing swim. After that we had a 'hair of the dog' and some food. I still found it very difficult to concentrate, and after I'd cleaned up my shoregoing clothes we both turned in for a snooze.

When Joe woke us a couple of hours later there was a note of urgency in his voice. "It's time we got moving," he said. "We've just under thirty miles to go. That's about three hours' steaming and an hour's sailing. Lend a hand, will you?"

We all turned to, and in a few minutes *Dawn* was heading south-east under power. Three hours' steaming should bring us to the entrance of Tallinn Bay just as the sun was going down, and an hour under sail would see us at the Vake shoal—with luck—just at dusk. So far, our timing was excellent.

We had had so many problems to deal with in the past twenty-four hours that we hadn't been able to think much about the details of the rescue. Now we went over our plans point by point. The girls would probably be pretty exhausted when we picked them up out of the water and we equipped the dinghy accordingly. We rolled up their clothing in two separate waterproof bundles and stowed them carefully under the dinghy's stern seat. We put in several towels, some food, a thermos of coffee and a flask of brandy. It was agreed that Joe should stay with *Dawn* at the anchorage and that Denny and I should row in.

The old tingling excitement was coming back now as the crisis approached. I couldn't help casting apprehensive glances round the horizon and wishing that these last hours of daylight were over. Providence had so far been kind. The sea was quiet and warm, the breeze was gentle but sufficient, the beat of our engine was steady. If only our luck held!

Just before half past seven I tuned in to Steve's Leningrad wavelength. There was almost certain to be a message and we waited even more tensely than usual for him to come on the air. He wasn't so very far away from us and he came through as clear as a bell. Sweat gathered on my forehead as I heard the word 'Today' and I scribbled furiously to get the message down. My hand had acquired an alcoholic tremor, or else it was excitement that made me take a lot longer than usual to transcribe my shorthand.

"Today in Leningrad," ran the broadcast, "I have been privileged to go and examine post-war reconstruction work, which is far ahead of my expectations. First, it is only proper to recall the fearful bombardment which made Leningrad a hell in the war years. The shelling had consequences with which Leningraders have mainly dealt, though it left marks on the city. Some effects of that long and ghastly ordeal are still visible. Occasionally in the angles of buildings you can see even now heaps of old weed-covered debris which the citizens have been too busy to clear away. . . ."

That was all of it that mattered. With my heart pounding and the other two breathing down my neck I ringed the significant words. They were GO AHEAD TO HELL WITH MARKS AND ANGLES.

I loved Steve for that message—not merely for his pleasing ingenuity in conjuring Marx and Engels out of such unpromising material, but for the buoyancy and assurance, which did us more good than any conventional *bon voyage*. He had evidently played his part—the girls would be there to meet us. Now it was up to us.

Just before sundown we got our first and last glimpse of Tallinn, but it faded quickly as dusk spread over the sea. We were still well on schedule. Joe had been ceaselessly occupied with the chart and the engine and his watch. He had guaranteed to get us to the Vake shoal by nine, and he was going to do it. With dusk upon us there was nothing but the harbour lights to guide us, and pilotage required the utmost concentration. So far we were all right. On our starboard bow there was a flashing white light high up on the northern tip of Nais Island which we had no difficulty in identifying. Right ahead were the red and white flashes of the Aegna light.

As darkness fell Joe switched off the engine, and once more we helped him make sail. With the engine silent we felt more secure. The wind was little more than a zephyr just forward of the beam, but we were making fair progress. The atmosphere aboard was now electric. There was nothing to do but wait, and nothing useful to say. Better to leave it to Joe. His eyes were everywhere, watching the sails, peering out at the buoys, checking the compass. His taut features, faintly illuminated by the binnacle lamp, were a mask of concentration. Far ahead, in the darkness of the wide bay, lights were winking out on the low shore and from buildings high up in the three-tier town.

Suddenly Joe gave a sharp exclamation. "There it is," he cried, pointing landwards. "See it? The Vake shoal. Time the flashes." I strained into the darkness, following the line of his pointing finger, and in a moment I saw a white flash which disappeared and then flashed again. I counted, and the interval was four seconds. Our first objective was in sight.

"Good old Joe," I said softly. "We'll be on the dot." Now that we had spotted the buoy it beckoned us insistently. There was no possibility of losing our way; there were no navigational hazards. With our grey hull and our tanned sails we were quite invisible a few yards away. The only danger was that we might be run down in the dark, but that risk would pass as soon as we reached the shoal.

We were all keeping our eyes open now for the most vital of our direction-posts—the Viimsi leading lights. Again it was Joe who spotted them first, far away on the port bow. They were not, of course, in line yet—that wouldn't happen until we took the dinghy south of the shoal. But they were readily identifiable—one light was flashing every second and the other occulting every four seconds as the chart indicated.

The night seemed very still as we slid slowly and silently into the depths of the Bay. Out of the distance, faint shore noises came stealing over the water—a train whistle, a motorcar engine, and every now and again the strains of music. Judging by the illuminations along the beach below the town there was a lot of activity going on. Over on Viimsi, however, all was dark, apart from the leading lights. It seemed that our rendezvous had been well chosen.

Just before nine Joe said quietly, "Stand by to let go," and I went forward to tend the anchor. I could see that we were almost abreast of the Vake light, and could make out the shape of the buoy. We sailed on for a hundred yards, nearly ramming one of the four coloured beacons which marked the limits of the shoal. I felt *Dawn* swinging into the faint wind and just caught Joe's hushed instruction to "Let her go". I lowered the anchor over the bows with infinite care as we began to gather sternway, and paid the cable out as quietly as I could. Joe heaved the lead and I heard him say "Three fathoms". I veered twelve fathoms of cable. There was almost no current, and barely enough wind to pull the chain taut.

I scrambled down to the cockpit. Joe said: "I'll look after the sails. You'd better get going—it's five to nine." He helped us to launch the dinghy, and Denny and I clambered in. It was a moment that imprinted its details permanently on my mind—Joe's tense face as he leaned over the gunwale holding our painter; Denny's quiet matter-of-factness as he arranged himself for the long trip and made sure the luggage was safely stowed; the buoy flashing just astern of us; the warm air and hushed stillness and bright stars.

Joe gripped our hands. "I'll expect you when I see you. Good luck! Good hunting!"

I said: "Thanks, Joe. We should be back about eleven. Okay, let her go."

Joe slipped the painter and I pushed off into the darkness of the Bay.

Chapter Eleven

This is the moment, I think, when I should break off the narrative and briefly record the fortunes of Marya and Svetlana up to this point.

As soon as Steve had got back to Moscow from London he had taken the girls out to Sokolniki park on the outskirts of the town—where he could talk without fear of microphones behind the wallpaper—and had told them our plan. Their feelings were very mixed; they were terrifically excited, but apprehensive. It took Steve a long time to convince them that it was a practicable undertaking. He agreed that it was dangerous, but when they realized that the plan was not just an idea and that it was already half undertaken they were eager to make the attempt. Svetlana, matter-of-fact and rather fatalistic, was soon getting down to details as practically as though she were compiling a shopping list. Marya, lifted to ecstatic pinnacles of hope, was ready to dare anything, though with her keener imagination she was the more fearful.

Marya presented no great problem for Steve. She was about to leave on her long tour, and the Russians themselves would bear her surely and safely to the planned destination. Steve went over the details with her before she left, impressed on her the date and time of meeting, and gave her a harmless code message which she could cable to Svetlana if there was any last-minute change in her itinerary. Such a change seemed in the highest degree unlikely, since it would not be policy to disappoint any of the large towns which featured in the schedule.

Steve had told Marya to keep in touch with Svetlana by letter, and this she did. She wrote from Kharkov saying she had danced the lead in *Swan Lake* and had been tremendously applauded by the provincial public. She wrote from Kiev that she had slightly strained a muscle but that it was already better. She wrote from Odessa that she had found an amusing companion in the assistant Wardrobe Mistress, one Valentina Alexandrovna, and that they went everywhere together. She wrote from Minsk that she had received 'three offers of bigamy'. She seemed in high spirits.

With Marya off his mind Steve could turn to more difficult matters. The first problem was to contact Rosa, the Tallinn dressmaker. Svetlana found the woman's address in Steve's files—flat 36, house 12, Pushkinskaya. Steve knew that Rosa occasionally came to Moscow on business, but he didn't want to suggest a call at the hotel in a letter through the open post. But Svetlana found a way. The chief dress factory in Moscow happened to be holding a public exhibition of clothes for postwar mass production. Svetlana went along and managed to get friendly with a girl from Baltiski—the next town along the coast from Tallinn—who had brought samples of Estonian work to Moscow and was going back through Tallinn in a day or two. Svetlana gave her a carefully worded letter for Rosa, and some nylons.

There were some anxious moments after that, but within a fortnight Rosa called at the hotel. She said it had been fairly easy for her to undertake the journey, for the dress exhibition was still on. Svetlana met her in the hotel entrance hall and they talked there of the fur wrap which Rosa was going to have made for Steve's wife in America. This was for the benefit of the vigilant reception office, but a secret appointment was also arranged.

The three of them met in Sokolniki after dark. Steve didn't tell Rosa any more than he had to, but the drift of his purpose must have been fairly plain. He had to trust her that much, and felt he could do so, for the letter she had sent to her people in America by him had been of a kind to get her a life sentence if it had been found. A thin, bony woman of thirty-five or so, Rosa was highly intelligent and emotionally intense. She was very intrigued when Steve asked her to stroll out to Viimsi as soon as she got back and look at the leading lights and the Vake buoy, but she agreed at once to do it. Steve gave her a little sketch-map which she was to destroy as soon as she had studied it. She promised that if it were humanly possible she would meet Svetlana at Leningrad station with a spare ticket on the night of August 13 and accompany her back to Tallinn. Steve offered her a substantial sum of money, but she refused to accept it, saying to him, "One day *you* will set *us* free."

Both Steve and Svetlana now began to cultivate the goodwill of the Press Department, and particularly of the second censor, Bankov, who usually arranged the correspondents' trips. Steve contrived to give the impression that he was undergoing a change of heart, and his broadcasts became increasingly friendly towards Russia. In July he approached the Head of the Press Department with a request that he should be allowed to go to Leningrad and do a couple of broadcasts on the successful reconstruction of the city. He suggested that the middle of August would be the best time because that was always a dead period for news at home, and he enlisted Bankov's co-operation—a censor was always glad to get out of Moscow on a trip. Svetlana made the final arrangements. Bankov was ardent and susceptible, and she had no difficulty in persuading him that the middle of August was a convenient time. In the end the Press Department decided to lay on a trip for all the correspondents, as Steve had no objection, and on August 11 a band of newspaper men some fifteen strong, with four or five secretaries, arrived at the biggest hotel in Leningrad for a three-day stay. Precisely two weeks before, Svetlana had received a brief note from Rosa saying that the fur wrap would soon be ready and that she was looking forward to meeting Svetlana as arranged.

At about the same time as Svetlana was settling into the Leningrad hotel Marya was climbing with her friend and admirer Valentina Alexandrovna to a seat under the old castle ramparts in Tallinn. Their train had come in that morning and they had a free day. Marya had rather wanted to wander off alone and get her bearings in the town, but Valentina had begged to be allowed to come along too. They sat down at a spot which gave them a wonderful view of the Bay. Valentina was chattering away as usual, but Marya hardly listened to her. She was thinking how incredible it was that somewhere out on that still sea—not very far away—*Dawn* must at that moment be approaching. Away on the right she could just make out the hazy line of the Viimsi coast, where she would soon be keeping tryst. She felt terribly excited and wondered how she would get through the next three days.

Valentina said: "How quiet you are today, Marya darling. What are you dreaming of?"

Marya pulled her wandering thoughts back and answered with a laugh. "I was thinking how wonderful it would be to dance before Joseph Vissarionovitch in the Bolshoi. One day, perhaps I will, Valentina."

"Of course you will. You looked so sentimental, I thought perhaps you were thinking of your husband."

Marya was startled. "My husband!" Then she smiled sadly and shrugged her shoulders. "What is the use?"

"You still love him, don't you?"

"Let us not talk of him," said Marya, with some impatience. But Valentina persisted.

"You know," she continued, "you are very foolish to waste yourself. I know what I should do if I were as young and beautiful as you. I should choose a new husband—very carefully. Soon, Marya, they will all be at your feet—generals, commissars, everyone. You will be able to take your pick. I envy you."

Marya could stand no more. "Valentina, please leave me alone for a while—I don't feel well."

"Then I certainly shan't leave you, little dove. You look pale. You must come and have a glass of tea."

Marya, afraid to behave in anything but a normal manner, rose reluctantly and followed her insistent companion.

Three days more to get through!

Back in Leningrad the Press trip was following a well-established routine. On the first day the correspondents made a tour of the city, interviewing planners and architects and talking to the leading civic authorities. In the evening the Mayor gave them a banquet. On the second day the whole body of correspondents and secretaries went out to Peterhof to see how the famous palace was being restored and in the evening there was another banquet at which the leading intellectuals of Leningrad were produced.

Steve had done his broadcast, and having taken leave of Svetlana with a quick handclasp and a 'Good luck, baby!' was now giving himself an alibi by repeatedly drinking 'bottoms up' with a still unpurged Soviet poet. The party was hilarious, for work was over and tomorrow they were all returning to Moscow. Svetlana had no difficulty in slipping away by ten o'clock, for by that time no one knew or cared where anybody else was. She had to meet Rosa at ten-thirty for the eleven o'clock train, and the station was only about ten minutes away.

At a quarter past ten she went downstairs to the entrance hall. She had, of course, no luggage. She wore a light summer frock and carried a handbag. She had had just enough to drink to take the edge off her apprehensions. She pushed through the swing doors and was about to walk away when someone called her. It was Bankov, leaning heavily against the wall. He managed to get himself upright and stood swaying. "Svetlana Mikhailovna!" he cried. "What good fortune!" He put a hand on her arm. He was much more drunk than a censor ought to be.

Svetlana brushed him off with a disapproving "*Oy yoy*, Alexei Alexeivitch, aren't you ashamed of yourself?" She began to walk along the street, but Bankov followed her.

"Where are you going, Svetlana Mikhailovna? You shouldn't be out alone, my dear, as late as this."

Svetlana turned on him angrily. "I am hot—I want to walk. Go away, Alexei Alexeivitch, you stink of vodka."

"How unkind you are," said Bankov, putting his arm round her. "You need a husband, Svetlana, my dear."

"I've got a husband," she said fiercely, trying to free herself.

"Oh no," said Bankov, leering at her, "you *had* a husband."

Svetlana said desperately, "I shall report you for drunkenness." But Bankov continued to paw at her.

"Just one kiss, Svetlana, my dove."

She smacked his face hard. Instead of sobering him it made him violent and he began struggling with her. Luckily he was a small man, barely a match for her. She clenched her fist and hit him with all her strength. Bankov staggered back, tripped and fell—and at that moment Svetlana heard a whistle being blown. She began to run, but a militiaman intercepted her.

"Why the hurry?" he growled. "What's happening, *tovarisch*?"

"I was out for a quiet walk," Svetlana gasped, trying to fasten her torn dress, "and a man attacked me. He's drunk."

"Come back with me," said the militiaman, taking her arm.

Svetlana dared not refuse. They went back to where Bankov was just getting up from the gutter. "You little bitch!" he shouted when he saw Svetlana, and made a grab at her. The militiaman let go of Svetlana and blew his whistle as he tried to restrain Bankov. Svetlana turned and took to her heels. She raced up a side street and continued running for two blocks, as hard as she could. Then she stopped and listened. Nobody seemed to be following her. She gave a little sob. Everything had gone wrong. She was hot, dishevelled and out of breath, and the time was nearly half past ten. She had run in the wrong direction for the station and dared not go back past the hotel. She made a detour, walking fast and trying to tidy herself as she went. Presently she saw the big clock above the station. The hands pointed to ten forty. Svetlana nearly wept; she was late for her meeting with Rosa, and in twenty minutes the train would leave. The last train—the only train that would get her to Tallinn in time!

She rushed through the vast waiting hall, where hundreds of people lay with all their worldly possessions and a crowd seethed like a besieging army around the closed ticket offices. She ran to the train indicator, her heart pounding. Surely Rosa had waited—for ten minutes, for fifteen minutes? Desperately Svetlana gazed around, searching for Rosa's thin, tense face. There was no sign of her.

Now what to do? To scour the station?—but Rosa might come, and miss her. To wait there passively?—and let the train go. To search the platform?—perhaps Rosa was making sure of the seats.

The Tallinn train was filling up in noise and bustle. Svetlana could see the usual milling crowds on the platform—the travellers, the would-be travellers and the non-travellers. The minutes ticked by. Svetlana knew she was losing her chance for ever. It was ten to eleven—she must search for Rosa. Quickly she darted up the whole length of the barrierless platform. But it was hopeless to find anyone. She could not see into the high train. At the entrance to each coach there was a harassed car conductor examining tickets, appealing for order, guarding his precious seats. There were clearly more people without tickets than with. Voices were raised, strident, urgent, appealing. A militiaman patrolled the platform in case argument became more than verbal. He seemed quite undisturbed by the babel. He knew that in a few minutes the train would draw out and the rowdy shouting throng would melt away.

A bell rang. Svetlana rushed wildly from carriage to carriage. She could think of nothing but that Rosa had failed her. Suddenly she saw a young Red Army man with a bandaged foot and a crutch stumping up to a hard-class carriage. He was carrying a large parcel wrapped in newspaper, sweat was pouring down his face, his lank hair was in his eyes. Svetlana saw that between his thumb and finger was a ticket. She rushed up to him as the bell sounded for the second time. "Let me help you," she said. He gave her a grateful glance and she took the parcel. "Make way there!" she cried. "Make way! Aren't you ashamed of yourselves, blocking the way for a wounded hero? Look at his foot, the poor boy." She hacked and elbowed, cursing and being cursed. "Conductor," she cried, "make them stand back. This boy has a ticket." The conductor shouted "Make way!" She was nearly there now, with the soldier close behind her. She was touching the rail by the steps. As she struggled up and held out a hand to the soldier the conductor said sharply, "Your ticket, citizeness?"

"I'm not travelling," said Svetlana, hauling the soldier up and pulling the crutch after him. "If no one else will help this fellow, I must."

"Be quick, then," the conductor warned her. "We're just going." He took the soldier's ticket and tucked it into a little pouch. "Place

135

number twenty-seven. Stand back, there." The bell clanged for the last time. Svetlana was in the carriage. The train gave a sudden jerk. The soldier said: "Quick, you must go. Thank you, thank you." The conductor rushed in. "We're moving. Hurry, citizeness, hurry." Svetlana looked through the window and saw the platform lights slowly slipping by. The conductor was half dragging her towards the carriage door. There was only one thing to do. The whole ten stone of her sagged to the floor and she lay there inert with her leg carefully crooked round a seat support.

By the time she had had water dashed in her face and was ready to come round, the train was leaving the outskirts of Leningrad. She scrambled to her feet. People were gazing down at her with benevolent interest from the tiers of hard wooden bunks. The soldier was leaning on his crutch and regarding her with concern.

"I fainted," she said, unnecessarily.

The conductor was muttering bad-temperedly. "A fine thing!" he said. "I have known many people travel without tickets, but this was the cleverest trick of all."

Svetlana gave him a withering look. "Fool! Do I look as though I'm travelling? No coat, no blankets, no luggage, not even food!" She glanced round to see if public opinion was with her so far, and found that it was. "Idiot! If you had kept proper order at the entrance it would have been unnecessary for me to get in." There was a murmur of approval. "It's disgraceful that you should let a howling mob make travel impossible for decent people."

The conductor was sulky and unconvinced. "All the same, you must get off."

"Get off! What do you expect me to do? Jump out?"

"You must get off at Narva."

"And pray when shall I get a train back from Narva?"

The conductor shrugged. "Perhaps tomorrow morning. Perhaps tomorrow night."

"And perhaps next week! I shall go on to Tallinn. There I shall go to the Press Department of Narkomindyel, for whom I work, and they will get me a ticket. And you, my friend—*bozhe moi*, for you there will be trouble!"

136

The conductor regarded her doubtfully. She was a talker, this girl—she could put a case. She had a confident air—and a gold wrist-watch. She seemed, indeed, a person of authority—not a person who would travel hard-class. Perhaps she *would* make trouble. He said, "Let us go and talk quietly." He took her to his own cubby-hole where he slept when off duty.

"And now, *tovarisch*," said Svetlana amiably. "Let us stop arguing and be reasonable. The harm is done. Let me have your bed, and we will say no more." She took a hundred rouble note from her handbag and his fingers closed over it.

It wasn't a very clean bed, but Svetlana was tired out and managed to make herself very comfortable. The conductor, relieved of anxiety and financially fortified, could not do enough for her. He even made her a glass of tea. Svetlana dozed a little, but mostly she lay awake wondering about Rosa. How was it possible that they had missed each other at the station? Well, it didn't matter now. In a few hours she would be in Tallinn.

It was a fine and sunny day on the Baltic coast and as they steamed into Tallinn Svetlana's spirits rose. It was nearly midday, and she was hungry. She went into the station buffet and ate two rolls. Then she washed and tidied herself. When she finally stepped out into Tallinn she was neat and smart again. If she attracted attention now, it would only be on account of her good looks.

It had been agreed that she should meet Marya on the beach by the leading lights at a quarter to ten that night, so she had many hours to kill. She took a tram out to Pirita and walked along the coastal track until she could see the tall mast on which the foremost light was fixed. There would be no difficulty at all, she decided. Having reconnoitred the ground she returned to the town, had a good meal, and relaxed. She wondered if her absence from Leningrad had been discovered yet. It had been Steve's intention to be ill after the banquet and to lie low in bed as long as possible. Bankov, however, would probably be looking for her, if he wasn't in jail. She knew he would want to apologize. She felt sorry for Bankov, who would undoubtedly lose his job, if nothing worse. She sighed. In every operation there must be casualties.

Her thoughts swung back to Rosa. Perhaps the woman was ill or in trouble. Svetlana could not forget her taut, harassed face. If she were ill it would be ungrateful to go off without at least trying to see her, and Svetlana had much to thank her for. There could be no harm in calling at her house, if it were done with caution. The visit would help to fill in the hours of waiting.

A passer-by directed her to Pushkinskaya, a new road on the outskirts of the town. She decided to walk, and in less than half an hour she had found the street, which was composed entirely of newish blocks of flats, tall, ugly and commodious. She approached house 12 with care, but there were no signs of anything unusual happening. Children were playing and women were talking, but there were no suspicious loiterers or waiting cars. Svetlana slowly climbed the concrete stairs to the second floor. Three flats shared the same landing and all seemed quiet. She knocked at Number 36. There was no answer and she knocked again, very loudly.

Beside her the door of Number 37 opened a fraction and a voice said sharply, "Well?" Svetlana saw a worn-out wisp of a woman peering at her with hostility and suspicion.

Svetlana said, "I wanted to see Rosa Meingal."

"Who are you? What do you want with her?"

Svetlana was frightened and wished she hadn't come. But she said: "I'm a customer of hers. She was making me a dress."

The woman opened the door a little wider, looking Svetlana up and down. Then she said in a milder tone: "You won't see her. She's in hospital."

"In hospital! What's the matter with her?"

The woman's face was hard. "*They* came for her—a week ago."

"*They* . . .?"

"Yes," said the woman. "Rosa wouldn't open the door. When they broke it in, she threw herself out of the window."

Svetlana turned pale. "*Oy yoy*," she said in a shocked tone. "Will she recover?"

The woman shrugged. "She was very badly hurt. It is a big drop from the window. They took her to the municipal hospital. *They* went with her."

Svetlana slowly descended the stairs, clinging to the rail and feeling sick. Poor Rosa! A phrase that the woman had used came into her mind. "*They* went with her." Svetlana could imagine them, sitting by the bedside, waiting. What did they suspect? Why had they arrested her? Had it anything to do with Steve and herself? Had they searched the apartment and found something?

Svetlana's thoughts flashed back to that grim ordeal she herself had had to face at N.K.V.D. headquarters—the small hot room, the straight-backed chair, the bright light shining in her eyes, the shadowy figures, the questions and the questions. And she had been lucky. They had let her go. There was nothing special they had wanted from her. But if they *had* wanted anything and she had remained silent. . . . Svetlana shuddered again. It was horrible. But a woman who had fallen from a window, who was desperately ill—they wouldn't take her away. . . . They wouldn't torture a sick person. Or would they?

Svetlana felt she must set her mind at rest. At this very moment they might know about Steve and herself, about their interest in the lights and the buoy. They would soon know about her own disappearance from Leningrad and they would put the bits of the puzzle together. They might be setting a trap. If only she could talk to Rosa! But that was impossible. They might still be at the hospital, and they would certainly question visitors. There was still the telephone, though.

She walked nearly a mile before she found a telephone booth. She rang the hospital and a man's voice answered.

"I'm inquiring about Rosa Meingal, who was brought to your hospital about a week ago. An accident case. Please tell me how she is."

"Are you a relative?"

"Yes, yes. I'm her sister. I've only just arrived in Tallinn."

"Wait, please."

Svetlana leaned heavily against the side of the booth.

Presently the voice said: "Are you there? Rosa Meingal died the night she was brought in. I'm sorry."

"Did she leave any messages?"

"I'll ask," said the man. Presently he came on again. "I'm sorry, *tovariscb*. Rosa Meingal left no messages. She died without recovering consciousness."

"Thank you," said Svetlana slowly.

Chapter Twelve

Dawn had become a vague black shape against the stars, and gradually we lost sight of her altogether. I rowed south, away from the shoal, till Denny called softly that the Viimsi lights were now in line. Then I swung the dinghy almost at a right angle and began the long pull to the peninsula. We had oiled the rowlocks and muffled the oars, and our progress was almost silent.

We had about four miles to row and just under an hour to do it in. The wind seemed to have died completely and I had seen heavier seas on the lake in Regent's Park. I concentrated on the rowing. After much practice I had learned to judge roughly how far I had rowed by the number and strength of the strokes. To arrive a minute or two early wouldn't matter, but if we were late the girls would turn back and we should have the risky pull in to the beach. We were both keyed up. If all had gone well ashore success seemed within our grasp. At this very moment Svetlana and Marya were, we fervently hoped, sitting on the beach only three miles or so away. In less than an hour they'd be in the dinghy with us—we'd be able to talk to them, to touch them. My pulse raced at the thought.

Denny was keeping his eye on the Viimsi beacons, for I had my back to them. Every now and again he said softly, "Starboard a little" or "Port a little" and I made a slight correction until they were in line again. Without them we could never have made the right landfall. The rest of the coastline was either quite dark or a confusion of lights. I thought I could distinguish brightly-lit Pirita over on my left, but I wasn't even certain about that. Away in the harbour there was some activity and once we heard the distant splutter of a motor-boat engine. Our part of the bay was quite empty.

I rowed on steadily, rhythmically, counting the strokes. About half-way Denny suggested taking over, but I didn't want to spoil the timing. A clock somewhere over by Pirita chimed a quarter to ten, and we checked our watches. Denny whispered "We shan't be long now," but the journey seemed endless to me as I continued to pull. When I thought we were close inshore I sounded the water with an oar, but it was still too deep to find bottom. My watch showed two minutes to ten. I rested on the oars, and we both listened tensely. My heart was thumping. Denny was motionless. I took three or four more strokes and then unshipped the oars. The lights were bang in line and I could just make out the tower of the foremost light against the sky. We couldn't be more than a quarter of a mile from the shore. If the girls had entered the water sharp at the appointed time they must be approaching the dinghy.

The strain of those few minutes was indescribable. I was almost choking with excitement and a clutching fear. I paddled the boat forward with my hands and we listened again, staring out into the darkness. Denny was leaning over the stern. There was no sound but the faint lapping of the water against the boat. We paddled a few feet further in. Even a few feet might help. There was still no sound, and dreadful thoughts began to race through my mind. It was four minutes past ten. What could have happened? Could we have missed them? Ought we to row right in?

Then I heard a splash that was not made by the dinghy and there was a hiss of warning from Denny. He had seen something—someone. I leaned over the bows. Yes, he was right—there was a movement in the water a few yards away. We paddled quickly towards the bobbing head and in a few seconds had hauled a dripping panting figure over the stern. It was Svetlana.

"Where's Marya?" I whispered with desperate urgency.

"She didn't come," Svetlana gasped. "She wasn't on the beach. I haven't seen her."

"Oh, God!" I murmured, sick with apprehension. "You're *sure* she wasn't there?"

"Certain. I looked everywhere for her."

"What was your arrangement with her—tell me quickly."

"To meet her on the beach by the lights—that was all."

"She knew the time—ten o'clock?"

"Of course. Oh, poor Marya!"

"Sh!" We were much too near the bank to talk safely. For a moment I gazed towards the shore in blank despair. Everything seemed hopeless. Yet when I thought of going back to *Dawn*, to England, without her I knew what I had to do. This was destiny. I said softly: "Denny, I'm going ashore. She must be in the town. I'm going to look for her."

I couldn't see his face, but I could hear the alarm in his voice. He said: "You're crazy. You can't do that."

"I must. I can't go back without her."

"But she might be anywhere. You won't know where to look. You've no documents. You'll be pinched and jailed."

"I can't help it. I've got to take a chance. I've got to."

Svetlana said: "The N.K.V.D. were after Rosa. She committed suicide a week ago."

I scarcely heard her, and certainly didn't take in what she said. I grabbed and unfastened one of the bundles of clothing, threw the garments across to Svetlana, stripped off all my own clothes and wrapped them securely in the waterproof cover. Then I lowered myself naked into the milk-warm water and held on to the gunwale.

"Denny," I said, "listen carefully. You're to take Svetlana to *Dawn* now. Ask Joe to bring the dinghy back here right away, by himself, and to wait until one o'clock. That's the deadline. If we're not here by one, he's to get back to *Dawn* as quickly as possible and you're to sail for Stockholm. Is that clear?"

"But, Philip——" He was in great distress.

"Don't be a damn' fool, Denny. If you hang about we shall all go down the drain. You know that. I'm off now. Good-bye, Svetlana. Good luck, both of you."

"Good luck, old man," Denny whispered. "Good luck. We'll keep our fingers crossed."

I let go the dinghy and swam slowly ashore, pushing the

waterproof bundle in front of me. My feet soon touched a sandy bottom. I crouched in the water for a moment, listening, and then waded cautiously in to the beach. I felt horribly white and visible, but there wasn't a soul about.

I struggled damply into my clothes and pushed the waterproof under an overhanging rock. I hadn't the slightest idea what I was going to do except get into Tallinn somehow and look around. I felt curiously exalted and indifferent to consequences. At least we had half-succeeded. We had snatched Svetlana away. Now I would go home with Marya or not at all. I don't think I doubted at that moment which it would be—the time was too short, the odds were too great. But I had to try.

I picked my way along the beach for a hundred yards or so, stepping carefully to avoid dislodging any stones, and then I climbed up a low steep cliff and found myself on a rough path. Below me and about two miles ahead I could see the lights of Pirita, with the glow of the town behind. I set off along the track at a smart pace. As I walked I tried to guess what might have happened. I remembered now what Svetlana had said about Rosa. The N.K.V.D. might have found out something. Marya might have been arrested. But if so, why hadn't they arrested Svetlana? Marya might have been taken ill—seriously ill. I couldn't imagine that anything less would have kept her away. Perhaps she had had an accident. I didn't think she could have mistaken the time of meeting, but she might have been delayed. I might even meet her on this very track. I kept a sharp lookout.

The shore was surprisingly empty—there didn't appear to be even a coast patrol. It began to look as though we might have overestimated that danger. I increased my pace. If only I had more time! I tried to think of a plan. I must know what I was going to do when I reached Tallinn—I couldn't just walk about in the darkness. The ballet company must be staying at a hotel—I could try the hotels in turn. Or perhaps it would save time to go first to the theatre and ask there. Even if the theatre were closed there was still the public restaurant in the same building, I remembered.

Somebody would be sure to know where the ballet people were staying.

I tore over the ground now. The path was a good one. Out at sea the flash of the Vake shoal buoy seemed to mock me. Very soon Denny and Svetlana would be there. To me, *Dawn* seemed as remote as the South Pole.

As I swung downhill I passed one or two couples in the dark, but they were intent on their own affairs, and no one spoke to me. The track was widening. On the left some ruins stood out starkly against the sky and I guessed they were those of the monastery I had seen marked on the chart. I was dropping down now into Pirita. I could see the gleam of the little river. Across the bridge was a large pavilion on the beach and I could hear dance music and the chatter of people enjoying themselves. The guide-book had been right about all Tallinn coming out here on hot summer nights. In the road behind the pavilion several sleek and official-looking motor-cars were parked in a row. The idea of taking one flashed through my mind, but the risk seemed too great. The chauffeurs couldn't be far away and the last thing I wanted was a motor-car chase. I heard the tinkle of a tram in the distance. That would be safer. Then I remembered, with a horrible pang, that I hadn't a *kopeck* of Russian money. I hadn't been very smart. Svetlana must have had some—no doubt she had left it with her clothes on the beach. It was too late to go back now. I should have to walk into Tallinn, wasting a precious half-hour. I knew I should probably be terribly handicapped without money when I got there, and I cursed my short-sightedness.

I walked round to the front of the pavilion. There were tables on a verandah under coloured lights. Half a dozen Red Army officers with their girls were drinking beer and eating pastries. Inside the pavilion, people were dancing. The sandy beach in front was floodlit from the verandah and several groups of young people were sitting about on coats and rugs, apparently picnicking. There was an old crone selling ice cream, and a plump young militia girl talking to her. I heard cheerful voices and laughter down by the water's edge and saw that people were swimming.

At the edge of the floodlit area was a public convenience—a long wooden building backing on to some bushes. I thought there might be a path from it to the road and the trams, and I hurried along the beach, avoiding scattered parties of bathers. Half-way down the beach from the convenience a man was sitting alone on what looked like a motor rug and keeping guard over a pile of clothes on the top of which was a Red Army cap. On a sudden impulse, I said as I passed him: "There's a bit of trouble back there. Someone tried to pinch a car."

It was a shot in the dark, but it found its target. He was on his feet in an instant. "What sort of car, *tovarisch*? Not a black army ZIS?"

"That's right," I said. "It's not yours, is it? The militia are making trouble about a missing chauffeur."

The man caught my arm in panic. "*Tovarisch*, help me, I beg you. Just keep your eye on these things while I go and see. If the colonel comes out of the water tell him I've gone to the convenience. *Bozbe moi, bozbe moi!*" And he raced off, muttering, to the pavilion.

I didn't hesitate. As soon as the man had disappeared I grabbed the bundle of clothes and made for the convenience. I paused for a second at the entrance and listened, but the ramshackle shed appeared to be unoccupied. I walked in quickly and closeted myself.

I changed as fast as sweat and excitement would allow. Happily the colonel was a tall man or I shouldn't have been able to get into the uniform at all. As it was I had to brace the trousers down. I was evidently slimmer than the colonel, for his tunic was loose on me, but the flat peaked cap was a perfect fit. I reflected, as I belted myself in and fastened my neck-band, that I should soon know now if Marya had been right when she said I could pass for a Russian. I was fairly confident, which was half the battle. There was something comforting about the revolver in the holster against my hip. There were medals on my left breast, but I hadn't time to examine them. I rolled my own clothes into a tight bundle and stuffed them under a pipe. They would certainly not be found before morning. I gave a final hitch to my tunic, threw my shoulders back and was just about to step out when I heard a noise from the beach which was anything but a shout of joy. I found a hole in the wooden wall where a knot had fallen out and applied my eye to it. As I had feared, the owner of the clothes had finished his swim and discovered his loss. He was standing by the rug shouting "Thief! Thief!" and waving his arms in a fury.

What happened next was so very Russian that it would have seemed funny if I'd had any thought in my head but to get away. The plump militia girl came panting up from the pavilion shouting "What's going on here?", or words to that effect. Dancing with rage and using frightful language, the colonel declared that his chauffeur had stolen his clothes. Except for abbreviated swimming trunks he was stark naked, of course, and altogether he cut a most undignified figure. The militia girl seemed unimpressed when he said that he was a Red Army colonel, and tactlessly asked to see his documents. That naturally made him more furious than ever. He called her several unprintable names and she indignantly blew her whistle. A crowd began to collect, a big militiaman pushed his way into the noisy throng, and then the chauffeur came panting up. The colonel at once seized him by the throat and began shaking him, and the next moment colonel and chauffeur were both being marched away under police escort.

For the moment, at least, the hue and cry was postponed. It would take a little time for the colonel to cool off and get his story corroborated, and I didn't think the chauffeur had seen enough of me in the darkness to give much of a description. If I knew anything of Russian red tape it would be an hour or two before the search for a bogus colonel got fully under way. In that time a lot could happen. I slipped round to the back of the convenience, found a path, and cautiously climbed to the road. I discovered that I had a fat wad of documents, a bunch of keys, and a pocketful of small change. Looking down at my chest I saw that I had become a member of the Order of Suvorov and a Hero of the Soviet Union. No wonder the humiliated colonel had been beside himself with rage!

Now I must make up for the time I had lost. There was no sign of a taxi, so I marched smartly up to the tram stop. My heart sank when I saw the long queue of trippers already waiting there. Two tramloads, at least. Then I remembered, just as a tram came in, that people wearing decorations were allowed in the Soviet Union to go to the head of a queue. As the tram drew up I planted myself squarely in front of two old women and four children who had probably been waiting fifteen minutes. They glanced at my medals and muttered something uncomplimentary, but nobody protested. I boarded the tram and got a seat.

It was quite like old times. There was the same unmistakable smell of the Russian tobacco substitute, *makhorka*, which the Red Army carried with it into every conquered country. There was the same familiar rattle of dilapidated trams over worn-out lines, the same jostling and squabbling of people whom hardship had deprived of good manners. I would have known I was in Russia again if only by the sack of potatoes and the hoe handle which were being prodded into my ribs by a little old peasant woman. Nobody bothered about me. There was a man in the seat beside me but he was worn-out with fresh air and sun, and almost before the tram had left Pirita he was snoring with his head against the window. When the shrillvoiced conductress cried "Take your tickets" I handed a rouble to the old peasant woman and watched it being conveyed down the tram by willing hands above an impenetrable mass of bodies. In due course a handful of *kopecks* and a shred of flimsy paper torn in the middle came back by the same route. No, the place hadn't changed!

While the tram clattered and jerked its way into the town I looked at my documents. I discovered that I was Colonel Vladimir Kirilovitch Skaliga, of the 12th Guards Division. When I looked at the photograph pasted on to his identity card I wasn't surprised that he had won medals. He had a fierce stare and a prognathous jaw and looked extremely tough. I hoped I should never meet him.

After about twenty minutes the tram stopped at what I took to be the terminus, for the fifty or sixty people who had managed to cram themselves into it suddenly flung themselves as one towards the exit and there struggled noisily with an even greater mob waiting to get on. I battled my way through with the rest. I found that I was in a large square which I didn't recognize. What I did notice at once was a clock in the face of one of the buildings, its hands pointing to eleven. Desperately late though it was for my purpose there were still masses of people about. Indeed, all round the square there was a shuffling promenade of young men and girls in cotton shirts and white frocks taking the night air. It was oppressively hot. I stopped under a lamp and asked a man to direct me to the theatre. He pointed ahead, addressing me very respectfully as "Comrade Colonel". That was reassuring.

The theatre building was in the next square, and it was just as I remembered it. It had two wings—one of them a concert hall—with a restaurant in the centre. There were a lot of people standing outside the theatre entrance, most of them in uniform. A performance of some sort was obviously being given and this, no doubt, was the last interval. My eye caught an announcement on the wall near the main doors, and I walked up to read it. It was a hastily scrawled bill, and it said that a special performance of the *Sleeping Princess* was being given that night exclusively for the Red Army garrison and its chief guest—Colonel General Zhdanov. Marya was billed to dance Aurora. She must be in there now, getting ready to dance the final act.

I felt an immense relief. At least she was safe. Why she was dancing, why she hadn't managed to make an excuse, or to slip away during the day, I couldn't imagine, but no doubt I should learn. The problem now was to make contact with her, and quickly. I might try going round to the stage door, but I doubted if I could overcome the various obstacles before the last act started. With Zhdanov in the building there would probably be N.K.V.D. chaps all over the place and I was in no position to show my documents. I should have to send her a message.

I was fumbling in the colonel's wallet for a piece of paper when bells began to ring inside the theatre. The interval was just ending—I was too late. People who had been standing talking outside began to move in towards the doors. I was gripped with sudden panic. Somehow I must get inside the theatre. As I stood near the entrance, meditating some bluff, a young Red Army lieutenant came out with a girl on his arm. I caught his eye and then he glanced at my medals. He must have been struck by the look on my face for he saluted and said: "Do you want a ticket for the last act, Comrade Colonel? We have to leave."

I thanked him warmly and took the ticket. He smiled and saluted again and I saluted. Then I pushed my way into the lobby just as the second bell began to ring. I flung my cap on the cloakroom counter and took my check. My ticket was for the seventh row of the stalls. There was a kind of flower-shop at one side of the foyer and on an impulse I bought a great bouquet of roses with a fifty-rouble note from the Colonel's wallet. I just managed to squeeze inside the theatre before the doors closed. I felt pretty conspicuous as I marched down the centre gangway but hoped that the flowers would divert attention from any possible defects in my military appearance. The two empty seats were at the end of a row, and I fell into one of them with immense relief just as the orchestra struck up.

It is difficult to describe my feelings during those next few moments. I was dizzy with emotion. There was a tumult inside me—my head was pounding and my mouth was dry. I gripped the arms of my seat to keep my hands from shaking. The whole thing was like a dream. I couldn't believe I was really there, sitting in that outlandish uniform in that strange and yet familiar company. I couldn't believe, now that the moment was so near, that Marya would suddenly appear on that stage, and that after two aching years I should be looking at her again. Yet suddenly, with a burst of tremendous clapping—there she was. She looked so incredibly beautiful that for a moment I almost stopped breathing. I yearned for her across the gap that still parted us and it was all I could do to sit in my seat. I tried to read her expression but she was too far away for me to see clearly. Whatever misery might be weighing on her privately, she was dancing divinely—so much so that the audience kept breaking in with applause, slowing down the whole performance. For my part, I had never been less interested in the technical precision of a pirouette. Though the last act of the *Sleeping Princess* is pure delight, my sole desire was that it should end.

That was about the longest half-hour I've ever known, for time was our enemy. But the ballet could not be hurried, and an audience such as this would not be deprived of its few minutes of worship. When, at the end, the orchestra played its last triumphant chords and Marya came forward to take her curtain, I felt the sweat pouring down my back. I knew I had to do something to make my presence known to her, or she might slip away and be lost to me. A crowd of officers were on their feet near the curtain, clapping and 'bravo'-ing. There was tempestuous applause from all over the house.

I edged my way to the front until there was nothing between Marya and me but the orchestra. As she looked my way I threw the bouquet of roses at her feet and shouted as loudly as I could "Marya! Marya!" Several of the officers laughed in a friendly way and one of them slapped me on the back encouragingly. As Marya picked up the flowers with a smile and a little curtsey in my direction I shouted again, desperately. I didn't give a damn what people might think—they might suppose me a bit the worse for liquor but they'd certainly never think I was Marya's English husband. The second time I called she stared hard at me. I saw her hands tighten on the roses, and for a moment her eyes looked large and frightened. I knew then that she'd recognized me. I waved my hand and glanced over my shoulder towards the back of the theatre. She gave me a tiny nod even as her head went up to smile at Zhdanov and the other applauding people in the boxes.

A Red Army major was looking at me curiously. "Do you know her, Comrade Colonel?"

"I met her at Sevastopol," I said. "She was the last dancer to give a show there before we evacuated. I lost my heart to her."

The major smiled and shook his head. "You will have a lot of competition," he said. "I wish you luck."

As the curtain fell for the last time I shouldered my way up the sloping aisle to the foyer. Nobody there seemed in any hurry to go home. A band had struck up in the restaurant, which was packed tight with dancers. I didn't know how long it would take Marya to change, or where I'd meet her. I promenaded up and down, my nerves on edge, my thoughts in a whirl. I wondered what she'd be wearing. I couldn't keep still. Once I went outside the building, to see if by any chance she was there, then back into the restaurant, and yet again into the foyer. Suddenly I remembered that I hadn't recovered my cap, and I was obliged to join the animated queue of officers outside the cloakroom. A General of Artillery, the tips of whose grey moustaches I could see from behind, turned and gave me a friendly nod, noting my insignia. I wished the queue would move along more quickly, and felt myself grow cold as the general said, "It's a long way from Tiraspol, eh, Comrade Colonel?"

I made an effort to smile. "I feel a long way from everywhere tonight, Comrade General. Such dancing! Such grace!"

"Not so bad," he agreed. "Not so bad at all. But these chits of girls don't compare with the ballerinas of my day. Now I remember . . ." And he launched himself on a sea of recollection. I didn't have to say another word except an occasional affirmative "*Da*." The general had forgotten Tiraspol. He finally picked up his cap and said with a reminiscent twinkle in his eye: "I wish I were your age, Comrade Colonel. Good night."

I retrieved my own hat and rushed back into the foyer just as Marya was entering from another door, her hand lightly resting on someone's arm. With one horrified glance I saw that her companion was Zhdanov, the guest of honour!

This seemed the end. Zhdanov, saviour of Leningrad, Party boss in the north, one of the biggest of the big shots in the Soviet Union! Everyone else was keeping a respectful distance and I dared not butt in. It was a frightful moment. For all I knew he might be inviting her to supper. Marya looked very pale and I could guess what she must be feeling. Then Zhdanov gave a little bow and a smile, and an aide fell in beside him as he went out to his car.

In a moment Marya was the centre of a knot of high-powered Russian brasshats. I saw her look round a little wildly and knew that I should have to rush in. I tore across the floor, elbowing aside a general and a couple of colonels. "Marya!" I cried effusively, stretching out my arms to her. "After all these years! How are you, little dove? How is the family?" I kissed her resoundingly on both cheeks. "She is my sister," I explained to the company. "Please forgive me. I haven't seen her for five years. Marya darling, how is Shura? How is Mamachka?" And I took her arm possessively.

"You *will* forgive us, won't you?" Marya said with a dazzling smile all round. "We have so much to talk about." The brasshats made way for us good-naturedly, though I felt their interested stares boring into my back. The risks were piling up. I prayed that my uniform looked all right, that no one knew Marya's family history, that the people to whom I had told different stories were out of earshot. I put my arm protectively round her shoulders in what I hoped was a fraternal manner and we strolled away. I needn't have worried about myself—it was Marya that the whole place was watching. I was afraid that she would be caught up again in the press of her admirers. Firmly I propelled her to the exit while she kept up a most convincing chatter. A dark slim girl was standing by the door and Marya whispered quickly to me, "Be very careful." The girl, smiling, ran up and embraced Marya. "You were wonderful, darling," she said. She looked inquiringly at me.

"Valentina, this is my brother Serge. I haven't seen him for years. Isn't it marvellous? Serge, this is my dear friend Valentina Alexandrovna. She has been so kind to me during our tour."

I clicked my heels and gave a stiff little bow. I was itching to be off. Valentina's shrewd eyes were inspecting me. I saw she was impressed by my medals—not every colonel wore the Order of Suvorov.

I said: "No doubt we shall meet again. I am staying over tomorrow. If you'll excuse us now—Marya, and I have so much to say to each other."

"Of course, Comrade Colonel." Valentina smiled and stood aside.

"Serge will bring me to the hotel," said Marya. "Good night, Valya darling."

"Good night, Marya."

At last we were in the street. I set my cap firmly on my head and Marya threw a silk scarf round her hair. She wouldn't be recognized once we were away from the theatre-goers in the square. It was agony to loiter when the need for speed was so urgent, but until we reached the corner it wouldn't be safe to hurry. I murmured, "Darling, darling Marya," and held her tight against me.

"Oh, Philip darling," she said softly. "I can't believe it's really you. I'd given up hope."

"We're not out of the wood yet," I whispered. "Round that corner we've got to hurry for our lives."

"What about Svetlana? Is she all right?"

"Yes," I said. "She turned up at the beach. What happened to you? Couldn't you get away?"

Marya gave a nervous glance over her shoulder. "It was Valentina—she's an N.K.V.D. spy. I only found out today. She wouldn't leave me—not for a moment."

So that was it! I began to wonder how long it would be before Valentina discovered that she had handed over her charge to a bogus colonel. Not long, I suspected—they must have identified the real colonel by now and the net would be closing. I gripped Marya's arm more firmly and we turned the corner. The street seemed empty. I said: "Come on, now, as fast as you can. It's touch and go whether we reach the beach in time."

I had hoped there might be a tram at the terminus but there wasn't, and we couldn't afford to wait. The town clocks showed a quarter after midnight. We raced along the cobbled streets, under old arches and past pepper-pot turrets on battlemented walls. Whenever we saw anyone approaching we slowed down until they were well past. Four miles to cover and less than three-quarters of an hour to do it in! It was impossible. Marya was doing her best, but she was already tired after a strenuous evening's dancing. She was almost running to keep pace with my long strides, but soon I felt her begin to drag on my arm. If an opportunity had offered now I would have stolen any car, any conveyance, even bicycles. But there was nothing to be seen. The streets were almost deserted. If our own legs could not carry us to the beach in time, nothing would.

A car came rushing along, its headlights blazing, and I drew Marya into an alley while it swept by. I was very nervous now about my uniform, but could see no way of discarding it. The tunic smothered me and sweat poured off me in rivulets as we rushed along. By the time we reached Pirita it was ten minutes to one. The cars had gone, the people had dispersed, the restaurant was just closing. We hurried over the bridge and bent to the long slope uphill. Marya's breath was coming in little sobs and I knew she was just about all in. We couldn't have talked now if we'd wanted to. I knew how she must be feeling—my own head throbbed, my throat was sore and dry, each intake of breath was a rasp. Somewhere behind us a distant clock struck one, and it was like the first note of a passing-bell. Deadline! We still had a mile and a half of uphill track to cover.

The clock acted on me like a spur. To be so near and yet to fail—it was unbearable. But we had to rest. Marya was stumbling blindly forward and I knew she would collapse if we went on at that pace. We flung ourselves down for a moment, soaked with sweat, panting for air. I tried to exhort her. I said: "We're nearly there, Only another mile. That's all. Marya, don't give in! Just a little more."

I dragged her up and she swayed against me. I urged her on, half carrying her, murmuring little words of encouragement. I knew we could not regain our former pace. The Viimsi lights seemed very near, but even as I exhorted her I had no hope that we should reach them in time. I couldn't bear the thought of what was ahead. Marya had no reserves of strength to swim out—she would drown. I couldn't even let her try. Anyhow, the dinghy must have left by now. Despair overwhelmed me, and I no longer tried to force the pace. We moved forward mechanically and in my mind's eye I saw our brief lovers' meeting shattered by arrest and separation, questioning and worse.

Suddenly a figure loomed out of the darkness ahead. I whispered a warning to Marya and we became a spooning, sauntering couple. The figure stopped. It was a coastguard or police officer of some sort—I could see his uniform and holster. He flashed a torch on us, then on me, then on my epaulettes. He stopped.

"Good evening, Comrade Colonel. I apologize for bothering you.

A colonel's uniform has been stolen and we have orders to check all documents."

So it had come at last! A wave of anger possessed me. For a moment this one man seemed to personify all the things in the world that I most hated. I lashed out at his face with all my remaining strength and as he fell I hurled myself upon him. I'm not the commando type. I was more strongly built than he, but he was much more skilled in a rough-and-tumble. It was the darkness that saved me. He couldn't get to grips. We struggled noisily, violently, rolling over and over on the path. I was hardly aware of pain or blows. All I knew was that I wanted to get my hands on his throat and squeeze the life out of him. Once he got on top of me but I managed to heave him away with a tremendous effort and together we rolled off the path. I felt the sharpness of rocks as we slid and slithered down the slope of the cliff, still clawing at each other. The Russian seemed to have gathered new strength, but my own was nearly gone. As we struggled and plunged together down the beach, sometimes half upright, sometimes flat on the ground, my hand suddenly closed over a stone. I struck wildly at his bare head as he lunged at me. Two or three times his upraised arm protected it and then the stone crashed against his skull. He went down without a sound and I lay dizzy and exhausted, my wits scattered.

I must have lost consciousness, for the next thing I was aware of was Marya bending over me, pouring water on my face from her shoe. I tried to get up, but a violent pain shot through my arm, and I felt horribly sick. For a moment all went black again. I heard Marya, distantly, murmuring soothing gentle words of love. I managed to sit up, and agony of mind came back with a rush. I remembered, and wished I could forget. Despairingly I said, "Marya, darling—forgive me." I felt as though I'd destroyed her.

She kissed me and we clung helplessly together. Suddenly Marya whispered "There's someone coming," and she gripped my arm. There was a rattle of stones by the water's edge and once again a figure loomed up out of the darkness. But this time it wasn't a patrol. It was Joe.

Chapter Thirteen

For a moment he hung back as he saw my strange uniform. Then I whispered "Joe," and he leaped forward and gripped our hands in heartfelt relief. Marya and I could hardly speak, so great was our emotion. I imagine a condemned man doesn't chatter very much in the first few minutes after his unexpected reprieve. But after the first shock Joe acted on us like a blood transfusion. Hope and strength came flooding back, and with them a renewed sense of urgency.

We bent over the inert coastguard. His breathing was stertorous. He appeared to have some sort of concussion but we couldn't be sure. Anyhow, there was nothing we could do about him. We couldn't kill him in cold blood and we certainly didn't want him with us. We carried him to the shelter of the cliff, where he'd be less conspicuous at daybreak, and left him there.

Joe had the dinghy beached just below us. We soon had Marya in the sternsheets, and with my good arm I helped Joe push the boat off. In a few moments we were under way.

Until the dinghy was clear of the shore no one said a word. Poor Marya was shivering violently—the mental reaction was almost more exhausting than the physical strain. I sat with my arms round her stroking her hair, and gradually she calmed down.

When we were well away from the beach Joe said in his commonsense way: "Have some grub. It's under the seat."

It was just what we needed. I didn't know when Marya had eaten last, but I hadn't had a bite myself for seven hours and now that the tension was relaxed I felt ravenous. A large tot of brandy apiece did a lot to revive us. After sandwiches and coffee I felt a new man, apart from the wrist I must have twisted as I rolled down the cliff. Marya bandaged it for me. When she'd finished she began fumbling in the bag which somehow she still carried and started to tidy her hair and do things to her face in the darkness. I knew then that she was feeling better too.

Joe was concentrating on rowing, pulling with strong, expert strokes. The explanations could wait till afterwards, if there was an afterwards. The dark coast seemed quiet enough now, but I couldn't believe it would stay like that. Apart from the injured coastguard there was that girl Valya to give the show away. When Marya didn't return, and she heard about the stolen uniform, it wouldn't take her long to draw the right conclusion. We were still going to need a lot of luck.

The night was incredibly still and it was difficult to believe we were only a few miles from a big city. We seemed to have the whole Bay to ourselves. I could hear nothing at all except the chafe of oars and the gentle slapping of water under the dinghy's planks. It was a soothing sound. I remember whispering "Are you all right, Joe?" and when he answered, with a faint chuckle, that he was, I became drowsy. Actually, Marya and I must have slept for half an hour, for when we woke the Vake light was very close. I could see the buoy when it flashed. We slid by one of the unlighted beacons and soon I made out the line of *Dawn's* mast against the starry sky. At that moment Denny and Svetlana must have seen or heard the dinghy, for voices incautiously raised came echoing over the water. I heard Denny say excitedly "I believe they're all there," as Joe swung the dinghy under *Dawn's* stern. Then we bumped, and Marya was being helped aboard. For a few minutes our peril was forgotten. Denny shook my hand and shook Joe's hand and kept saying, "Praise the Lord." The girls were chattering and laughing and there was a lot of kissing all round in which Joe seemed to be sharing. But it didn't last long. Joe said: "We'd better save this till afterwards. Let's get under way." He became very businesslike. "Women in the cabin, please, and no lights. Denny, help me stow the dinghy. And let's have a little less noise."

The girls disappeared and Denny and Joe got to work. I couldn't do much except keep an anxious watch on the shore. We had precious little time if we were to clear territorial waters before daybreak—it seemed to me that there was already a hint of grey in the east. At last, too, there was more activity ashore. Two or three cars were racing along the coast road towards Pirita. Soon the whole place would be in an uproar.

There was only a capful of wind, but we daren't risk running the engine until we were out of the Bay. I took the tiller and sheet, Joe got the anchor, the mainsail caught a puff of air, and the Vake light began to fall away to starboard.

We were moving very slowly—you could see that by the angle of the two lights on Viimsi. It hardly changed. I looked at the compass and saw that we were headed almost due north. The main thing was to get out of the Bay. There was a shoal with a least depth of only two feet about three miles ahead and the chart showed one or two rocks awash. But there were distant buoy lights to guide us to the mouth of the Bay. Lack of wind was the chief anxiety. I couldn't see Joe's face, but he was whistling softly between his teeth, which was always a sign that he was deeply preoccupied. He kept looking up at the drooping sail and then over towards Viimsi.

Presently he muttered: "It's no good—we'll have to risk the engine. We're almost becalmed."

Denny reached for the handle and gave it a swing and the motor sprang to life at once. The sudden noise was shattering, but at least we were moving. Svetlana put her head out of the cabin to see what was happening but retired again immediately. Joe called for full throttle and Denny furled the useless sails. The sea was beginning to take on the luminous pewter colour that it gets at first light. We had undoubtedly left things very late.

Joe said, "How soon do you think they'll be after us?"

I thought of the clues we'd left behind. There'd be plenty of things pointing to an escape by sea—Svetlana's clothes on the beach, my clothes in the convenience, the battered coastguard, our footmarks in the sand, the marks of the dinghy on the beach. But it might be some hours after daylight before they came across these signs.

I said: "I can't see them catching us up much before midday unless they're very smart. But your guess is as good as mine."

Denny looked nervously back along our wake. "There's no sign of a 'hot pursuit', anyway," he said.

We were almost abreast of Aegna Island and in an hour we should be out of the Bay. Joe said: "You two had better get some sleep. If I need you, I'll shout."

That made sense. What with the hangover, the strenuous night and the reaction from immediate danger, I felt just about whacked, and in the first grey of morning Denny didn't look much better. And nothing would have made Joe give up the tiller at that moment. I said, "Thanks, Joe," and we went into the cabin. Svetlana was stretched out on one of the settee bunks in the main cabin with a rug over her, dead to the world. Marya occupied one of the two bunks in the fo'c's'le. She, too, was fast asleep. She lay like a child, with her small head cushioned on her hand and an expression of utter contentment on her face. I hoped fervently that nothing would shatter that new-found peace. I climbed into my own bunk, and in a couple of minutes I must have been asleep too.

I was wakened by a shout from the cockpit. I tumbled out automatically and rushed on deck with Denny just behind me. The scene had greatly changed. The morning had brought a fresh breeze and, all unknown to us, Joe had hoisted the sails and switched off the engine. The sea had got up a little and *Dawn* was pitching a bit as she thrashed to windward. Joe looked worn out and my conscience smote me. I realized that he had had no rest for thirty-six hours.

"There's a boat over on the starboard quarter," he said. "Get the glasses."

Denny snatched the binoculars from their hook in the cabin and handed them to Joe, who said to me: "Take the tiller, will you? My arm's breaking." Steering was about all I was fit for. Joe trained the glasses on the distant black speck. He said, "It's a boat, all right," and handed the glasses to me. The pitching made it difficult to keep them steady but I could see the outline of a hull.

I said, "Where are we, Joe?"

"About twenty miles from land and thirty from Tallinn. We're headed for Stockholm." He braced himself against the starboard gunwale and took another look at the boat. "She's making heavy weather of it," he said, "but she's nearer. I believe she's the *Neva*." That, of course, had been in all our minds. "She's moving pretty fast—there's a hell of a bow wave."

There was nothing for us to do except keep sailing. We held our course for ten minutes. Presently Svetlana stuck her head out of the cabin and gave us a wan "Good morning". She felt her way cautiously into the cockpit and looked around. "What's happening?"

"We have company," said Denny grimly.

Svetlana seemed more concerned about the vast expanse of tossing sea. She said "What a lot of water!" and staggered as *Dawn* gave a lurch.

"Better get back inside," said Joe curtly. "We're busy. And stay there till we call you." Svetlana gave him a sharp look, but did as she was told.

Joe had taken the glasses again. He said: "It's *Neva*—no doubt about that. I can see the lieutenant. We're on converging courses—she'll be alongside in a few minutes."

"She can't do anything to us here," said Denny hopefully. "I wonder what she wants."

It was fairly clear that she wanted something. She was coming very purposefully our way. I could make out the lieutenant plainly now without glasses, and presently we saw the little man come out of the cabin and join him in the cockpit. I saw him take the wheel from the lieutenant and then a bright light winked at us across the water. They were signalling with an Aldis lamp.

Joe gazed out over the water, his eyes narrow with concentration. It must have been a short message—some international signal that I didn't know. Joe's face became grim. He said, "They want us to heave to."

"Who the blazes do they think they are?" said Denny. "Don't

take any notice." It wasn't like Denny to give instructions, but the indignant flush in his cheeks showed that he was roused.

We watched the launch race towards us, rolling and pitching in the slight chop. The lieutenant was back at the wheel and Kleinman was leaning over the side, gesticulating in our direction. In a few minutes she was abreast of us, ten yards away, and had slowed to our speed. The lieutenant was pale and stolid; Kleinman was agitated. He cupped his hands and shouted: "You must stop. You have been ashore. You have contraband aboard."

Joe shouted back, "Go to hell!" He was getting angry too.

The little man danced up and down. He looked beside himself with rage. "You are in Russian waters," he bawled. "You are breaking the law. I command you to stop."

Joe yelled back: "We're on the high seas. We're twenty miles from land. You've no right to interfere with us. Get out of our way."

Denny joined in. He shouted, "It's you that's breaking the law!"

It didn't seem at all clear how the shouting match was going to end. At that moment, however, Svetlana appeared again at the cabin door. Her face was a dirty green, and her need for air had been stronger than her sense of discipline. She sprawled over the side and was violently sick. Kleinman gave a yell of triumph. "You see! You have Russian women aboard your ship. You must give them up." *Neva* swung in as though to come alongside. Joe muttered, "Stand by to repel boarders." Denny was bursting with anger, and as the gap closed he seized our long boat-hook and waved it threateningly in the air. "You bloody pirates!" he shouted. "Come and get them!" And he brought the boat-hook down with a crack on their gunwale a foot from Kleinman's head.

The little man looked startled and I heard him give a sharp order to the lieutenant. *Neva* sheered away and stood off from us at about twenty yards' distance.

"Good work, Denny," Joe said calmly. "Keep her on her course, Philip. What's their next move, I wonder?"

We knew Kleinman wouldn't let the girls go—he had enough blunders to account for already. We guessed he was preparing for a real crack at us, and we weren't far wrong. *Neva* kept her course abeam of *Dawn* for a few minutes and then began to close in again.

I gripped Joe's arm. "Look," I said. "Kleinman's got a gun."

Joe stood motionless, staring. I think he hardly believed that they would dare to shoot. Kleinman was shouting again, "Heave to, or we'll fire at you!" He said something to the lieutenant, who rather slowly undid his holster and took out his own gun. The situation was about as ugly as it could be. They might have difficulty in hitting anyone, pitching as both boats were in that short sea, but they could do a lot of damage and might kill someone with a chance shot even if they didn't intend to.

Suddenly I remembered the gun that was still with the colonel's uniform in the cabin. If we could shoot back it would keep them at a distance. "Denny," I said urgently, "the gun—in the colonel's holster!" Denny rushed into the cabin and came back with the gun. He examined the chambers with a quick expert eye and gave an exclamation of disgust. "Empty!" he said, and threw the gun on the deck. "Just for show."

Neva was coming in for the attack. Kleinman shouted, "You've been warned!" I saw him raise his gun and fire, and I heard the whine of a bullet quite close. He fired again, and the lieutenant too. A couple of holes appeared in our mainsail. Kleinman had an evil grin on his face. Denny jumped on to the cabin-top and hurled an empty bottle which shattered on *Neva's* counter. The launch swung away out of bottle range and they went on firing. I heard a crash in the cabin and a sudden cry. I couldn't leave the tiller but Denny was inside in a moment. He emerged a couple of seconds later and gave me a quick 'thumbs up' sign, but he looked shaken. It only needed one unlucky shot ....

Now *Neva* put on speed and started to cross our bows. I suppose our sail was in the way and they wanted to get to windward of us so that they could see better what they were doing.

I felt utterly impotent and Joe told me afterwards that he'd felt just the same. This kind of thing was right outside his sailing experience. We couldn't fight, we couldn't run, and we certainly weren't going to hand over. We'd done too much damage—there'd be no mercy for any of us now if we were caught—least of all for the girls.

Then I saw that Denny was up by the mast, feverishly stripping the oilcloth from the old punt gun. I had completely forgotten it, and I think he had until that moment, when he saw *Neva* crossing our course. Anyway, it didn't take him a second to whip the cover off and I saw him fumbling in his pocket for a cap. I held *Dawn* steady and watched *Neva*. Joe clambered on to the cabin-top, an iron bar in his hand. As *Neva* cut across us, broadside on and almost under our bowsprit, Denny waited for our bows to dip and then snapped the heavy trigger. The gun was pointed straight into their cockpit.

I wouldn't have been surprised if nothing had happened, but somehow Denny had managed to keep that powder dry. He must have put in a massive charge, too, for the explosion was far louder than the one we'd heard in the Thames estuary. Denny's recoil apparatus collapsed under the strain and the whole bowsprit came adrift. Joe was hanging on to the lifeline, which he'd never removed, but Denny himself came flying over the cabin-top into the cockpit. He was lucky not to be knocked into the sea.

Joe rushed forward to haul in our slatting jib and make the punt gun fast where it had torn loose near the mast. I peered anxiously through the smoke. *Neva* was almost stationary and a little to port, and I steered towards her. Kleinman, who had been leaning against their starboard bulwark, had disappeared. The lieutenant had left the wheel and was gazing overboard. After that things became confused. I felt *Dawn* scrape the side of *Neva* and I let the mainsheet go. I saw Joe take a flying leap from our deck into *Neva's* cockpit, looking like a fighting Norseman with his iron bar raised. Denny was right behind him. The lieutenant, bleeding, shaken by the unexpected explosion and unnerved by the disappearance of Kleinman, was in no condition to put up much of a fight. As he turned and saw Joe coming at him with the lump of iron he recoiled against the side of the boat, lost his balance and fell into the sea. He swam round to the stern and with some difficulty Joe and

Denny hauled him aboard. He slumped on the floor of the cockpit—the most bedraggled and miserable-looking lieutenant I'd ever seen. Denny took his gun away from him, just to make sure.

Joe quickly switched off *Neva's* engine and shouted to me to throw him a rope from *Dawn*, which had begun to drift away. In a few minutes *Neva* was made fast to us. With a sharp instruction to Denny to keep his eye on the lieutenant Joe jumped back aboard *Dawn* and lowered the mainsail, which was flapping like mad in the stiff breeze.

Then we began to search for Kleinman. *Neva's* engine, left just ticking over by the lieutenant, had continued to propel the boat slowly through the water while the fight was on and *Dawn* had had quite a lot of way on her. The *mêlée*, though short, had been so fierce that no one now had much idea how far we'd travelled or from what direction. The lieutenant said Kleinman could swim, so there was still a chance we might pick him up. I started *Dawn's* engine and we began slowly to circle round, with *Neva* in tow, scanning the water for any sign of life. There was enough of a sea to make it difficult to spot a bobbing head. We searched for nearly half an hour but with no success. It seemed likely that Kleinman had been hit by some of the heavy pellets—perhaps knocked unconscious—and that he'd drowned right away.

We now had to decide what we should do about *Neva*. The thought had flashed through my mind that we might all transfer to her and make a quick dash for Stockholm at fifteen knots, but I soon realized that there was too much of a sea, and anyway we found that there wasn't enough petrol aboard her to reach neutral territory. We discussed the advisability of taking her with us, but we had one perfectly good boat and there seemed no point in burdening ourselves with another. On the other hand it would clearly be a mistake to leave her floating and derelict, for the Russians would find her and guess that we had encountered her.

The only thing, then, was to scuttle her. We brought the lieutenant aboard *Dawn*, and I mounted guard while Joe and Denny prepared *Neva* for her last trip. The lieutenant watched our preparations glumly. It seemed to me that he was more concerned about *Neva's* fate than about Kleinman's. He appeared to be losing quite a lot of blood from the pellet wounds in his left hand and arm, and I called to Svetlana to bring bandages. She made quite a passable job of the dressing and the lieutenant looked grateful.

Meanwhile, Denny had transferred *Neva's* cans of spare petrol to *Dawn* and had helped Joe stow in *Neva's* cabin every object that might float and so provide a clue to her fate. When all was done Joe unscrewed the water inlet pipe from the engine and let the sea rush in. It seemed ages before she began to settle, and I kept glancing back towards Tallinn, expecting that at any moment another hull would appear on the horizon.

When it became clear that *Neva* would last only a few minutes longer, Joe gave the order to get under way. I put *Dawn* on her old course and opened the throttle. We had gone barely half a mile before the launch was engulfed by the waves and quietly disappeared. None of us had liked sinking her, but this wasn't a time for sentiment. I hoped we should have no occasion to need the turn of speed she might have given us.

We ourselves had been very fortunate. Apart from the broken bowsprit, which we should have to repair before we could do any more sailing, the only injuries we had suffered were a few holes in the sail and in the sides of the cabin and some smashed crockery. It was a bullet going through one of the cupboards that had made Svetlana cry out.

The first thing now was to get Joe into bed. He was rocking on his feet and I think he was asleep before his head hit the pillow. I kept the tiller and Denny stayed out in the cockpit to keep an eye on the lieutenant. Denny seemed a bit shaken. He certainly hadn't intended to drown anybody and the thought of it depressed him. I pointed out that if it had been necessary for someone to drown Kleinman was the ideal man, but he didn't seem to think that was very funny.

He leaned against the bulwark and gazed with cold anger at the sodden lieutenant. I saw that we should have to do something about Stepan. Whatever shock we had had, his shock had been much greater. Though the day was warm he was beginning to shiver. His face was bluish-white and he looked the personification of misery.

I suggested some brandy, and after he'd taken a stiff shot he began to look a bit better. "I suppose we'll have to give him some clothes," said Denny grudgingly. He seemed to be holding the lieutenant responsible for everything, including Kleinman's death. "'Don't start anything," he said warningly as he turned to go into the cabin—though the warning was certainly unnecessary. Presently he emerged with the colonel's uniform which I had taken off the night before. Stepan stared at it in some astonishment—I dare say he thought we'd murdered a colonel in order to get it. I could see he didn't much like the idea of putting it on, and anyway it proved too tight for him. In the end the only thing we could find to fit him was one of Denny's own khaki shirts, which he had to leave unbuttoned down the front, and a pair of khaki shorts. Denny flung him a towel and he stripped, dried himself off, and struggled into the khaki. He looked much better that way. Denny bundled up the old uniform and threw it overboard. He had come to dislike it very much.

Stepan, looking rather wistful, watched it disappear in our wake. He was still very subdued. I had seen the same look on the faces of German prisoners on the Don, dragged up in the middle of the night by the Russians to be interviewed by a bunch of correspondents. They had expected to be shot, and couldn't quite believe that they were not going to be. I don't think Stepan foresaw anything quite so drastic, for we'd shown a measure of goodwill by giving him some clothes, but he couldn't be sure. There was plenty on his conscience, in any case, for it wasn't his fault that we were still alive. He kept looking from one to another of us as though trying to read our intentions, and every now and again he gazed with renewed perplexity at the fore part of our ship which had done so much damage so mysteriously. He couldn't make us out at all, and his bewilderment had increased when Denny had started talking to him in Russian. We must have seemed very different from the two English gentlemen whom he and Kleinman had entertained on board *Neva*.

Denny didn't help to set Stepan's mind at ease, for he was still fuming. He said: "You're a damned pirate. You deserve to be hanged." Stepan eyed the masthead gloomily.

"I believe we've a *right* to hang you," said Denny, working himself up.

"We could look it up in the book," I said. Now that the crisis was past I couldn't feel any great animosity against the lieutenant.

But Denny's sense of justice was outraged. "You deliberately tried to murder us all. A cut-throat, that's what you are." He was delving deep into the recesses of his Russian vocabulary and I was surprised at the number of recondite words he knew. That, no doubt, was what came of sleeping with a teacher of languages.

Stepan shifted his big bulk uneasily on the deck. He said, "I obeyed orders."

"At Nuremberg," said Denny, "that was no defence. You're guilty of a crime against humanity. Piracy!"

"Kleinman said you were breaking the law yourselves," said Stepan obstinately. "And if I had disobeyed him he would have had me shot."

"Was he N.K.V.D?" I asked.

The sort of look came over Stepan's face which I had often seen before in Russia; a sort of conscious blankness, an automatic defensive mechanism against the sound of the unmentionable. Finally he nodded.

I thought I'd better explain. I said: "We never intended any harm to your country, you know. These women are our wives—Russian girls. We married them when we were in Russia during the war. Denny, here, was a soldier—an ally of yours. Do you remember that we were allies? I was a correspondent—and a good friend of your country. Your Government wanted to keep our wives in Russia. We thought we were entitled to fetch them out. That's what all the trouble's been about."

Stepan seemed to be thinking that over. He stared at the deck. Presently he said, "No doubt it is natural to want one's wife." He smiled, showing a lot of white teeth. "Russian girls are very attractive." He was beginning to sound more like the Stepan we had known in *Neva's* cabin. He said, "How did you succeed in getting them away?"

I couldn't tell him that. "You'll go back to Russia and tell your beastly N.K.V.D." I said, "and then more innocent people will be sent to Kazakstan."

He shrugged. "Perhaps."

"You tell *us* something," said Denny. "What did you do when you found all your petrol had gone?"

Stepan grinned. He said: "We went back to our base near Porkkala and got some more. Kleinman was very angry."

"I bet he was," said Denny, thawing a little. "That was a good party. Did you have a headache in the morning?"

"A small headache. Kleinman had a bad headache. He was very ill. He was afraid, too, about what might happen to him."

"Because he'd let us go?"

"Yes."

"How did you find us so soon?"

Stepan threw out his hands. "It was simple. When we woke in the morning and discovered you had gone Kleinman said you were foreign spies. We had thought perhaps you were. There are many boats in the Gulf from Sweden and Finland which try to make contact with enemies of the Soviet people, and it was our work to prevent them. We did not know what part of the coast you were going to, but we knew that you would have to come out through the Gulf. We patrolled where we thought you would have to be, and there you were. Perhaps it was luck."

"It was bad luck for Kleinman."

Stepan looked down his nose. "He could be spared."

"You didn't like him?"

Stepan shook his head. "We have a saying, 'Watch the goat from the front, the horse from behind, and the bad man from all sides.' He was that bad man."

"You seemed friendly enough."

He shrugged again. "A wise man does not quarrel with his chief. I did not like him and I did not like his work." He smiled. "I prefer coal-mining. It is cleaner."

We were getting a new light on Stepan's character. Unless he was a good deal deeper than he appeared there was no real malice in him at all. He was just one of the millions of Russians who'd got caught up in a machine.

It was almost noon. Far ahead I could just make out the hazy outline of the Finnish coast near Hango. In another couple of hours or so we should be out of the Gulf. We were making fine progress, though I didn't like the idea of using up so much petrol.

I said, "After lunch we'll have to get that bowsprit mended."

Stepan looked with renewed interest at the broken spar. He said: "What was it that hit us? You have a gun—or bombs, perhaps?"

"Not bombs, Stepan. We *had* a gun." I told him about the bowsprit and he was fascinated.

"Perhaps I can help you to mend it," he said.

"So that we can shoot at another Russian boat?"

He considered. "Well," he said, "perhaps not."

"You've got to keep your record clean," I told him. "It's not our worry, of course—you're just an old pirate to us—but you'll have to have a good story for the N.K.V.D."

He said. "What are you going to do with me?"

"If you give us any trouble, we shall probably throw you overboard. If you behave yourself we shall hand you over to the Swedish police at Stockholm. After you've been held in jail for a while they'll probably get in touch with the Soviet Embassy and you'll be repatriated. I don't see what else we can do. We can hardly land you on Russian soil."

Stepan nodded. He looked a bit gloomy and I supposed that the prospect of cooling his heels in prison while the diplomats got busy didn't much appeal to him. But he had no other suggestions to make. He sat with his head in his hands, apparently in deep thought.

Presently Marya came out into the cockpit and said that Svetlana was still not feeling very well, but that she herself was hungry. Denny said that he was, too, and went in to prepare a meal. The sea was a good deal quieter than it had been in the early morning, and cooking presented no great difficulty. Before long an appetizing smell was coming from the galley and Stepan raised his head, sniffed, and grinned.

"I'm not sure that we feed pirates," I said. His face fell and Marya said, "*Oy yoy*, Philip," and looked reproachful. Stepan was as teasable as a small child.

I felt it would be a pity to wake Joe, but it seemed that he was already stirring. His sleep had been satisfying, if short, for after he had sluiced his face he looked as fresh as ever. He came into the cockpit and I gave him a short report. He took a look at the distant coast through binoculars, gazed all round the horizon, and glanced at the petrol gauge.

"No more trouble?" he asked. "No more Russians?"

"Not a sign. It's too good to be true."

I lashed the tiller and we crowded into the cabin for a good meal. We put Stepan between the two girls and he looked after both of them. With a pang of something ridiculously like jealousy I noticed that Marya seemed more at ease with him than she did with me. I was beginning to hate these cramped quarters and total lack of privacy.

We'd hardly begun to eat when the note of our engine seemed to change—and then I realized that it was the drone of a 'plane I could hear. Joe told the others to sit tight, and he and I crept cautiously into the cockpit. The 'plane came straight at us, and for one dreadful moment I thought it was going to drop a bomb. But as it flattened out at little more than masthead height I saw that it was an old single-seater reconnaissance monoplane without armament. I could see the pilot leaning out to look at us. He banked and flew round us twice, and then he turned and made straight for the Estonian coast.

That took our appetites away completely. It had been such a businesslike sortie. The Russians had obviously fitted all the bits of the simple jigsaw together and had known exactly where to look for us.

Stepan didn't make us feel any more cheerful. He said soberly: "Before evening they will come for you. If you resist you will be sunk."

On such matters Stepan clearly spoke with authority. I said, "What do you think they'll do?"

He said: "I think they'll send a gunboat out of Riga, perhaps, and cut you off before dusk. In the morning there'll be no trace of you."

"There'll be no trace of you, either," said Denny.

"That is so," said Stepan.

Denny was getting hot under the collar again. "It's an outrage. I don't believe they'd dare . . ." The sentence tailed off lamely. The facts were as plain to Denny as to the rest of us. If they'd only used pistols before, it was because that was all they had had.

Stepan was realistic. He said: "Who can stop them? If you had a destroyer in the Gulf, that would be different. But you have not. It is safe enough for them. You will not be able to complain. You will be dead. They will naturally not write to the newspapers about it. It has happened before."

I looked at him curiously. It was his constant use of the word 'they' that caught my attention. I had heard it so much in Russia. 'They' was Authority, remote and rather terrible. It seemed to me that Stepan spoke of it with no great affection. He had become a different man since Kleinman's death.

Denny said: "We're in a trap. If we keep going, they'll catch us. If we go back into the Gulf it's only a matter of time before they find us."

"We can't possibly go back," I said. "They can spot us anywhere with that 'plane, and the deeper we are in the Gulf the more free they'll feel to shoot. Our only chance is the open sea, even if it's a slim one. What do you think, Joe?"

Joe motioned towards Stepan. "Ask him what he'd do if he were in our place."

I put the question to Stepan, who was looking far from happy. He thought a little and then he said: "I would go north and hide. To the islands."

"And run into another *Neva*!" said Denny. "No thank you."

"What does he say?" asked Joe impatiently. I translated, and Joe slowly shook his head. "I don't much like it, either. Those islands looked pretty tricky to me. We don't know the channels and we shouldn't know where to lie up. They'd spot us from the air."

I told Stepan what Joe had said. He crumbled a bit of bread thoughtfully and said: "I know the islands well. For six months I have been patrolling there. Once you are deep inside the archipelago you are safe. It is necessary only to approach the right spot."

I said, "Look here, Stepan, whose side are you on?"

"I have no choice," he replied. "Like you, I do not want to be sunk. To be in the water once in a day is enough."

"Let's have a look at the chart," I said. We opened it up and spread it out on the table. I pencilled in our position, very roughly. Due north of us, and perhaps twenty miles away, the islands lay off the Finnish coast in a belt seven or eight miles deep. There were a few big ones, near the mainland, that were named; there were hundreds of unnamed smaller ones, and in addition there were innumerable dots representing no more than large rocks.

Stepan took Joe's pencil and drew a circle about three inches in diameter. "Inside this circle," he said, "there are perhaps a thousand islands. Except for an occasional yacht, no one ever visits them. They are inhabited only by birds. Some are wooded, some are bare, but I know where there is good cover. I am a skilful sailor—you need have no fear."

I don't think any of us doubted his sailing abilities, but his good faith was another matter. He had been detached from one set of loyalties—could we trust his conversion? Then I remembered that he was only trying to save his skin. For all I knew there might be a Russian base inside the islands, but it would hardly help him to take us to it. He had good reason to know that we should put up a fight with whatever we'd got handy. He could hardly expect to get away himself in a scrap, for we should be three to one against him, and if he led us into a trap we should obviously deal with him whatever happened to us and the boat.

Apart from the question of his trustworthiness the plan had everything to commend it. We were less than three hours' steaming from the islands, and with luck we should be snugged down before dark. Besides, there was no apparent alternative. Stepan might be exaggerating the danger of a gunboat, but that 'plane had certainly looked very purposeful.

We discussed the problem for a while. It wasn't an easy decision to take. For once Joe didn't seem to be able to make up his mind. His faith in the freedom of the seas had been shattered, and yet I knew he couldn't quite believe that we would be attacked again. He suggested that we put it to the vote.

I explained the alternatives, with what I thought was horrible clarity, in English and in Russian. Marya said she thought Stepan could be trusted, and he gave her a little bow. Svetlana said the sea made her feel ill, anyway. Denny was for the islands, and I thought that on the whole they were the lesser risk. Joe agreed.

"So the islands it is," I said. I went out into the cockpit and altered course for the north.

The greatest danger now was that the 'plane would come out again and report our change of course. It would have been an obvious precaution, but it wasn't taken. No doubt the Russians realized that we couldn't get very far in an hour or two, and felt quite confident of their ability to intercept us by sea at their pleasure. Still, it was an anxious time for us. All afternoon we were straining our ears for that tell-tale drone in the sky, and there were several false alarms. The sound of an aeroplane engine is the easiest thing to imagine when you are expecting it.

After we had been steaming north for an hour we crossed astern of a Finnish cargo boat homeward bound, and someone waved to us from the taffrail. We were glad when it was well past us. Otherwise, we saw nothing. Now that the Soviet Union controlled the greater part of its coastline the eastern Baltic seemed to be almost empty of traffic.

We could already make out the dark line of the outer islands. They looked, and were, very similar to those we had skirted and slightly penetrated a couple of days before. Stepan and Joe were studying the chart and Denny was translating. Stepan said the chart would be quite useless once we got inside the archipelago, but he was anxious to make the right landfall. As the water began to shoal Joe gave him the tiller and we cut down speed to a couple of knots.

For the next hour Stepan gave us as fine an example of pilotage as I've ever seen in my life. Joe was enthralled. He stood motionless in the cockpit with a faintly anxious smile on his lips while *Dawn* slipped between jagged rocks with only a foot or two to spare on either side. Sometimes it seemed that we were heading for a closed shore, and then at the last moment a new channel would open out and we would turn and glide between two more islands. We held no set direction for long, and often it seemed as though we were going right back on our tracks. But the islands were visibly closing in behind us, and with every twist and turn of the maze we felt a greater sense of security. Stepan had been right—it was possible to count the islands in hundreds. Some were flat and bare and marshy, like the islands off the Essex coast. Others were much higher out of the water, and thickly wooded with pine and oak and birch. They ranged in colour from brilliant green to the hazy blue of the far distance on a hot summer day. Every now and again we passed a withy or a spar, planted in the water to mark the safe channels for those who could read their meaning. Stepan didn't seem to bother much about them. He gave the impression of knowing precisely where he was going all the time and he never faltered. The real danger was the sharp rock just awash, and such rocks were everywhere. As I sat perched up in the bows I could often spot them by the yellowing of the water, sometimes right ahead, but before I could call out Stepan had made the necessary change in our course. It was evident that he had a natural love for this kind of exploration, and that he had made the islands his playground, combining pleasure with duty.

After we had been rock-dodging for well over two hours he suddenly gave an exclamation and pointed ahead. "That is our destination," he said. As far as I could see the piece of ground he was pointing to looked exactly like any of the other islands we had passed. It was about a hundred yards long on the side we were approaching, and half-way along, close to the water, was a copse of small oak trees. Stepan steered for the trees. We rounded a thin tongue of land, beyond which was a narrow inlet which ran in among the trees.

"Engine off," called Stepan, and Denny threw the switch. We came to rest a few yards from the shore. Everything was very still. The surface of the water was like a mirror and there seemed to be almost no current.

"Now we must get the mast down," said Stepan. That was a job that required all male hands, for *Dawn's* mast was a considerable spar. We had a little trouble with the broken bowsprit, but in about fifteen minutes we had the mast safely lowered into the crutches which Denny had shipped, and the standing rigging and halyards all neatly lashed up and secured under the big green canvas cover which we'd brought with us but had certainly never expected to use. Then Denny started the engine again and we glided into the creek among the trees. Leaves were parted by *Dawn's* bows, and small twigs cracked off. At last we came to rest against a dry bank in six feet of water.

Stepan beamed, and Joe gave him a friendly pat on the back—the tribute of one virtuoso to another.

"Here," said Stepan confidently, "we can remain safely for weeks."

Chapter Fourteen

At least we had gained a much-needed breathing space. We were all worn out with excitement and fatigue, and there were a few hurts to patch up. Stepan still had some pellets in his flesh, which Svetlana competently gouged out. My wrist was badly swollen and wouldn't be usable for some days. *Dawn's* bowsprit had to be repaired before we could sail again. All told, the respite had come just in time.

That it was only a respite soon became apparent. Half an hour after our arrival another aeroplane came zooming low across our island, barely fifty yards away. It certainly couldn't have spotted us, for the trees in full leaf provided a perfect canopy, but it was an unpleasant reminder that our troubles were not over. By now the Russians must be feeling extremely sore. They had lost two girls, one uniform, a launch, a naval lieutenant and a possibly valued member of the N.K.V.D., and they had had a coastguard knocked on the head on their own soil. I hadn't the least doubt they would make the most determined efforts to catch us, and that if they saw us again they'd show no mercy.

For the time being, however, we were all too tired to worry. After we had eaten a meal from cans we lay relaxed on the dry bank and exchanged accounts of our experiences. Svetlana and Marya told the stories I have related elsewhere. Marya said she had been informed of the special performance for Zhdanov only in the morning. She had thought of pleading illness, but at her first hint of a headache the solicitous Valentina had settled herself so comfortably in Marya's room that the idea had had to be hurriedly abandoned. In the afternoon Marya had tried to slip away, but

Valentina had stuck to her like a leech. It was only then that Marya had realized the girl's function. Her efforts to get away alone—which naturally became more obvious as she became more desperate—had all been frustrated, and at last there had been no alternative but to dance. It must have been utterly nerve-racking for poor Marya and she didn't seem anxious to dwell on her experiences.

I described my own sortie, and Joe wound up the tale. He had rowed in to Viimsi immediately Denny had told him the news, taken up a position fifty yards or so out to sea, and waited. He had realized that the deadline I had set was about the limit for safety, but when the time came he just couldn't bring himself to leave. He stuck around, debating wretchedly with himself, and then he heard what sounded like a fight along the beach. He had rowed cautiously to the spot and found us. We had all been very lucky. Poor Rosa had come out worst in the whole affair, but it seemed fairly clear that her arrest would have taken place anyway and was not specifically the result of helping us. She was very much in our thoughts as we turned in.

First thing after breakfast the next morning we discussed our plans. We had to assume that the Russians knew where we were, to within a few miles. The first 'plane must have reported our position at sea and the second our disappearance, and there was no place we could have disappeared to in the available time except the islands. But finding us would be a different matter. It was most unlikely they would be able to spot us from the air if we were careful, and they would need a large expedition to comb the islands by sea. In the end, we decided that our best course was to lie low for a few days and see what happened.

That was no hardship for any of us. After our exertions, this peaceful island seemed like Paradise. It was small but sufficient. Except at the edges, where tall dry reeds rustled, it was covered with short fine grass and studded with little rocks, bright with moss and orange lichen. There were no big trees except for the oaks which sheltered *Dawn*, but there were masses of prickly juniper and sweet briar and wild rose bushes. Near the centre of the island was a small hill from which it was possible to see the channel all around and to watch the wildfowl which abounded. The weather was warm, and we could swim or laze to our heart's content.

Joe became very detached and independent. I think he was being tactful. Whenever I caught his eye he seemed faintly amused. He was very much the confirmed bachelor, watching with tolerant sympathy the difficulties of his less fortunate brothers. When he wanted company, he and Stepan got together. They both liked messing about in the open air and they plunged actively into island life. As for Denny and Svetlana, no one would have known they had ever been apart. They were a matter-of-fact couple and had slipped back into their old relationship with a smoothness which I envied. Their feelings were very evident. Svetlana hugged Denny publicly and violently and called him 'honey'. She must have learned that from Steve.

Joe and Denny lost no time in getting to work on the broken bowsprit, and Stepan helped. Denny had hoped to be able to re-load the gun but the springs were smashed beyond repair. When the bowsprit was serviceable again Stepan asked Joe for a coil of light rope, and presently I saw his bronzed body stripped to the waist and looking like Laocoon in the toils. It appeared that he had had enough of sleeping on the hard boards in *Dawn's* cockpit and was rigging himself a rope hammock between two of the oak trees. He had gone to work with Stakhanovite energy and very soon the hammock began to take shape. Joe watched for a while and then followed suit.

Stepan hummed little snatches of Ukrainian songs as he knotted up the rope. He had many childlike characteristics and one of them was the transience of his moods. For the moment, the shadow of a jail in Stockholm seemed to have lifted. He looked as though he hadn't a care in the world, and it was difficult to believe he was the same man we'd hauled out of the water only the day before. All the time he kept up an admiring commentary on his own work, and as he struggled to keep ahead of Joe he said something about 'Socialist competition' which I didn't bother to translate. Joe liked his competition straight.

All work had to be suspended during the afternoon when the

roar of approaching aircraft burst upon our ears and we were forced to take cover. Judging by the noise, the Russians were making a reconnaissance in force over the whole length and breadth of the islands. No 'plane passed directly overhead but several swept by very close at little more than tree-top level, and away in the distance there was a steady drone. It was less terrifying than a raid, of course, but it was far from pleasant to feel that all these machines had been brought together for the sole purpose of hunting us down. We all felt a little shaken when, after an hour or so, the last sounds had died away, but we were confident that we hadn't been seen.

Further reconnaissance seemed unlikely for the time being, so Marya and I went off in the dinghy to explore. Marya looked very slight as she took the oars, but I knew how misleading that fragile appearance was. You can't be fragile and a ballerina as well. Actually she didn't row far. We had bundled our swimming things into the stern and when we were away from the island we put them on and sunned ourselves, while the dinghy drifted in the barely perceptible current. It was the first time Marya and I had really been together since the escape. There were so many things we both wanted to say, but somehow this didn't seem the moment to say them. I found the sight of her most distracting as she lay back in the smart two-piece which Denny and I had bought in London, trailing her fingers in the water and smiling at me. For a while we just looked at each other and then by a common impulse went ashore to a sheltered fragment of lichen-covered rock which had just enough grass for a couch and made love to each other.

When we got back to *Dawn* we found the hammocks finished and Stepan looking for new jobs on which to blunt his energies. He was as indefatigable as though he were trying to earn a remission of sentence by good conduct. He had helped Joe tidy up the cockpit and swab the decks and air the bedding. He had filled the kettle for tea and collected a large pile of dry sticks to keep the fire going. I noticed, not for the first time, that if either of the girls wanted anything he seemed always to anticipate their need. He was clearly going out of his way to be helpful and obliging, and it was impossible not to feel friendly towards him. Svetlana and Marya both kept up a sporadic, bantering conversation with him, and he and Joe were definitely buddies. Even Denny had by now almost forgiven him for his misdeeds.

After the tea things had been cleared away, Stepan said slowly, "One thing I don't understand."

He was looking rather accusingly at me, so I said "Oh?"

"You told Kleinman and me that Joe was your servant. You do not treat him as your servant."

I'm afraid we all laughed—Joe most of all when I translated what Stepan had said.

"It was a trick," I told him, "like your pretending to lose your anchor. We had to leave Joe behind to sail the boat after we'd got drunk. He's our comrade, you see. You believed what we said because you wanted to believe it."

"Now I understand," said Stepan slowly. "It was clever." He brightened a little. "So you are not capitalists, perhaps?"

"Would it be so wicked if we were?" I asked.

"It is a bad system," said Stepan.

"Perhaps."

"Where there are capitalists the workers are exploited. I know that it is like that in England. We have learned it in political lectures."

"I know," I said. "I know exactly what you've been taught. About five per cent of it is true and the rest is mostly lies. Anyway, *we* don't keep girls from their husbands. *And* we don't send people off to slave in camps just because we don't agree with them. *And* we don't beat them up in jail."

"But if they plot against their country . . ." began Stepan. I could see we'd really started something, and since we'd nothing else to do I thought we might as well have it out. Stepan wasn't a political animal. He'd been born honest, but he was as credulous as most Russians and he'd swallowed everything he'd been told. I asked him to tell us what he thought England was like, and during the next few minutes he gave us a fascinating caricature of our country. It was a place racked with poverty and unemployment, riddled with anti-semitism and class hatred; a country at once decadent and aggressive; a country still hungry for colonial exploitation; a country where culture was *bourgeois* and rotten and where even sport was commercialized. His very phrases were the ones you could hear any day on the Moscow radio. It was the old gramophone record, and we let him run through it.

Then we got Joe talking. I suspected that Stepan thought I was a bit too fluent, but he was ready enough to listen to Joe, and the translation gave time for ideas to sink in. Joe wasn't politically-minded either, and he answered Stepan's questions without guile. He described his workshop, and the way people lived at Southfleet, and what their houses were like, and the sort of work they did, and the sort of wages they got. It was little things that interested Stepan—the fact, for instance, that Joe was against the Labour Government although he owned nothing in the world but his workshop and his hands, whereas Denny was rather in favour of it although he seemed anything but exploited and was considerably better off than Joe. Stepan was puzzled, too, when Joe told him that a lot of ordinary working families in England had a whole house to themselves, often with a bathroom—until he remembered that that was because we lived on the wealth produced by our colonies. Then we had a long discussion about the respective sizes of English and Russian rations, which involved much pencil work changing pounds into kilograms. We talked a bit, too, about Parliament and *habeas corpus*, upon which Denny and Joe had strong views. What tickled Stepan most of all, I think, was our telling him that as soon as a Government was elected in England we began paying the Leader of the Opposition £2000 a year to try to turn it out at the earliest possible moment. He thought that was really crazy.

By the time we'd got round to where we started, which was about two hours after we began, Stepan obviously didn't know what to think. He was like a man emerging into the sunshine from a dark cave, and you could almost see his mind blinking.

He said, very seriously: "I shall think about it. In Russia we have a saying 'There is no rope strong enough to hang the truth.'"

"What a pity it's only a saying," I remarked. I had become a little weary of the discussion, for it had covered well-trodden ground. Also, I felt that in the circumstances it would be no kindness to Stepan to send him back to Russia full of heretical notions. He'd probably have quite enough trouble with the N.K.V.D. as it was. But Stepan's appetite was whetted and he had all the persistence of the Russian. Half an hour later I saw him sitting on the bank with Denny and Svetlana and they were having no end of an argument.

Towards evening we had a further discussion about our plans. It was soon apparent that no one had any desire to stick a nose out of the archipelago just yet. Life on the island was very pleasant and appeared secure; the perils outside in the Gulf would hardly increase and might grow less as the days, passed. Stepan, naturally, was all for staying; Joe said we should have to watch our stores, but that we were all right for the moment. In the end we decided to wait for at least another day. "After all, it isn't as though we haven't plenty to occupy us," said Denny cheerfully as he and Svetlana walked off into the gathering dusk, their arms round each other as usual.

Next day was quiet, with no 'planes over at all. Joe thought it would be wise to keep watch during the daytime just in case a hostile boat should creep up on us, so Marya and I spent most of the day on top of the little hill. Joe and Stepan overhauled all *Dawn's* rigging, just for something to do, and then painted the whole of her topsides. There was no doubt that Stepan was a glutton for physical labour. To fill in any odd moments, he had sawed a chunk of wood from an old oak stump and was proposing to carve himself some chessmen. He said he would carve a piece a day, and seemed under the impression that he would be able to finish the whole set before we moved! I think he was enjoying the first real freedom he'd ever known in his life. Nobody tried to push him around, nobody expected anything of him, nobody asked him to break any records. He rarely spoke of Russia and he never mentioned *Neva*. He didn't start any more arguments, but in the afternoon he wheedled Svetlana into giving him his first English lesson. There was no longer the least restraint between him and the rest of the company.

We all became very lively that evening. We had to put out the fire after dark for safety's sake, but we sat round its embers telling stories and singing in low voices. It was incredibly romantic, sitting on the bank in the warm and scented night, listening to Russian songs sung in harmony by Stepan and the girls. How we missed Stepan's *balalaika*! No one had given it a thought when we scuttled *Neva*, but then who could have foreseen the present gathering, or dreamed that it could be so friendly?

It must have been about six o'clock the next morning when I stirred in my bunk. I looked round the fo'c's'le and saw that Marya was still sleeping peacefully. I got up and peeped out of the porthole to see what sort of day we were going to have. It was then that I noticed the dinghy had gone! I looked across at Stepan's hammock and saw that it was empty.

With a pang I realized how criminally negligent we had been. I threw on some clothes and, without waking the others, climbed quickly to the top of the hill. Perhaps, after all, Stepan had only gone for a short row, though as it was barely daylight the hope seemed slight. I peered anxiously out over the encircling grey water but there was no sign of him.

It seemed only too plain what had happened. Stepan had fooled us. He had traded on our readiness to forgive and forget. All his friendly helpfulness had been a blind. While we had been babbling about England and thinking that we were improving his mind he had been quietly planning his escape. He'd slipped away in the dinghy during the night, along those channels that he knew so well, and at this moment might be on his way back with a launch and an armed party. Our little idyll was shattered. My mind was suddenly filled with a nightmare picture of what would happen if we were captured.

I woke Joe and told him what had occurred. He looked grave. The girls were shocked and incredulous, and Denny could obviously barely restrain himself from saying, "I told you so." We had a quick council of war. Joe thought we had no alternative but to shift our berth at once and try to find a new hiding place as far away as possible, before Stepan's party caught us. Denny and Joe began to make *Dawn* ready for departure and I climbed the hill again to keep watch for a hostile launch. I felt pretty sick. We had overcome so many hazards, and now it looked as if we had run into the worst one of all. I couldn't imagine what we should do if that launch did appear. Stepan would have all the advantages on his side when it came to a game of hide-and-seek around the islands. Even if we didn't hit one of the many submerged rocks in our hurry we might well be spotted by boat or 'plane before we'd found shelter.

At least it seemed that we should have a few minutes' start—there was still nothing in sight, and though the morning was quiet I could hear no engine. I was just going to set off down the hill again in response to a halloo from Joe when I thought I saw something move at the tip of the neighbouring island. It was a very slight movement and I couldn't make out what it was. For a moment I stood tense, watching. Yes, something was coming. I could see the bows of a little boat . . . . Then I sat down and laughed hysterically with relief.

It was Stepan, drifting in the dinghy. He had a long rod over the stern and he was fishing!

He must have heard my shouts of laughter for he turned and waved cheerily, and then pulled in his line. He rowed across the creek and gave me a beaming "Good morning" in English as I joined him on the beach.

I hardly knew what to say. I felt pretty ashamed of myself, partly for jumping to the worst possible conclusion and partly for behaving in a way I now felt had verged upon panic. I said: "We thought you'd run away, Stepan. We were just getting ready to leave. Another five minutes and we'd have been gone."

His blue eyes opened wide. I have never seen a man look so utterly astonished. It was clear that the idea had never crossed his mind. He looked at the dinghy and then at me and at his home-made rod, and suddenly he threw it to the ground and stalked off without a word, like an offended prima donna.

There didn't seem much point in going after him till he'd cooled off, so I took the dinghy and went back to *Dawn*. The others had got her out into the channel and were waiting impatiently for my arrival. When I told them what had happened there was a moment's complete silence. Then Marya burst into tears and Svetlana stood shaking her head in self-reproach. Joe and Denny were too relieved to be upset, and philosophically eased *Dawn* back into her berth.

I thought I'd better go and look for Stepan. We couldn't have him sulking about the island—it would make life unbearable. I found him sitting dejectedly on the beach, chewing a piece of grass and gazing out to sea.

I parked myself beside him. "Look here, Stepan," I said. "We're all sorry. Forget it."

Stepan was still looking mortally affronted. He said slowly: "I thought we were friends. How could you think I would betray you and Svetlana and Marya, who have been so kind to me?"

I said: "Now don't be unreasonable, Stepan. You'd gone and the dinghy had gone. How could I know you'd suddenly decided to go fishing in the middle of the night?"

"If you had waited a little," said Stepan doggedly, "you would have seen that I came back."

I decided that this exhibition of Slav temperament was getting us nowhere and said: "Look, Stepan. Everybody makes mistakes. Three days ago you were shooting at us—remember? With real bullets. You might easily have killed Marya or Svetlana. That was a pretty bad mistake. If you'd known us better perhaps you wouldn't have done it. If we'd known you better perhaps we shouldn't have thought you'd run away this morning. I think we're quits. Let's shake hands on it."

I watched that sink in. Presently he turned, and a disarming grin spread slowly over his face. "Very well, we are friends again. You forgive me—I forgive you." We shook hands on it.

As we made our way back to *Dawn* I said, "Anyhow, what made you go fishing in the middle of the night?"

Stepan shrugged. "It was the right weather. I had made the rod and prepared the line. Svetlana said yesterday she was tired of eating fish from tins. Also, I could not sleep."

"Mosquitoes?"

"No. I was thinking what I would do—at Stockholm."

"Oh." I could see more trouble ahead. "What did you catch, anyway?"

He shook his head sorrowfully. "The fishing was not as good as I hoped." He led me to the dinghy, in the bottom of which I now noticed two small flounders. I tactfully said that we could fry them for breakfast.

Stepan said with a rueful smile, "We have a saying, 'Where there is no fish even the crayfish is deemed to be a fish.'"

That closed the incident. At least, I thought so at the time. In fact, the relationship between Stepan and the rest of us had subtly changed. A misunderstanding, a misjudging, either breaks or strengthens friendship. In this case it drew us closer together. There was a sort of assumption that Stepan had been proved, and was now one of us. The girls in particular tried to make up for their earlier disbelief by being extra nice to him.

Our fright had made us restless, and after breakfast we had another long discussion about what we should do next. The air reconnaissance seemed to have been called off altogether. Stepan's interpretation was that 'they' had realized they couldn't hope to locate us in the islands and had switched their patrol to the fifty-mile-wide mouth of the Finnish Gulf, through which at some time we should have to pass. That certainly made sense.

Our problem was how to get out of the Gulf in one quick dash without being seen from the air and intercepted. We were about fifty miles from the mouth of the Gulf. With a maximum speed of eight knots we couldn't hope to clear the danger zone in one night's travelling, and in daylight we should immediately come to grief. What we needed was a safe jumping-off point much nearer the mouth of the Gulf. The chart showed that the archipelago extended westwards along the coast to within about fifteen miles of Hango, so we ought to have no difficulty in finding a suitable spot. But we had to decide how to make the journey. If we put to sea, and sailed boldly outside the islands by night, there was a risk that we might be caught at daybreak before we had found a safe anchorage. If we worked our way westwards through the archipelago, in daylight, there was the risk of being spotted from the air. Joe thought we should be safe enough if we camouflaged the boat and kept a sharp lookout. Stepan made little contribution to the discussion—he still didn't want to move at all.

In the end we decided to take the inner route. We covered *Dawn's* deck and cockpit with branches of oak leaves until there was barely room left for us to move, and soon after breakfast we pushed her out of her narrow berth and started the engine. Once again Stepan took the helm. Denny went forward to look for submerged rocks and the rest of us acted as aircraft spotters. It was a tortuous, time-wasting passage that we made through the rocks, but at the end of the day we were nearly ten miles further to the west, and found a safe berth under the lee of a thickly-wooded islet.

It had been exciting to be on the move again, but by the end of the third day we were all tired of rock-dodging and were keyed up for the break-out. The islands had now become so scattered that there was no point in going further, especially as during the morning we had again heard a distant 'plane in the direction of Hango. We had reached our jumping-off place. We berthed in the afternoon on the inside of an island close to the open sea, having decided to leave at dusk and to steam at full speed for Stockholm. There was still a great risk, for by morning we should be little more than fifty miles outside the Gulf—near enough, certainly, for the Russians to claw us back if they found us. The risk had to be taken. There was no other way.

I shall never forget those last few hours. The sea was quiet and there was little wind. *Dawn* was ready, and there was nothing to do but wait. The girls were subdued and Stepan didn't talk at all. He was whittling away moodily at one of his chess pieces. I was as tense as on the night we went into Tallinn, and I know Denny felt the same. Only Joe looked and behaved as usual.

Just before it got dark we took *Dawn* round to the seaward side of the island. In this race, minutes might count. Night had still not quite fallen when we cast the last of the camouflage overboard and Joe gave the order to leave. We motored cautiously out into the Gulf. There was a ship's light over towards Tallinn and another in the direction of Hango. But they were both far enough away not to worry us. Having made sure there were no patrols about, Joe put us on our course and we gave the engine full throttle.

That was a night of horrible tension. I found myself yawning repeatedly, which is how fear takes me. Nobody, of course, had any desire for sleep. We talked, when we talked at all, in undertones. Joe at the tiller was whistling softly but interminably between his teeth. Denny and I kept him company in the cockpit most of the time. Stepan stayed in the unlit cabin communing with himself. From time to time one of the girls brought out sandwiches and coffee, and the hours passed.

We were steaming without lights, and twice we had to alter course to avoid shipping. The steady beat of our own engine made it impossible to hear any other. We brought Hango abeam in the middle of the night, keeping well out to sea. There was still no wind, but there must have been a tidal stream against us through the mouth of the Gulf, for we were falling a little behind schedule. Towards morning we again had to alter course, for we seemed to be slowly overhauling a vessel going our way. We gave it a wide berth, for it might be a Russian steamer, and daybreak was near.

We were now at the crucial point. The next couple of hours would decide our fate. As the grey light spread across the sky we all gathered in the cockpit to see what the morning would bring. Even Stepan stationed himself at the cabin door. His expression was as wooden as the chess piece he was still whittling. He cocked an eye at the steamer which was now far away on our starboard bow, and turned to his carving again.

Then, as the sun rose, we saw a 'plane. I suppose we had all felt pretty certain it would come. From the Russian point of view it was a simple and obvious precaution. A single dawn patrol each day across the mouth of the Gulf was all they needed to keep tabs on us.

The 'plane was flying at about three thousand feet and didn't see us at first. Soon, however, it turned, and began to come straight towards us. History was repeating itself. Joe watched it through the glasses. Stepan stepped back into the cabin. With a zoom the machine passed low overhead and then began to fly round us in a tight circle. No doubt the radio operator was already at work.

Joe said, "Ask Stepan how long he thinks we've got."

When I translated Stepan shrugged. "Perhaps half an hour—perhaps an hour. It depends from which direction the gunboat comes." He asked if he might have the glasses, and when Joe passed them over he turned them, not on the horizon as I expected, but on the distant steamer. He handed back the glasses and whittled for a bit. Then he said: "Why don't you overhaul that ship? She is not Russian. It is your only chance."

I told Joe. He said, "Suppose she *is* Russian?" but he altered course just the same. I gazed at the steamer through the glasses. She was an odd shape.

I said to Stepan, "There seems to be two of them."

Stepan looked at me almost with indifference. "It is a steamer and a tug," he said. "That is why we are faster than they. I know her. She is the *Vittorina*—Swedish. She was damaged in a collision outside Helsinki last week. Now they are taking her home."

Again I translated. There was a new light in Joe's eye. He said, "If she *is* Swedish I think we might just make it." Already the steamer seemed a little nearer. Excitement filled the cockpit. Even the Russians would hardly attempt high-seas piracy under the eyes of witnesses. The 'plane was still circling but there was no sign of any gunboat. Ten breathless minutes passed. The girls were standing with their arms round each other and Denny was watching the engine as though that would encourage it to put forth greater efforts. Suddenly Joe, who was still holding the glasses, shouted: "She *is* Swedish! I can see her ensign."

Stepan must have understood. He looked a little sardonic, but he said nothing.

We were coming up quickly now. We must have been a good two knots faster than the *Vittorina*. Soon we could make out some of the steamer's crew, lounging against the stern rail. They were watching us with interest. Presently one of them waved, and the girls waved back.

Joe pointed to the gaping hole in the steamer's stern, just above the waterline. Stepan regarded it thoughtfully. He said, "In Russia we have a saying, 'It is a poor wind that blows no one good.'" He couldn't understand why we laughed. We were closing the *Vittorina*, rocking through her stern wave until we found calm water abeam of her. There we slowed to her speed.

Joe looked up at her towering rusty side and blew her a kiss. "You lovely ship!" he said.

The aeroplane continued to circle us for a few minutes, then turned and flew away to the south.

We kept close to the *Vittorina* all day, but the danger was over. Towards evening Joe lashed the tiller amidships and we began a hilarious party in the cabin. Even Stepan brightened up for a while but presently he lapsed into moody silence once more. I said: "Cheer up, Stepan. You'll soon be back in Russia. I'm sure you won't be kept long in Stockholm."

Stepan was toying with his glass. He said, "In Russia I think I shall be shot." After a little reflection he added, "Or perhaps just sent away."

A sudden constraint fell on us all. Marya's hand crept into mine. She said, "I think he will, too, Philip."

I said, "What do *you* think, Denny?"

Denny said solemnly: "I wouldn't be in his shoes, now I come to think of it. Remember how the Russians treated their own men who'd been taken prisoner by the Germans?"

I remembered very well. I had seen some of them in Kharkov after they'd been 'liberated'—white, ill and ragged, creeping round the market-place trying to beg a crust of bread. They had been left to fend for themselves because the authorities didn't regard them as trustworthy any longer. It had sickened me at the time.

A sterner view might well be taken of Stepan's case. I was beginning to realize how greatly he'd compromised himself and how difficult it would be for him to explain. He would be blamed for Kleinman's failures as well as for his own. I could imagine the charge sheet. He had omitted to keep us under proper observation as a result of getting drunk; he had lost his ship, although he and Kleinman had got guns and we had not. His story about a wild-fowling gun would never be believed. Last but not least he had actually guided us to safety through channels which we would otherwise not have known. He had been on friendly terms with us, the enemy. He had made no effort to get away. Indeed, the N.K.V.D. might well think that Stepan himself had killed Kleinman and joined us in the hope of escaping from Russia. The more I thought of it the more certain I became that he hadn't a chance. I gazed unhappily at his frank good-natured face. I had a vision of him after he'd spent a few hours in an underground room with a couple of Kleinmans working on him, and I didn't like it.

For Joe's benefit I outlined what I conceived to be the probable case against Stepan. Joe was the one who knew least about Russia and he might think our anxiety about Stepan was exaggerated. But in fact he agreed that the case was pretty damaging.

Stepan himself said nothing. I realized now that he'd known from the beginning what his fate would be and that it wasn't the Stockholm jail he'd been worrying about at all. Looking back over the past day or two I marvelled at his cheerfulness and courage.

I said: "All right, Stepan, let's agree you'll be shot. What do you suggest we do about it?"

He said, without any great hope, "Can I not, perhaps, come to England with you?"

"The authorities might refuse to let you land in England," I told him. "They might send you back."

Stepan shrugged. "Only the evening can show what the day has been," he said. "It is a Russian saying. If they sent me back I should be no worse off than now."

Denny said: "I don't see why our people shouldn't let him stay. After all, he's helped us. We should never have got out of this mess without him."

I couldn't help saying, "We should probably never have got into it without him."

"We aren't obliged to tell them that," said Denny seriously.

"Anyway, I bet they'll be glad to have him. He's a coal-miner—they need miners."

Joe said, "What are you all talking about?" He listened gravely while Denny translated.

"There's another thing," I said. "Haven't you got a sweetheart in Russia, Stepan? And parents? What about them? You'd never be able to go back."

"I have many sweethearts in Russia," said Stepan. "Ten, twenty—but they will all marry someone else. My parents—they were killed by the Germans in Poltava."

"What about relatives? The N.K.V.D. may punish them instead of you."

"I have a sister in Irkutsk," said Stepan. "But perhaps if I come to England the N.K.V.D. will never know about me. The aeroplane did not see me. I can have a new name in England. They will not know what happened to *Neva* or to me." He gave a fleeting smile. "Perhaps I shall receive a posthumous decoration."

Marya said: "Please let him come, Philip. We shall never be happy if we send him back. We shall always think of him."

"It's all very well," I said, "but how are we going to get him to England? If we touch at Stockholm or any other port on the way he'll probably be taken off and shipped back to Russia. Don't forget he hasn't any papers. I can see no end of trouble. We can put up a case to our own people—we can't argue with the Swedes. It seems to me our only hope is to sail straight to England without touching anywhere. What about it, Joe? You're the skipper."

Joe stubbed out his cigarette and gave me an odd look. He said, "You really want my advice?"

"Of course."

He said: "We'd be crazy to try. It's more than a thousand miles. We've been lucky with the weather so far but it probably won't hold. There are the girls to think of."

No doubt Joe knew best, but it wasn't the answer I had hoped for. It *was* crazy, of course, though no crazier than everything else we'd done. I said, "You really think we ought to dump him in Stockholm?"

Everybody looked at Joe—Denny with anxiety, Svetlana with reproach, Marya pleadingly. Poor Joe wriggled uneasily. He said, "Well, if you put it like that—I don't." He seemed to ponder for a moment. I knew what he was thinking about—high winds, torn sails, strange waters, inexperienced passengers, *Dawn* a wreck on some wild shore in the Skagerrak or the Sound. Surely we had tempted Providence enough.

Then he gave a little shrug and a slow smile spread over his face. He wetted his thumb, held it up and blew on it. The smile broadened. "There's a fair wind," he said. He got up and gave Stepan a friendly pat on the shoulder. "I'll go and alter course."

Chapter Fifteen

As it turned out, the weather favoured us. We had light fickle winds and a slow passage, but never a hint of danger. We were overcrowded, and towards the end we had to ration our water, but these were minor discomforts. The days slipped by very happily in almost a holiday cruise atmosphere, and just over a fortnight after we had parted company with the *Vittorina* we were sailing past the Nore.

It was indescribably thrilling. The girls and Stepan were agog for their first sight of England and we all gave a cheer as Joe pointed to the hazy outline of Sheppey and Canvey. My thoughts went back to the early summer, when what we had now successfully accomplished was no more than a crazy idea. I remembered the grim nights I'd spent alone on the saltings aboard *Wayfarer*, and my desperate hopeless longing for Marya. I remembered vividly that depressing day when Denny had been seasick, and the catastrophe of his torn hand. I reminded him of that incident as we passed almost the very spot where it had happened, and he smiled. We could afford to smile now, but neither of us would ever forget those moments of utter despair.

We motored up the creek on a flood tide. Joe's eyes were sparkling and he was sniffing the strong salty air as though it were a precious perfume. He said: "You can have the Baltic. Give me Southfleet." His eyes travelled from one high wall of mud to another, remembering the shape of the banks, recalling the channel. Stepan watched Joe rather as Joe had watched Stepan during our penetration of the islands. All this mud was something quite new to him, and so was the three-knot tidal stream and the great rise and fall of the tide. Marya and Svetlana were studying with interest the little houseboats which lined both sides of the creek. There were quite a lot of sailing-boats and launches out at Southfleet itself, and as we approached we were inspected—as all boats are always inspected by enthusiasts—and then hailed. Joe waved back—it was almost like a royal procession. A few minutes later he turned *Dawn's* head into the tide and I let go her anchor exactly opposite the old workshop. We were home again. Solemnly we shook Joe by the hand. It was a great moment for him as well as for us. I think he was proud of the job he'd done, and he had a right to be.

Then, of course, the excitement started. The return of a boat to its home port after a long cruise always makes big local news in a place like Southfleet, and we hadn't had our anchor down ten minutes before the saltings began to seem very crowded. The news spread quickly that we had a boatload of passengers, including two women, and I thought I'd better go and see the police and immigration people before they came to see me. I left Denny to deal with the Press while I went along to the police-station. I wish you could have seen the face of the station sergeant when I told him I had come to report the presence aboard *Dawn* of three people without papers of any sort. He'd never had anything like it happen to him before. A slightly hurt expression came over his features, as though I'd been a bit inconsiderate in not waiting until he was off duty, and then he reached for a pad and began writing down particulars as calmly as though I'd been offering a reward for a lost wallet.

Naturally, we had a lot of trouble, and at much higher levels than the local police-station. Denny and I had to rush up to town and call at the Foreign Office and the Home Office and see a lot of V.I.P.s. We told them the whole story, just as it had happened, naturally stressing the part Stepan had played in getting us out of a jam and the fact that he was now a political refugee. The upshot of it all was that he was given a permit to stay in the country temporarily while further investigations were made, and was taken off to a Ministry of Labour hostel where Poles and other displaced persons were being given an English language course. We managed to keep his name out of the papers—which was quite a feat in the circumstances, for the story really hit the headlines—and I doubt if the Russians ever connected the arrival in Southfleet of an unidentified foreigner with the strange disappearance of the launch *Neva* in the Baltic Sea.

We didn't have our grand reunion on Steve's birthday after all. We had it much earlier. The moment I reached London I asked his office to send him a tactfully worded cable, for I knew how anxious he'd be. The next thing was that Donovan rang me to say that Steve had been ordered to leave the Soviet Union and that he was already on his way out. Marya and I met him at the airport and took him straight back to the flat. I must say no one ever looked less like a deportee—he was in the highest spirits and as thrilled as a schoolboy over our success. We got Denny and Svetlana along for a celebration that very evening and we really 'went to town'. The meeting between Steve and the girls was quite touching, and then of course we had to have his story in detail.

He told us how the correspondents were rushed back to Moscow after Svetlana's disappearance, and how a day or two later he'd been summoned to appear before Mangulov, the Head of the Soviet Press Department.

"Mangulov's new since your time, I guess?" said Steve. "He's nothing much—just one of those suave diplomatic guys doing what he's told. He tried very hard to pin something on me but he hadn't a chance. He didn't know anything. I told him Svetlana was a big grown-up girl who pleased herself what she did, and that I hadn't seen Marya in months. He went on asking questions, trying to tie me up, and in the end I got sore. When he said, 'So I take it, Mr. Quillan, you've really nothing at all to tell us about this regrettable affair?' I said, 'Only that I'm mighty glad they got out of Russia, Mr. Mangulov.'"

Steve took a sip of champagne and his eyes sparkled. "Then he thought he'd be smart. He came right back at me. 'And how do you know they've left Russia, Mr. Quillan?' I said, 'Hell, they're both sensible girls.'"

I laughed. It was always good to hear of anyone who'd answered back in that country. "But they wouldn't have thrown you out for that," I said. "They must have suspected you all right."

"Oh, I guess they did. They knew someone on the inside must have had a hand in it, and who else was there? I reckon they'd already decided to deport me whatever I said. Anyway, when Mangulov finally got up and bade me a stiff 'Good-bye' without offering to shake hands, I felt sure they'd put the black spot on me. So I said, 'Good-bye, Mr. Mangulov. See you after the liberation!'"

Steve raised his glass. "Maybe I will at that. Let's drink to it, anyway."

There's not much more to tell. Steve was finally assigned to Paris, so we continued to see him from time to time. I made Joe a present of *Dawn* so that he could raise a mortgage on her and build the larger workshop that he'd planned. Denny had no difficulty in getting his old job back and before long he and Svetlana were leading a quiet suburban existence in rooms at Streatham. I reported at the office, and after a few days of intense excitement Marya and I settled down at the flat, absolutely determined to live happily ever after.

Oh, there's just one other thing. About a month after the party a letter arrived at the flat from Stepan. It was postmarked Merthyr Tydfil, South Wales, and was written in very creditable English. It said that his permit had been extended on condition that he worked as a miner for an agreed period, that he was very happy and hoped we were too. There was a postscript that made us laugh. It said, simply, *You will like to hear number three shift overfulfilled his norm five per cent for this week. Next week we do better.*

THE END

www.ingramcontent.com/pod-product-compliance
Ingram Content Group UK Ltd.
Pitfield, Milton Keynes, MK11 3LW, UK
UKHW040104010325
455690UK00002B/10